DEVIL

JOEL ABERNATHY

Copyright © 2022 by Joel Abernathy

All rights reserved.

No portion of this book may be reproduced in any form without written permission from the publisher or author, except as permitted by U.S. copyright law.

BLURB

The hunter will become the hunted...

I'm a monster. I've done things that can't be undone. Things that can never be forgiven.

When I saw him, I thought he was an avenging angel who had come to punish my sins.

Instead, he captured me and brought me into his world of saints and hunters. Righteous predators who prey on monsters like me, using the power of the cursed blood that runs through our veins.

I'll do whatever it takes to become one of them. I'll give him my blood, my body, and my soul. Whatever it takes to prove to Castor that I can be more than the bloodthirsty beasts he hunts, and stand at his side as his partner.

Even if I want to be so much more than that.

When my sire comes to collect what's his, everything I thought I knew about my monstrous nature is called into question. But it might just explain the dark cravings Castor's touch awakens within me.

I

VALENTINE

"We've got another one, DiFiore. Be ready to meet them in the ambulance bay," Chris, my supervisor, called from across the ER. He was the physician overseeing my first year of residency, and also the antichrist, I was pretty certain. About ninety-three percent sure, give or take.

"Yeah, I've got it," I muttered. I was up to my eyeballs in patients tonight, and the last thing I needed was another one.

"Good," Chris said. "And don't forget, I need your report on my desk by the end of the night."

"Yeah, yeah, I'm coming," I said as I scrubbed quickly at the sink and pulled on a fresh pair of sterile gloves. It was a full moon, so there was no telling what was coming in on that stretcher. Last month, I'd treated a kid with a compound fracture, a guy who was convinced he was the Queen of England's nephew, and a frat bro who'd "accidentally" sat on a soda bottle, all in the span of a few hours. Truly what I'd had in mind when I applied for med school. It was great to know you'd found a calling.

I hurried down the hall to the ambulance bay, where the stretcher was already being off-loaded by the EMTs.

"What have we got?" I asked as the first paramedic made it out of the ambulance.

"Twenty-eight-year-old male, gunshot wound to the chest, loss of consciousness, and severe thoracoabdominal and proximal bleeding," he answered, passing me the clipboard with his write-up. "We found him in an alley off Mulberry Street. Someone heard shots about ten minutes ago and called it in, but he's lost a lot of blood."

Well, that was one way to start the night. "Blood type?"

"No idea. Other than trying to cut me with a switchblade when we first showed up, he's been unconscious most of the time. I just know his age from his license," he replied. "He's all yours."

"Gee, Andy, you spoil me," I said dryly. Andrew flipped me off half-heartedly and disappeared, but the sight of the patient on the stretcher rendered my mind blank for a second or two.

"Rob?"

Anna, the RN assigned to babysit the residents, gave me a look as she took the railing on the other side of the stretcher and we rushed the vic into the med bay. "You know this guy, DiFiore?"

I opened my mouth to respond but hesitated a moment. Learning to pause before I spoke had been a hard-won skill, but it was necessary if I wanted to keep my day job while keeping the less-than-legitimate family business in its proper compartment. Or survive, for that matter.

"Yeah," I finally said, since I knew Anna's bullshit radar was second to none, and she was kind of scary when she was mad. "We grew up together."

That was an understatement. We'd grown up together, gone to school together, fought together. We were the kind of friends who never had to say anything because we always knew what the other was thinking. Our adult lives had shaken out so differently that we'd just slowly drifted apart. I should've known he was in trouble when I hadn't seen or heard from him in over a year, but so much had happened lately that a year might as well have been a month. Ever since my big brother, Enzo, had gotten romantically involved with our fixer, culminating in our father's death and the collapse of the only normal I'd ever known, everything and everyone else had taken a backseat.

Hell, I'd barely scraped through the last couple of years of med school without losing my mind, and it was mostly the fact that I desperately needed a distraction that kept me going.

"I need O-negative in the ER, now," I shouted to the tech who was still milling around outside of the trauma room, hitting on a CNA. "And a chest X-ray."

He jolted and stepped away from the doors. "Got it, Doc," he replied, before disappearing through the door.

"I already paged Dr. Adams. What do you need?" Anna asked calmly, as she started an IV and began prepping Rob for emergency surgery. The paramedics had already cut open his shirt, a once-white button-down that was now stained red with his blood.

"Ten milligrams of tranexamic acid," I answered, forcing myself to numb out to everything but the task at hand. "We need to stop the bleeding and get him stabilized."

The prep team got to work while she finished setting up the IV, and I did my best to stabilize him, all the while cursing Chris, wherever the fuck he was.

I jolted as Rob's eyes flew open and his hand shot out, snatching my wrist. He was a hell of a lot stronger than someone who had lost that much blood had any right to be, and when I saw the crazed, half-gone look in his eyes, I wasn't quite sure he was conscious in any meaningful sense of the word.

"Valentine?"

His voice cracked with uncertainty, like he wasn't sure if he was hallucinating. His life really must've taken a downturn if I was the best thing he thought his mind could conjure up at a moment like this.

"Hey," I said, trying to sound nonchalant and reassuring. "You're gonna be okay, Robbie. Just relax and try to stay with me."

"That's bullshit," he said with a cough that seemed like it might've been an attempt at a laugh, if a pitiful one.

"Well, you always were a pessimist," I said flatly, keeping the compression firm against his chest. "Shit. Uh, Anna? What's the ETA on Dr. Adams's arrival?"

She hesitated, backing toward the door. "I'll go check."

"Listen to me," Robbie said in a pleading tone, an urgent look coming into his eyes. He gripped my wrist tighter as if he was trying to pull me closer and grabbed my hand with his other one, forcing it open. When I looked down, I saw he had placed something small and cylindrical in the center of my palm. "You have to take this. Put it somewhere safe."

I picked up the small object, so bloody I only realized it was a capsule when I had wiped it off with my thumb. "I don't understand... what is this?" I asked, knowing there was a high likelihood that he was just delirious.

"It's proof," he muttered. He was wheezing now, his eyes no longer sharp and full of panic but rather glazed and growing dim with confusion, like he was having a hard time keeping his train of thought.

"I need help in here!" I cried at the top of my lungs.

Rob's grip on my wrist tightened, and he was sharp again in an instant, pulling me closer.

"Demon," he said, his voice rough and his breathing raspy. It sounded like the beginning of a death rattle. In my relatively short time of residency at the hospital, I had heard that sound more than enough times to know.

"Demon?" I echoed. "What? Robbie, there's no demon, you're just confused."

"No!" he spat. "It's a person. He's part of our world, and he's going to be after this. He knows I have it. I killed the first guy he sent after me. You have to make sure he doesn't get it. Promise me."

As I stared down at him, my hands and forearms slick with his blood, which was still pouring profusely from the wound in his chest, no matter what I did, I felt like I had just been transported back in time. Back to the treehouse in the woods between our properties, back to when his parents had lived next to mine. Back to the time Robbie had stolen two cigars from his father's study and brought them for us to try, and he made me promise him I wouldn't tell a soul.

"Swear it," he said, every bit as eager as back then, even though it was fear rather than excitement that tinged his eyes that particular shade of blue. "Just promise me you won't tell anyone. Swear it, on your life."

"Robbie, I—" My voice broke.

"Promise me, Val," he gritted out.

Before I could say anything, Chris rushed into the room with Anna close behind.

"Where the hell were you?" I seethed.

He turned on me, scowling, but there was a hint of guilt in his eyes as he worked. "Dealing with a car crash vic down the hall," he said, which probably marked the first time he had ever explained anything in his damn life. He went over to the tray of surgical supplies a few feet away from the bed as Anna placed an oxygen mask over Robbie's face. He tried to push it away at first, but he was losing momentum fast.

"Hang on," I pleaded with him as the others worked, doing my part on autopilot. There was so much fucking blood. "I promise, okay? I swear, but you have to stay with us."

Chris gave me a strange look, but Robbie didn't answer. His eyes were glazed again, looking far away at something on the ceiling, or maybe through it. I knew that look, just like I knew the sound rattling in his throat.

And the shrill, mechanical scream that followed when it finally went silent.

No, no, no. Please, God, no.

"Shit," Chris muttered. "Starting defibrillation."

I quickly moved to grab the defib unit and brought it over. He looked up at me, suspicion glinting in his cold eyes. "You know this guy?"

All I could do was nod. I couldn't take my eyes off Robbie. I forced myself to move back as Chris grabbed the chest paddles and held them to Robbie's chest.

"Clear!"

Robbie's body trembled violently before going as still and flat as the line on the heart monitor.

"Clear!" Chris cried, trying again.

And again.

Nothing.

"CPR," I said urgently. "You gotta try CPR."

Chris gave me a weary look. He wasn't moving fast enough, so I moved in myself, pressing the palm of my hand beneath Robbie's sternum. I pushed down hard until I felt the telltale snap of his ribs disconnecting from the sternum and started compressions.

More nothing. Just the shrill, relentless scream...

I kept going. I refused to stop. I couldn't. Even though I could hear Chris and Anna talking to me in the background, their voices were far off, meaningless.

"DiFiore!" Chris bellowed, putting a hand on my shoulder. The ringing in my ears dulled as he came back into focus. "I said that's enough. He's gone."

"I'm not giving up," I said. When he tried to pull me away, something in me snapped. Before I even realized what I was doing, I whirled around and my fist connected with his jaw, a bloody smear now left along his chin from the brief contact.

The room went dead silent. Everyone and everything except the heart monitor, but its shrill scream was being drowned out by the ringing in my ears that had picked up right where it left off.

For a moment, I stared at Chris, and he stared back, bringing a hand up to touch his face. He pulled it away, looking down at the blood on his fingertips.

"Shit," I muttered. "Dr. Adams, I—"

"Get him out of here," he said gruffly, and the security guard I hadn't even realized was there approached me, looking like he was walking up to a cornered animal.

He was looking at me the way everyone had when I first started. When my name on the roster was cause for scandalized whispers and nervous glances. I liked to think that in my two years of residency, I had allayed those fears and proved that I wasn't who they all thought I was, just because of my family name.

One fuck up, and all that was out the window.

"Come on," the guard said, looking like he thought it was going to be a fight.

I nodded, following him out of the OR without a word. I glanced back at the door, though, in time to see Chris leaning over the clipboard he was holding.

"Time of death, 8:36 PM," he muttered out loud.

My heart sank into the pit of my stomach. This didn't feel real. Even as I changed out of my bloodied scrubs and gloves and slipped the capsule into the pocket of my pants, I felt numb. Like I was in a waking dream, and I couldn't get out of it.

I went out back around the side of the hospital to smoke. Holy shit, this sucked. A ghost from my past had just showed up out of nowhere, and just like that, he was gone.

I reached into my pocket for the joint I kept there, since I was pretty fucking sure I wasn't going back to work anyway. I needed something to take the edge off.

My fingers brushed something in my pockets, and I pulled out the capsule. I didn't even remember putting it in my pocket, and I'd forgotten about it until then.

I looked down, twisting the capsule open. It was just large enough for what it contained, a tiny strip of plastic with metal bits on the end. A microchip? It wasn't like any I had ever seen, but I couldn't think of what else it would be. I had just enough presence of mind to avoid touching the metal parts, since there was blood on my fingertips from the outside of the capsule, and sealed it away again.

What the hell was this? And why had Robbie given it to me?

That much was obvious, after a second of thought. Who else would he have given it to? I didn't know what was on the chip, but I knew one thing—it was the reason Robbie was dead. And I knew the moniker of the guy who killed him, assuming he wasn't just hallucinating that a literal demon was after him.

Now I just had to figure out why.

"You need a light for that?"

I shoved the chip back into my pocket and looked up sharply to find Chris standing a few feet away, watching me, and realized I still had the joint dangling from my other hand.

Enzo was right. I wasn't observant enough for the family business. Not by a long shot. And apparently, I wasn't cut out for this one, either.

I followed Chris's gaze down to the joint. "Might as well, since you're already writing me up for insubordination," I said with a shrug, glancing at the red mark on his jaw, which was already a bit swollen. That was going to be one hell of a bruise come morning. "Or are you going to press charges?"

He blew a puff of air through his nostrils, walking over to me. "Even if I did, I doubt it would stick. Rumor has it, your brother-in-law is the chief of police."

My eyes widened as he pulled a lighter out and flicked it on, his hands somehow perfectly steady while mine were still trembling, and waited expectantly. I reluctantly popped the joint between my lips and leaned in, letting the flame eat away at the tip. I took a drag, breathing the smoke in deep. One hit wasn't near enough to do anything more than take the edge off my frayed nerves, but the habit was comforting.

"How did you know that?" I asked. "It was a small courthouse wedding, and something tells me you don't run in the same circles."

"I did my research when I heard one of my resident applicants was a DiFiore. Your brother might not like the publicity, but your family has certainly garnered enough of it over the years," he remarked.

I frowned. "Enzo isn't like our father. Neither am I, for that matter."

"I know," he said, taking the joint from me. I watched in shock as he took a drag from it, too, before handing it back. "If I thought that, I never would've chosen you. But I don't believe in holding people accountable for the sins of their fathers."

"You probably regret that decision after tonight," I mumbled, taking another puff. I offered it to him again, but he held his hand up, so I crushed the embers out on the brick wall behind me.

"It's certainly the first time I've gotten decked in my own OR," he mused, rubbing his jaw. "Probably won't be the last, though. You know, if you get tired of medicine, you could have a decent career as a prizefighter. That's a mean right hook."

I snorted. "Comes with the territory."

"What, being a mob boss's kid?"

"Being the scrawny awkward kid in school who everyone wanted to beat up," I corrected.

He raised an eyebrow. "I'm surprised your brothers didn't kill them."

"They would have," I admitted. "Which is why I never told them. I can fight my own battles."

"I can see that," he said thoughtfully. After a moment's pause, he asked, "So, that guy. You were close?"

"Once upon a time, but we grew apart," I answered, folding my arms over my chest and looking out at the rain falling on the plastic awning over the smokers' lounge. Soon enough, the rain would wash away all the blood on the streets, and any evidence of Robbie's unfortunate ending along with it. There would be no family left to mourn him, either. Just me, and whoever else had been a part of his life these last couple of years.

"I guess you don't know what happened, then," Chris said. He sounded nonchalant, but I knew better than to think that. I wasn't used to him being anything other than a dick, and I knew him not to be the kind of man who did anything unnecessarily. Certainly not cozying up to me.

"No," I said. "I don't."

He watched me for a few moments, and I wasn't sure if he believed me, but he didn't call me out on it, either way.

"That's good. Then there's no reason for you to be here when the police come."

I watched him warily. "Police?"

"I'm a mandated reporter. I have to call in any violent gun crime. Especially when it results in a homicide," he explained. "I haven't called it in yet, but I can't wait too much longer."

"You waited because of me?" I asked, frowning. "Why?"

He paused as if he was considering it. "Did I ever tell you where I spent my residency?"

"No... you didn't."

"St. Francis."

"The one downtown?" I asked. "That's a rough hospital."

"It's a rough area," he remarked. "I'd know, considering I grew up two minutes away from it."

"Oh," I said awkwardly.

He snorted. "I saw a lot of shit during my time at St. Francis. A lot of shit growing up, too. I learned there are things you don't say, and people you don't say them to. Cops especially. There were plenty of times I should've called back then, but I didn't. Cops have a way of making things worse, especially in a place like that."

"Yeah... I know what you mean."

"In a place like this, though... rules can only be bent so far."

I nodded in understanding. "Thank you. I'll be out of here long before they show up." I hesitated. "Am I going to have a job to come back to Monday morning?"

"You will," he said. "But I think you should take the weekend to consider some things. Namely, whether this is something you really want to do. Whether it's something you *should* do."

My heart hammered against my chest in panic. "Of course it is. Look, I'm sorry for hitting you. I know I fucked up, and it won't happen again."

"I'm not talking about the punch, Valentine," he said, holding my gaze. It was hard to hold his, in the same way it was hard to hold Silas's. Chris's eyes were a frosty blue compared to my brother-in-law's gunmetal gray, but they both had a hardness to them. A coldness. "This is about you being honest with yourself. About what you're capable of, and what you're not, and if someone like you should even be trying in the first place."

I bristled at his words, and I kind of regretted promising that punch would be a one-time thing, since suddenly, I wasn't sure that was a promise I could keep anymore.

"A person like me?" I challenged. "What happened to not blaming someone for their family's mistakes?"

"I'm not," he said with a shrug. "This is all about you. Tonight was your first time losing a patient, right?"

His question caught me off guard. "I've seen patients die before."

"That's not what I asked," he pressed. "I asked if it's the first time you've lost a patient."

I clenched my jaw and answered, "Yes."

"There it is, then," he said. "It's your chance to reassess, now that you know what this job really entails. Now that you know what it's like, the good, the bad, and the ugly. And trust me, as someone who's been doing this since you were in junior high, there's a whole hell of a lot more of the ugly than there is anything else."

"What, you think I'm too soft to be a doctor?" I asked, still trying to make sense of his words. I was used to people thinking I was some psycho who was bound to fly off the handle at any moment, and I couldn't really blame them for that. Everyone who actually knew me thought I was a flaky dumbass, and I couldn't blame them for that, either. I still wasn't entirely sure where I stood with Chris.

"A doctor? No," he replied. "There are a lot of specialties I think you'd excel in. You're a team player, you're compassionate—sometimes to a fault—and despite what a lot of people seem to think, yourself included, you're smart. You'd make one hell of a pediatrician."

"A pediatrician?" I muttered.

"Or a cardiologist, endocrinologist... hell, even family practice, if you feel like being bored out of your mind," he continued. "Might not be the worst thing in your case. Some field where compassion is an asset rather than a liability."

I frowned. "Isn't that all medicine? People come here at the lowest points in their lives. They want someone who's understanding."

"No, they want to leave this place alive," he countered. "There's a reason the bleeding hearts get weeded out sooner or later. Getting emotionally attached isn't going to help you treat your patient any more effectively. All it does is cloud your judgment. What these patients need is someone who's calm, rational, and authoritative. Do you think you can manage that when the shit hits the fan? You think you can handle looking into the eyes of a mother of three and telling her that her husband of twenty years isn't going to make it? You think you can handle trying to resuscitate a dying child while the parents are screaming at you, all the while knowing there's not really any point because it's hopeless?"

I stared at him in stunned silence for a moment, which probably was just proving his point in his mind. "I've seen shit. I've lost people I love. You make it sound like I'm some sheltered kid who's never had anything bad happen to him."

"Oh, I know you have," he said. "I can tell, because you carry those things with you. Every one of them has left a scar on you, and tonight's just another one to add to the collection. I can't tell you what to do, but I can tell you to take some time to think about it. Think about it and be honest with yourself. Really ask yourself whether it's worth it."

With that, he turned on his heel and started to walk back toward the entrance of the building. I stared after him for a moment, irritated.

His words stuck with me, though. It wasn't like it was the first time someone had questioned my choice of career. Even though my brothers were supportive, I knew they didn't really understand. They probably just thought it was another phase, like being goth or the time I decided I was going to start a garage band.

I sighed and put the joint away, pulling the chip back out to examine it in my palm for a moment. Chris was right about one thing, at least. I needed to take the weekend to figure things out. Robbie—my Robbie—was gone, and he had entrusted me with the last secret I would ever keep for him. A secret that had gotten him killed.

I had made a promise, though, and I intended to keep it. "I swear, Robbie," I murmured. "On my life."

2

VALENTINE

As I walked through the front door at home, the sound of the door falling shut echoed across the empty halls. I had lived here all my life, but lately, it didn't feel like my home at all. Now that Luca lived down the street with his new wife and their three-month-old baby, Timothy, and Dad was... gone, the house was empty more often than not. Sure, Enzo was still here, but he was plenty busy running the family, and as for his husband, well... "Ghost" was a fitting codename, considering I hardly ever knew if he was around or not.

That suited me fine, though. I was happy Enzo was happy, but Silas still gave me the creeps.

Maybe it was time I got my own apartment. I wasn't the biggest fan of change, but it had to happen at some point.

With both of my brothers married, I was starting to feel like the fifth wheel on the rare occasion we all got together at all.

I went upstairs and opened the locked box I kept under my bed. It had been secure enough when I was a teenager wanting to store my weed and a couple of tiny bottles of vodka, but it felt childish now, especially considering how important the object I needed to store was. I decided it would have to do for the moment, until I could ask Enzo for the code to the safe.

Hell, I wasn't even sure where the safe was.

Once the chip was in the box, I hopped into the shower. I turned the water pressure up until my skin was reddened and the heat was almost intolerable, but it was better than the alternative.

As I got dressed, I could hear voices downstairs. Judging from Enzo's laughter, I assumed he and Silas were both home. For some reason, he found the guy's bone-dry humor absolutely hilarious. How he managed to get along with a complete psycho like him, let alone go to the same bed every night, I had no idea.

To be fair, I was pretty sure Silas was a threat to everyone *but* Enzo.

I took a deep breath and walked downstairs, having every expectation that this was going to go disastrously. When I rounded the corner to the kitchen, I saw Silas had Enzo pinned against the counter, groping him, his tongue halfway down my brother's throat.

"You know, other people have to eat on the counter," I remarked.

Silas looked up, shooting me a frigid glare that put me on edge even though I knew Enzo wouldn't actually let him do anything to me.

Hopefully.

"What do you want, Doogie Houser?"

I wrinkled my nose. "Who?"

He rolled his eyes as Enzo slipped out from under his arm. "What's up, Val?" my brother asked.

I hesitated a moment. I wasn't sure how to bring this up. I didn't really want to think about it myself, and somehow, it felt like maybe if I didn't say it out loud, it wouldn't be true. It was clearly delusional, wishful thinking, but I wasn't exactly in a logical frame of mind right now.

"Something happened at work," I said, feeling like a kid trying to tell his parents about something that had happened at school. Only the one parent was the older brother I had always wanted to impress, and the other was a serial killer without a conscience.

"Yeah?" Enzo asked, sounding like he was trying to pay attention even though I could tell he wasn't fully, from the smirk he was trying to fight as he batted Silas's hand away from whatever he was doing behind the counter. I really did not want to know.

It wasn't the fact that Silas was a guy or anything. I would've been just as grossed out if Luca and his wife were acting like that in front of me. Fortunately, they weren't a physically affectionate couple, at least not in front of other people.

"You remember Robbie Caruso, right?" I asked.

"Sure," Enzo said absently, trying to cut the tomatoes on the wooden board sitting on the counter in front of him while his husband continued to molest him. "You guys used to be inseparable. Whatever happened to him, anyway?"

My throat tightened, so I tried to clear it. "We kind of lost touch until today. He came in as a patient, and..." I stopped. Even though I had just lived through it, for some reason, I couldn't bring myself to get the words out.

Enzo looked up from his diced tomatoes, and Silas turned to me as well, looking less irritated and more confused.

"What happened?" Enzo asked warily, even though I could tell from the tone in his voice he already had an idea.

I tried to swallow again, but my throat was bone dry.

"He's gone," I said, my voice sounding kind of pathetic, if I was being honest with myself. That was a dangerous game lately. "He got shot, and he lost a lot of blood on the ambulance ride. I tried to save him, but I couldn't. He's just... he's gone."

Enzo dropped the knife against the block. For a few moments, they both just stood there staring at me, and I couldn't bring myself to look either of them in the eye.

I knew what they were thinking. The same thing I was. I was as useless as a doctor as I was in the Mafia. The thing about Chris's words that had infuriated me the most was that they were true, and deep down, I knew it. I was not cut out for this kind of thing. Hell, I wasn't sure what I was cut out for, if anything. Maybe I was just destined to be a loser living in his brother's shadow his entire life. At least then I couldn't do any real damage.

"Holy shit," Enzo breathed. "Val, I'm sorry. Are you—?"

"I'm fine," I said quickly, even though the words felt as hollow as they were. I cleared my throat. "I will be. But that's not all."

Enzo listened intently, waiting for me to go on.

"He gave me something, before he... you know. A chip."

"A microchip?" Silas asked.

"Yeah, I think so," I said with a shrug. "He said it was important. Asked me to keep it safe. And I think it's what got him killed."

I didn't just think, I knew, but I really wasn't in the mood for Silas's semantics right now.

"Killed by who?" Silas demanded.

I was starting to wish I had asked to have this conversation alone with Enzo, but I knew even if he agreed, Silas would've just been listening in. He was omnipresent. Or at least, he wanted everyone to think he was. "Another mobster, I think. He said the guy's name was 'Demon,' but he was half out of his mind with blood loss and shock, so there's no telling."

"Demon?" Silas echoed. The look that came over his face as soon as I said the name made me second-guess myself.

"Yeah," I said warily. "I figured it was just a code name or something."

Enzo looked over at his husband. "What is it?" he asked. "You know that guy?"

"You could say that," he muttered. His attention fixed back on me, his gaze sharpening like a knife. "Exactly what did he say? Be very specific."

"I don't know, I was trying to save his life at the moment," I muttered. "He just said the chip was proof of something, I think. Something that could take this Demon guy down."

"And?"

"Silas, you're scaring me," Enzo said, frowning. "Who is this guy?"

"He was my student," Silas said quietly.

"Your student?" Enzo stared at him in disbelief. "Seriously?"

"It was a long time ago," Silas murmured. "Long before we met. James was a hired gun turned serial killer, and a general menace to the wrong people. I was hired to make him disappear, but he showed promise. He was brilliant, ruthless... completely devoid of a conscience."

"Yeah, sounds like a real winner," I remarked. "I can see why you guys got along so well."

"What happened?" Enzo asked, a jealous edge to his tone. It was subtle enough that anyone else might not have recognized it, but I did.

Silas looked away. His tone grew somber as he spoke again. "Like I said, he was brilliant. The kind of brilliant that goes hand-in-hand with madness. He became a liability. And I made the mistake of letting things get... personal."

"Personal?" Enzo asked, folding his arms over his chest. "So you fucked your 'student.'"

"As I said, it was a mistake. And it was a long time ago," Silas said pointedly. He reached out, brushing a dark strand of hair away from Enzo's forehead. "My tastes have come a long way."

Usually, Enzo would've gotten all melty, but he still had his guard up. Maybe he wasn't completely blinded by the rose-colored glasses after all.

Then again, the issue was that he was jealous, not that he was beginning to see how batshit insane his husband was. Or the fact that he had a past so dark, most shadows wouldn't touch it.

"So what happened?" Enzo asked. "Something tells me the breakup wasn't amiable."

Silas sighed, dropping his hand to his side. "Indeed, it was not. He was out of control. I had to put him down."

Enzo frowned. "I don't understand. If you killed this guy, how is he still out there?"

"He can't be," Silas said firmly. He glanced back over at me. "Which means someone is mistaken."

"What, you think I'm lying?" I demanded. "Until five seconds ago, I didn't have a fucking clue who this guy was, never mind that you used to bang him."

"No one said that, Val," Enzo said, ever the peacemaker. "We're just trying to figure out what's going on."

"What's going on is my friend is dead, and apparently, it has something to do with you," I said, turning back to Silas. Normally, I would be too chickenshit to get on his bad side—even though I seemed to live there regardless—but I didn't care anymore.

Silas just stared at me, like he wasn't going to dignify my accusation. "This microchip. Where is it?"

I hesitated, because all of a sudden, I wasn't so sure giving it to him was such a good idea.

"Where is it, Valentine?" Silas repeated, his gaze darkening.

Enzo nodded to me, and I clenched my jaw, reluctantly walking up the stairs. When I came down a moment later, I dropped the chip into Silas's waiting palm. He took it between his thumb and forefinger, studying it curiously.

"What is it?" Enzo asked.

"It's a microchip, all right," Silas said. "One that isn't even on the market yet. It's used by intelligence, primarily. It costs a fortune to manufacture, and not a small one."

"Can you read what's on it?" Enzo asked.

"Not with anything I keep in the house," was his cryptic answer. "I know someone who can, but the question remains as to whether it's wise to do so."

"Of course it is," I interjected. "That thing holds the answer to why Robbie is dead and how to get the guy who killed him."

Silas gave me a weary look I knew all too well. The one that said he thought I was just a child having a tantrum. "This is bigger than your friend. Anyone crazy enough to use that name in the underworld, let alone masquerade as him, is not to be trifled with. Certainly not by you."

"Bullshit," I growled, stalking forward. "If you won't help, just give it to me and I'll take care of it myself."

Silas looked pointedly at Enzo, as if expecting him to get me under control.

"Well, he's right," said Enzo. "We have no idea who this is, and enough people know you're connected to Silas that you getting involved is a risk we can't afford to take."

"Are you kidding me?" I seethed. "This is Robbie we're talking about. He was my best friend."

"I know he was," Enzo said, his voice infuriatingly placating. He treated me like a child, too, just not quite as contemptuously as his partner. "And I'm not saying we let it go, but we have to be careful. *You* have to be careful in particular. Just let us handle it."

"What, like I'm supposed to trust him?" I demanded.

"Valentine—"

"No!" I snapped, stepping back from him. "I'm sick of you taking his side."

Enzo heaved a weary sigh. "Come on. I know you're upset, but—"

"Upset?" I gave a dry laugh. "Yeah, I guess I am upset. I'm upset my brother would put someone else above his own flesh and blood."

Enzo's eyes narrowed. "I'm going to give you a pass on that, considering everything that just happened, but you need to get a grip."

"Fuck you," I spat, turning on Silas when I saw him tense, like he thought he had to protect his lover from me. "Don't worry," I sneered. "You win. I'm doing what I should've done a long time ago. I'm leaving."

"Valentine!" Lorenzo called after me as I made my way over to the door.

I ignored him, but I heard Silas say quietly on my way out the door, "Just let him go. He'll calm down."

I bristled at his words. He was the one I'd like to punch, but I wasn't enough of an egotistical dick to think I would actually stand a chance.

It would feel damn good, though. No doubt about that.

I got on my bike and threw on my helmet, since I had seen way too many people come in with their brains scrambled from a bad accident. I didn't give a shit if I looked like a dork.

I rode for a while, not really going anywhere in particular, when I realized I was close to wrapping back around to Luca's neighborhood again.

Well, I did need a place to stay for the night. I could just check into a hotel, but the truth was, I didn't feel like being alone. I sure as hell didn't feel like being home.

Both cars were in the driveway when I arrived at Luca's place, so I parked behind his car and walked up the small pathway through well-maintained shrubs and rose bushes to knock on the door.

I hesitated when I heard voices from within. Loud, angry voices. I couldn't make out what they were saying, but Carol was yelling, and so was Luca. I could hear the baby crying in the background.

Maybe it was a bad time. I decided to just turn around and get back on my bike. I really needed to figure out what I was going to do for the night, but zoning out felt too good to resist, so I let my mind drift and just drove around the back roads until the first violet tinges of twilight hit the pale gray sky.

I eventually made my way to Johnny's apartment, since he was usually home on a Friday night, social butterfly that he was. Sure enough, when I knocked, he opened the door a few moments later with a beer bottle in his hand and some action movie blaring in the background. Guess he didn't get enough of that crap at work.

I used to enjoy the same shit, to be fair. Working at the hospital had changed all that. Ever since I found out that in real life, bullets don't always leave clean little holes the good guys can just shake off, the novelty of gratuitous violence had been lost on me. If there had been any left, trying to perform CPR on my best friend when I could hardly see my hands through his blood would've soaked it up like a sponge.

"Hey, Val," Johnny said, looking surprised to see me.

I couldn't blame him, considering we had both been too wrapped up in our respective careers to really see each other much lately. We used to be inseparable. Me, him, and Robbie. We were the three youngest, so we'd always stuck together when everyone else got tired of the annoying kids hanging around. If anyone would understand what I was feeling, it was Johnny.

He took one look at me and the surprise melted into concern. "Holy shit, you look like crap."

"Thanks, Johnny," I said flatly. "Good to see you, too."

He was right, though. If I looked even half as bad as I felt, crap was probably an understatement. He was a sight for sore eyes, though. Johnny was a DiFiore on his mother's side, so he had the same dark hair, olive skin, and brown eyes as the rest of us, but unlike me, he'd actually grown out of the baby face thing. Even my attempt to grow out the scruff along my jaw hadn't done much to change that. But despite the fact that we were born only a few months apart and Johnny was almost always clean shaven, he looked older.

There was still just enough familiarity in his face to remind me of the boy who'd always been at my side, egging me on while I did the stupidest, most dangerous shit a kid could get into. He had changed, though. Not just physically, but in other ways as well. Once upon a time, I could count on Johnny to make me look good in the responsibility department. He'd always been a Grade A flake, but after a come-to-Jesus moment a few years back as a result of a lost shipment, he'd cleaned up his act. In a twist of fate worthy of a fucking Dreamworks movie, he had become Enzo's right-hand man and his most trusted soldier outside of the immediate family.

I was proud of him. But now I was alone in the glare of the fuck-up spotlight.

He stepped back and nodded for me to follow him into the apartment. It was trashed, as usual. At least some things hadn't changed. There was laundry on the floor and a huge pile of it rumpled up on one end of the sofa, like he'd dumped it out of the basket and just said fuck it halfway through folding. There were beer bottles littered all over the coffee table, and if it had been anyone else's place, an intervention probably would have been in order —but knowing Johnny, they had accumulated over weeks.

Not that I was one to talk when it came to responsible consumption of alcohol. I stayed sober during the week and whenever I was on shift, but ever since Dad's death, I had gone from being a social drinker to drinking myself into oblivion every chance I got. It was easier that way. Easier not to see Dad's wide, gaping eyes and his mouth stretched open every time I closed my eyes. Easier not to replay all the grisly scenes I saw on a day-to-day basis that I couldn't do fuck all about. Tonight was no exception.

"You okay, man?" Johnny asked, even though I could tell from his tone he knew I was pretty far from that.

I was already on my way to the coffee table where an open fifth of Jack Daniels was waiting with my name on it. I grabbed an armful of laundry and tossed it aside before reaching for the bottle. I gulped it down until I had to come up for air.

"Not really," I finally said, clearing my throat and wiping off the excess drops clinging to my lips.

"Yeah, I can kind of see that," Johnny said, reaching for the remote to turn off the movie. He eyed me worriedly. "You wanna talk about it, or...?"

I didn't. I'd never wanted to do anything less, but I knew I owed him the truth. At least as much of it as I could stand to croak out.

"Robbie's dead."

Well, so much for breaking it to him gently. I really was going to be a mess when it came time for me to be an attending physician. Breaking bad news to patients wasn't a resident's responsibility, and thank God for that, because I barely had it in me to keep my own emotions together, let alone anyone else's.

And what was the point, even? There was no amount of flowery language that could make it less of an atom bomb.

"What? Robbie Caruso?" Johnny asked, gaping at me for a few moments, like he wasn't sure I was serious. And to be fair, I had been as much of a smartass goof off as he was for most of our lives. That was probably why we got along as well as we did, but I couldn't remember the last time I'd laughed. Humor had always been a coping mechanism, but the shit I'd been neck-deep in lately was too fucked up for even gallows humor to touch.

"Yeah," I said hoarsely. "He came into the ER with a gunshot wound, and there was nothing I could do. He's gone."

"Holy shit," he mumbled, sinking onto the couch next to me. He just stared past the clutter on the coffee table for a long while in silence, and that was just as well, because I didn't know what to say any more than he did. When he finally spoke again, his voice was tentative. "I'm sorry, Val. I'm real sorry."

I glanced over at him, trying to smile even though it probably looked more like a twitch. It felt like someone had starched my entire body stiff, and my mouth was no exception. "Yeah. Me, too."

"Who was it?" he asked, a dangerous edge coming into his tone. The change that came over him was like a dark shadow, turning his shock and pain to something we all found easier to deal with. Rage.

"Some guy named Demon," I answered, spending the next few minutes recounting the conversation I'd just had with Silas and Enzo. At least I knew I wasn't alone in my mistrust of the former.

"So it's Silas's ex," he said in a tone of disbelief.

"I guess. Or someone pretending to be him. Either way, it's sketchy as hell."

"Yeah, no doubt about that," Johnny muttered. He paused. "You think Silas had something to do with it?"

I shrugged, polishing off the rest of the bottle. Johnny brought another one over and poured us each a glass, as if to encourage slightly more moderation.

"I don't know," I admitted. "But I do know that Enzo is incapable of being objective where he's concerned. And now I don't even have the chip."

"Yeah, could've told you that was gonna happen," Johnny scoffed. When I gave him a look, he smiled apologetically, but it didn't touch his eyes. "Sorry. I know 'I told you so' isn't what you need to hear right now."

"You're right," I conceded, leaning back against the couch. I stared up at the popcorn patterns on the ceiling. I was drunk enough they were already starting to look like some white trash version of Starry Night. "I fucked up, but what else is new?"

"Hey. You can't blame yourself for what happened," he said in a gruff tone.

"Can't I?" I challenged.

Johnny sighed, taking a long swig of his drink. "This is what I was worried about when you told everyone you were going to med school, y'know."

"What, that my incompetence would kill someone we both cared about?" I asked, my voice sounding slightly slurred. It probably wasn't a good sign it had taken that much whiskey to achieve that.

"No," he said, shooting me a scolding look. "That you'd end up raking yourself over the coals for shit that wasn't your fault."

I gave a noncommittal grunt of acknowledgment. He was half right. I had done everything I could, but that was the problem. Maybe I wasn't good enough. Maybe I never would be. And this wasn't just a matter of lost shipments and deals gone bad. This was life and death. What business did I really have to be in that position, anyway? Everything I touched got fucked up sooner or later, and now it would be people, not drugs and arms, serving as the collateral damage.

"C'mere," Johnny said, draping an arm around my neck to pull me against his side. He smelled like beer and cheap cologne and musk, a familiar and surprisingly pleasant combination that was more comforting than it had any right to be. I tried to shirk out from his grasp half-heartedly, but he held me in place easily enough, tousling my hair with his other hand.

His voice was rough with sadness as he spoke. "Beating yourself up isn't how Robbie would want you to honor his memory. You want to hate anyone, hate the motherfucker who killed him. Hate's a powerful thing. You don't waste that shit on yourself, you let it fuel you to do something."

I gave up struggling and slumped against him, my head dropping onto his chest. His heartbeat was a steady, soothing rhythm. A reminder that we were both still here, and he was right. As long as I was alive, I could do something. I could try.

"Yeah," I murmured. "I guess."

"Good," he said, pushing me away suddenly. "Now get off me. This is getting gay."

"Oh, fuck off," I muttered, elbowing him in the ribs. "You're the one who pulled me in."

Johnny just snorted a laugh and got up, snatching the mostly empty bottle from my hand. "You can crash here however long you want, but I'm not gonna watch you drink yourself into a coma. Get some sleep, okay? It'll all feel better in the morning."

I groaned, flopping onto my side with my head on the armrest. "I doubt that, but... thanks, Johnny. And not just for letting me crash."

He seemed surprised by my words, and this time, his smile did touch his eyes, faint as it was. "We're family. That's just what family does. Now get some sleep, you lush," he said, flicking out the lights in the living room before he went into his bedroom.

I rolled onto my back, staring up at my hands in the darkness. In the hazy grain of my vision, I could still see the blood dripping from my fingers before I dropped my hands onto my chest and closed my eyes, shutting them tight until the alcohol-induced hallucinations disappeared in the geometric patterns behind my eyelids.

That's just what family does.

Yeah, I used to think that, too. You fell, family picked you up. You made a mess, they helped you clean it up. You killed a guy, they helped you hide the body. That was how it'd always been, but what if that wasn't enough?

"Family is forever" was Mom's favorite thing to say, but she was the glue holding it all together. Ever since she'd been gone, we hadn't been whole. I was a piss-poor substitute, but I'd been trying desperately to hold it together in her absence.

It wasn't enough, though. I was starting to think it never would be.

3

VALENTINE

I stayed with Johnny through the weekend, dodging Enzo's attempts to reach out since I knew he hadn't actually changed his mind on anything. He was just going to do whatever Silas told him, so what was the point in even talking?

Sooner or later, I was going to get the damn chip back, but I very much doubted it would be because Enzo was actually willing to help me.

While I'd had plenty of time to process what happened, that certainly hadn't made it any easier to come to terms with things. Not by a long shot. I knew Johnny was right about letting my anger motivate me, but it did nothing to displace the guilt that so easily existed alongside it. I felt like shit, and that wasn't going to change anytime soon.

Certainly not until I managed to actually do something to avenge my friend's death.

If my brother and his husband had their way, it was probably never going to happen.

Going back to work came with plenty of issues on its own, but at least I was doing something.

Fortunately, Chris was busy when I first went in, so I wound up taking a few patients before I actually came face-to-face with him.

I could feel someone watching me, and turned around to see it was him.

"You showed up," he said, not even bothering to hide his surprise.

"You thought I wouldn't?" I asked.

He snorted. "I had hoped you wouldn't," he said without missing a beat. "But I guess it's a good thing you're here, since that means I don't have to replace you."

I blinked. "That's touching."

He just smirked, shoving a clipboard into my hand. "We're short, so get to work. The new intern is coming in later, and she'll need you to give her the rundown. Oh, and keep an eye on her."

"And here I thought you were still keeping an eye on me."

"I am," he said, already on his way out the door. "That's not going to change anytime soon, so get used to it."

"It's good to be back," I said dryly.

Time to get started.

Halfway through the morning, I had greeted the new intern and told her everything from where the good coffee was to who to avoid, Chris being near the very top of that list. Even if he hadn't been as much of a dick as usual lately.

I still didn't exactly feel like I belonged here, but there had to be something to the whole "fake it till you make it" strategy. I was going to employ it, in lieu of any better ideas. Maybe it would work eventually.

As busy as I was, there was still something that caught my attention. There was a woman in the waiting room with short blonde hair and a suspiciously nondescript black business suit. She was there the entire morning, even when others who had been there after her came and went. And I couldn't get over the feeling that she was, in fact, watching me.

Something told me it wasn't my dashing good looks.

"Hey," I said, leaning in to talk to the triage nurse behind the counter. "You see that woman over there?"

She lifted her head and squinted. "Who, the one with the short hair?"

"Yeah," I answered. "What's she here for?"

She shrugged. "She hasn't come to the desk. Probably waiting on another patient."

"Yeah," I said. "Right."

I decided to brush it off and go back to my rounds, considering there was more than enough work to focus on without worrying about something so paranoid. The whole thing with Robbie had me on edge, but that didn't mean a complete stranger was stalking me.

Even if she did look like she belonged to a Family. They all had a look. Growing up the way I had, it was unmistakable.

What was I going to do, though, go up to her and say, "Excuse me, ma'am, are you stalking me for some reason?"

Yeah, no.

I had finally stopped for two seconds to sit down and eat a microwaved burrito in the break room when Chris leaned in and barked, "DiFiore! Major pileup on I-95. All hands on deck."

I dropped my food and grabbed a drink of water since I had nearly choked. Damn, could this place be boring for all of two seconds?

To my relief, most of the patients who had already come in were free of any life-threatening injuries, by some miracle. I knew better than to get my hopes up for the rest of the day, but I took what I could get.

I was stitching up a guy's knee, which had been busted open so badly I could see bone, when I heard the sound of a commotion coming from out in the hall. That was strange, considering the only patients who weren't already here had been taken to another hospital for more serious injuries, as far as I knew.

I looked around the curtain separating my patient's room from the hall and saw a few people backing up. The sound of gunfire, deafening and familiar, made my ears ring, and I cried out in panic, ducking back behind the curtain as everyone else took cover.

I was almost convinced I was having another nightmare. I'd certainly had enough of those lately. It was rare that I could close my eyes without some horror awaiting me, sometimes even before I got to sleep.

This was all too real, though. The trail of blood seeping onto the black-and-white tile floor was proof enough of that.

I could hardly breathe, at a complete loss for what to do. I wasn't armed. Enzo and Luca both had always bitched about that, but when I was here, I wasn't a member of the Family. I wasn't a killer, or a criminal, I was a doctor who'd taken an oath to do no harm, as ironic as that seemed to most people.

For the first time, I was starting to regret that decision.

Shit. What the hell was I supposed to do now? When I saw a pair of shiny black shoes stop outside the curtain, I realized it was a little too late for that. I staggered back, putting myself between my patient and the stranger, trying not to look like I was on the verge of passing out from sheer terror.

I found myself staring up at a man I didn't recognize, and yet, in another way, I did. He was every black suit Mafia mannequin I had ever come across in my life. He was tall and imposing, but that was beside the point when he had a damn gun in his hand. One that had already been fired, and for all I knew, one of my patients or colleagues was dead as a result. The panicked screams had never stopped, but they were hardly audible over the ringing in my ears.

"Are you Valentine DiFiore?" the man asked in a voice that sounded like it had been put through a cheese grater.

My throat was tight, making it impossible to speak even if I wanted to. And that was probably for the best, considering I was pretty sure if I answered that question honestly, it would mean certain death.

Before I could say anything, I heard another gunshot and my body jolted violently. I felt nothing, but I knew from my brothers' accounts that it didn't mean anything. Getting shot was pretty much a rite of passage in the DiFiore family, and I was the only one who was still a "virgin," as they put it. Enzo had described it as feeling like being stabbed with a blade of ice, while Luca had merely shrugged and said he didn't remember what it felt like, considering his adrenaline had been pumping at the time.

When I saw a red dot appear on my would-be killer's temple, I was filled with confusion. The man's face went blank and he took a staggering step forward before he dropped altogether.

Standing behind him was the woman who had been watching me all day from the waiting room, her gun still smoking.

"What the fuck?" I murmured.

I heard the sound of gunfire from further down the hall, and she turned on her heel, ignoring me. There was the sound of ensuing chaos, and maybe it was adrenaline, unbridled stupidity, or both, but I ran out. By the time I was in the waiting room, I could see another guy in a black suit exchanging fire with the woman who had saved me. She ducked a split second before a bullet struck the wall where her head had been a moment before, then straightened again to fire another two at him. He took off and she ran after him.

My heart was hammering in my chest so hard it felt like it would explode, but I forced myself to act. I went to the doors they'd both gone through and barred them shut so no one else could get in. I could already hear sirens in the distance.

I felt like I was going to be sick. Or pass out. Or both. Someone's hand rested on my shoulder and I jolted.

"Valentine?" a familiar voice called, his grip tightening on my shoulder.

I looked up, still dazed and in shock. "Chris?" I croaked.

His gaze softened in relief, but it was short-lived. "Are you hurt?"

I shook my head, but my movements felt jerky and uncertain.

He frowned, like something about my response concerned him. Maybe I looked worse than I felt.

"Come on," he said. "Let's get you out of here."

I nodded again, following him, but I was still in a daze.

The next ten minutes—or maybe it was shorter, or longer; my mind wasn't fit for such distinctions—happened in a blur. I was vaguely aware of the fact that Chris brought me to the break room and kept checking on me, and I kept assuring him I was okay, even if it was pretty fucking far from the truth.

The ambulances came, and so did the police. I was still dazed when they wanted to talk to me, and I could hear Chris arguing with them about me being in shock, but they weren't hearing it. I was too out of it to keep track of what they could possibly know, and what they couldn't. It didn't really seem to matter, anyway. I regarded it all with a distant kind of apathy, knowing I was much too numb to care.

"For God's sake, he's barely even conscious," Chris spat. "His statement can wait."

"I'm afraid it can't," was the officer's response.

I felt like I had just woken up from a dream, and I had no idea what was going on, but I found myself the center of attention.

"Valentine?" Chris asked warily. "You with me?"

I nodded shakily. Even I wasn't exactly sure what the question was.

He seemed relieved, either way. "They're going to take you downtown to give them your statement. I'll call your brother, okay?"

"Okay," I said listlessly. Under normal circumstances, I knew that talking to the police was just about the worst thing I could do, but it didn't really seem to matter now. It wasn't like I could formulate a response to get out of it.

I didn't know why they even wanted to question me, considering I was pretty sure I hadn't done anything illegal, at least not at the moment—but I was guilty all the same. If that was what they wanted to ascertain, they didn't need to take me downtown for that. We could settle the matter, here and now.

4

MALCOLM

If there was one benefit to being a complete recluse outside of work, it was that when my phone did ring, I knew it was important. When I saw it was Silas on my caller ID, I knew it was probably a matter of life and death, considering my younger brother was not exactly the type who called just to chat.

After going five years without seeing each other at all, we had been in touch more often than usual. Oddly enough, him getting married had brought us closer together. At least, as close as two apathetic assholes lacking in the conscience and social skills department were capable of being.

"Excuse me," I told the coroner, stepping out of the morgue to take the phone call. "All right, what do you need?"

There was only indignant silence on the other end for a moment. "I can't call my brother to say hello?"

"You can, but you never do," I reminded him. "So I'll ask you again, what is it? You need me to bail your lover out of jail again?"

"Close, but not quite," Silas admitted. "It's his brother."

I blinked. "The married one or the stupid one?"

"The latter," he answered without missing a beat.

I groaned. "What did he do? Are we talking drunk and disorderly conduct, or murdering a prominent politician's son? Seems to be a family pastime."

"Fuck you, too, Malcolm," Enzo said in the background.

Silas snorted. "He didn't do anything, technically speaking. Did you not hear what happened at the hospital?"

"The hospital? I've been at a crime scene all morning. Double homicide."

"Sounds fun," Silas said without a trace of irony. "Is your radio off?"

"For a few minutes. The coroner always bitches about the noise when we're in the morgue."

"Well, you might want to turn it back on."

I turned the volume back up and listened to the flurry of activity on what had been a relatively quiet channel all of five minutes ago. There had been a fatal shooting at the hospital where Valentine worked, and I picked out the name "DiFiore" being muttered no less than five times.

Just then, one of the rookies from upstairs came running down the hall with a panicked look on her face. "Chief, the hospital—"

"I know," I barked, because I had never really been able to kick the habit of lashing out at the closest available target. "Go get Smith."

She hesitated for a split second before nodding shakily and disappearing around the corner.

I turned my attention back to the phone and muttered, "This had better not be one of yours. This is the last thing I need with election season right around the corner."

It was bad enough that my connection to the family was the most poorly kept secret in the industry. Granted, no one knew Silas was Ghost, but they knew he was my brother—and Lorenzo DiFiore's husband. That was enough of a conflict of interest, especially given everything that had gone down a couple of years ago with the untimely deaths of Lorenzo's father and Mark Rossi.

Untimely in the sense that they both should've been offed a long time ago, but still.

"Do you hear yourself?" Enzo demanded, sounding closer to the phone now. "You could at least try to pretend like you give a shit about the fact that innocent people are dead. All you care about is your fucking reputation. Which is a crock of shit, by the way. You're the most corrupt motherfucker there is, and the fact that you can wear that badge without bursting into flames is a damn divine comedy."

I rolled my eyes. He wasn't exactly wrong, but I didn't find his childish naïveté quite as charming as my brother did. Not by a long shot.

"Well, I can tell your little scamp of a brother isn't one of the vics since you're still coherent enough to bitch me out. You've been with my brother long enough you probably should've figured all this out by now," I replied, getting my coat. "And if you haven't, I feel sorry for you."

Enzo fell into silence, but I could imagine the look he was giving me. I was a lot fonder of him than he was of me, and truth be told, if he had liked me, I probably wouldn't have been. He, like most people, was under the impression that I was less of a full-blown sociopath than Silas was.

And in a way, he was right. I wasn't a sociopath at all. Silas was the way he was because he was traumatized from the shit we had gone through as children. I was the way I was because that was just the way I had come out. It was the one and only thing I had ever inherited from our bitch of a mother, and probably the useless sack of shit who had fathered us, wherever the fuck he was these days. I didn't care then, and I certainly didn't care now at the age of thirty-nine.

Growing up, I had always figured that Silas was better off without me. That maybe he could escape our family legacy if I wasn't around to taint him. Turned out, whether the source of the infection was innate or transmitted, there was no escaping it. Not for him. Not for me. He ended up giving me a run for my money half the time, with an appetite for chaos that superseded even my natural predilection for it.

We both found our own outlets. Our own ways to be productive, if not upstanding members of society. Even if we lived on the outskirts of it. I went into the law, he went above it. We were two sides of the same coin; two broken, twisted things that weren't fit for polite society, no matter how well we adopted the trappings of it when it suited us.

I thought that was something we would always have in common. And then Enzo came along, and Silas did the one thing I never thought either of us would be capable of–he changed. He fell in love.

He found someone who at once understood the darkness within him and, rather than being intimidated by it, was willing to take his hand and lead him through it. Not out of it, not entirely. Enzo had enough shadows of his own, but what their domestic life lacked in convention, it made up for in meaning. In warmth and humanity, and all those things that had once been so far out of reach for Silas.

And always would be for me.

"What do you need me to do, exactly?" I asked on my way outside.

"One of my men is on the scene. He told me they took Valentine to the station for questioning," Silas answered.

"You mean one of *my* men," I gritted out.

"I just need you to go down there and get him out," Silas said, conveniently ignoring my remark.

"Roll back a second. What do you mean, they took him to the station for questioning? If he didn't do anything, and he was just a victim in this bullshit, he could've said no."

Silas fell silent for a moment before replying, "He volunteered, as far as I can tell."

"He volunteered?" I echoed in disbelief as I climbed into my car and started the engine. "Are you fucking kidding me? What, has he been living in a shoebox all these years? You guys didn't teach him to know better than to go with the cops willingly?"

"Of course we did," Enzo snapped. "It's Valentine. He could get peer pressured by a toddler. Why the hell do you think I was so eager for him not to join the family business?"

It was a fair point. I sighed, running a hand down my face. I hadn't slept in the better part of three days, and it looked like that wasn't going to change anytime soon. "Look, I'm already knee-deep in bad PR with both of you. If he's innocent, there's nothing they can really do, anyway. Me going in there to spring my brother-in-law isn't exactly going to help with the corruption allegations."

It would be one thing if Silas was in direct trouble, or even Enzo, considering I knew how willing my brother was to throw himself on the pyre for his husband. But this was too tangential to risk that kind of involvement.

"You son of a bitch," Enzo snarled. "I told you he wasn't going to do shit," he said to Silas, sounding further away again.

"There's something else," Silas said, his tone darkening. I expected him to be pissy I wasn't helping, considering he couldn't say no to Enzo no matter how self-destructive that impulse was. Something about his tone had me on guard, though.

"What is it?" I asked warily.

"This didn't just happen out of the blue. An old friend of the family was brought to the hospital. He died, but not before he gave Valentine something that belongs to an acquaintance of ours."

"What the fuck are you talking about?" I demanded.

"Demon," he replied.

That name was enough to cause a visceral reaction in me. Silas fell silent because he knew exactly the effect that name would have. Pure, unadulterated, blinding rage. It was more emotion than I had felt since I could remember, and the last time, it'd been stirred by the same apparition.

"That's not possible," I said, sounding much calmer than I had any right to. "Demon is dead. He's been dead for years, and if you're just using that name to try to get me to intervene, you should fucking know better."

"I do," he said quietly. "And I'm not. I don't know if it's him, but at the very least, it's a bit too much of a coincidence, don't you think?"

I fell silent, trying to gather my thoughts, which was a lost cause when it came to the subject. I wasn't really a creature of instinct, but every rule had its exception. "What exactly happened? And I need you to be very specific."

"Like I said, an old friend of Valentine's came into the ER the other night. He was bleeding out from a gunshot wound to the chest, and it seems he knew he was going to die. He gave Valentine a chip, the kind some low-level mobster doesn't just have lying around. He claimed it has information that would be Demon's undoing, and considering the fact that it got him killed, I'm inclined to think he was right about that. Today, two men showed up at the hospital to kill Valentine."

"If he's still alive, that should be proof it wasn't Demon," I reasoned.

"I had someone watching him, obviously," said Silas.

"Of course you did," I said. "What, another one of my people, moonlighting as your entourage?"

"Please, I learned that lesson with Donovan. No offense, but I don't trust your vetting process," he quipped. "Sloan is former FBI."

"Of course," I said again.

"She intercepted the attack and killed one of the assassins," he continued. "She managed to chase the other one down, but by the time she found him in an alley, he was dead."

"Another hit?" I asked doubtfully.

"Cyanide capsule. No ID on either of the bodies. No fingerprints. Sound familiar?"

I paused to consider his words, still feeling like I had to be missing something. Like this was all just too fucking bizarre to be true.

"That's certainly his style. Do you really think it's him?"

"I don't know," Silas answered. "But I don't believe in coincidence. Not where that name is concerned."

"Yeah," I said gruffly. "Neither do I. Where is this chip? And what's on it?"

"I don't know," Silas admitted. "Just reading it is dangerous. It could be used to reverse trace our coordinates, and I can't risk using any of the equipment I have that could run it in case it's a Trojan exploit. For all we know, it could set off a tripwire if this really is Demon we're dealing with. At the very least, it's someone who wants us to believe it is, which is concerning in its own right."

He was right about that. Demon had been Silas's protege, which meant my brother would have taught him all the tools of the trade needed to cover his tracks. "Fine," I said. "I'll get the kid out. But in return, I want that chip—and when the time comes, if this *is* Demon, Valentine is my witness."

Silas didn't answer right away, but Enzo was quick to chime in. "Bullshit," he snapped. The protective big brother, as always. I could relate to an extent, but it didn't make it any less annoying. "He's not going to be a pawn in your investigation. He's been through enough."

"Love, please," Silas pleaded in that gentle tone I had only ever heard him use with Enzo. Hell, I hadn't even thought he was capable of it, and the fact that it seemed genuine was all the more bewildering. Granted, that tenderness was still reserved for one man alone, but it was incredible, regardless. "If you trust nothing else, believe that Malcolm isn't going to let anything happen to Valentine if he thinks there is even a chance he could lead us to Demon."

He was right about that, too.

Enzo hesitated. "I know Silas has a history with this freak, but what's the deal with you two?" he asked me. "Did he name himself after you or something?"

"No," I snapped. The name came from his press during his serial killer days. Before Silas 'scouted' him.

So Silas had told Enzo the truth. Or at least part of it. That in itself was interesting.

My half of the truth was a bit more complicated.

"Demon killed his husband," Silas answered for me before I could tell him to shut the hell up. "Just trust me on this. Please."

More silence.

"Fine," Enzo muttered. "But if anything happens to Val, I'm holding you responsible."

With that, I could hear footsteps as he stormed off.

"Trouble in paradise, brother?" I asked dryly, still pissed he felt like he had the right to tell anyone—even his husband—about Owen.

Silas sighed, heavily enough to cause static on the phone. "He's just worried about his brother. So am I, for that matter."

"I told you, I'll get the kid out," I muttered. "Protecting him from himself is going to be the hard part, from what little I know of him."

"You're not wrong about that," Silas said in a flat tone. "But I was talking about you."

His words caught me off guard. "Just give me the chip, and try to keep your pet mobster and his family out of the papers for twenty-four hours if you think you can manage it," I said before hanging up.

The truth was, he was probably right to be worried. Not for my sake, of course, but because if Demon really was still alive somehow, I wasn't going to stop until he was gone.

Even if I had to tear the world apart in the process.

5

VALENTINE

I had been sitting in a spartan room surrounded by three suits for the better part of twenty minutes, maybe thirty, and so far, the questions had been more focused on my family than the tragedy that had just happened.

As shaken as I was, I had managed not to give them any damning evidence yet. The fact that the woman to my right in the light gray pantsuit—who seemed to be their superior—kept asking about Enzo's role in Dad's death and that of Geo's father was proof enough this was a mistake, though.

I had thought being Malcolm's brother-in-law would give me some slack, but that seemed to be the opposite of the case, if anything. And it wasn't like I could say, "Excuse me, do you know who I am?" Because for one thing, they definitely did, and that was the reason I was here. And for another, that was a surefire way to make them hate me even more than they clearly already did.

"Don't you think it's a little strange?" Gray Suit asked, folding her arms as she loomed over me from the other side of the table. I wasn't sure if the others were supposed to be playing good cop or if they were just there for backup. Maybe just to make sure I didn't make a dash for the door. "You, the youngest son of one of the most infamous crime families in the city, just so happened to be at the center of a mass shooting—and yet you have no idea what might've precipitated it?"

I swallowed hard. "Only one of the most? Man, we've backslidden."

Gray Suit did not seem to find that funny. Neither did her flunkies.

"I'm glad you can find a sense of humor in all this," she said with a dangerous smirk, planting her hands on the table as she leaned in. "But I guess I'd be laughing, too, if I had the police chief in my back pocket."

"Yeah, I don't think we're as close as you seem to believe," I told her. The whole 'angry lady interrogating me with handcuffs dangling off her belt' situation was definitely a scenario I had been in before, but it was only in my fantasies, and she was usually wearing more leather. It was a lot more fun in my head.

Before she could say anything else, the door flew open. I wasn't sure who I was expecting, really. Part of me was kind of hoping for Enzo or Luca, and hell, I would've even been relieved to see Silas.

Okay, maybe relieved was an overstatement, but I wouldn't have hated it as much as usual.

At the moment, though, I was starting to feel like I was in some police procedural drama as Malcolm burst into the room, wearing a three-piece suit minus the matching beige jacket. Only he could make suspenders look cool. To be fair, it helped that the guy was built like a brick house.

Or was that just for women? Pretty sure he resembled a literal brick house more than any woman I had ever met, considering the guy was six and a half feet tall and wall-to-wall solid muscle. He looked like he could snap me in half, and when his eyes landed on me, he kind of looked like he was thinking about it.

I gulped.

"What the hell is this?" Malcolm demanded, looking between us. I could tell the question was directed at Gray Suit, though, not me, so I stayed quiet, not eager to make either of them more aware of my presence than I had to.

"Chief Whitlock," she said, rising back from the table. "What a surprise."

Her voice wasn't just dripping with sarcasm, it was saturated.

Malcolm stared her down, giving her a look so filthy I was kind of impressed she managed to withstand it without cringing. I wasn't quite that stalwart.

"You want to tell me why I've got my top detectives questioning a shooting victim like he's a fucking suspect when there's a double homicide and a drug raid going on downtown?" he demanded.

The other two detectives both stood from the table and backed up a little, looking warily between their superiors. Neither said a word, though, and I decided it was wise to follow their lead.

"Shooting victim who seems to find himself at the center of a lot of the city's biggest crimes," she said pointedly, folding her arms. "I can't help but be a bit curious."

"The city doesn't pay you to be curious," Malcolm said, stalking forward until he was toe-to-toe with her. "It pays you to do your fucking job, so I suggest you get out there and do that. All of you."

There was a further stare-down standoff, but the others seemed to see the writing on the wall before she did and quickly exited the room. Gray Suit looked over her shoulder, scowling at the comrades who had abandoned her.

Ouch.

"I'm sorry, did I stutter?" Malcolm asked in a seething tone. "Do I need to repeat myself again, Detective Miller?"

She clenched her jaw, anger burning in her eyes. "No, Chief. You made yourself perfectly clear."

With that, she stomped toward the door and threw it open. She paused to look back at me, giving me a dirty look. "You've got yourself friends in all kinds of places,

DiFiore. You better keep it that way," she said before leaving, slamming the door behind her.

Yeah, that wasn't menacing at all.

"Malcolm," I said, standing. "How did you know I was here?"

"That was easy," he said, taking a few menacing strides toward me. That was all it took for him to clear the room. I backed up, but found myself trapped against the wall beneath his withering stare. "I was just thinking to myself, what would be the dumbest possible shit Valentine DiFiore could've gotten himself into today? And it led me right here."

I shrank back, feeling my throat growing tight. "My brother?"

"No shit," he snapped, pushing on my shoulder hard enough to pin me back to the wall. "What the hell were you thinking, going with the cops? Are you a two-year-old, or a fucking mob boss's son?"

I didn't answer, because I was pretty sure he didn't actually expect me to.

He blew a puff of air through his nostrils like an angry bull. He continued to stare at me for a few long moments before he said, "What did you say to her?"

"Nothing," I said quickly. When I could tell he didn't believe me, I added, "I swear, I didn't. She just asked me a bunch of shit about my brother, and Dad, but I played dumb."

"Yeah, I imagine that would be easy for you," he snapped.

I grimaced, but it wasn't like it was anything I hadn't heard before. I wasn't sure if he was expecting me to defend myself or what, but when I didn't, he just heaved an exasperated sigh.

"Come on," he said, jerking his head for me to follow him as he opened the door. "Let's get you out of here."

"I can leave?" I asked doubtfully.

"You were never being held," he said pointedly. "What, did you think they were just going to admit that?"

"I don't know," I mumbled, feeling like an idiot as I followed him out of the station, trying not to look at anyone even though I could feel all eyes on us. I could understand why Malcolm was so pissed. This was definitely attention he wouldn't want. I was sure he had enough qualms about being connected to our family in any way. There were enough rumors about him as it was, and corruption was just the tip of the iceberg. He had friends in high places and in low ones, and even though no one knew what Silas did, Malcolm had garnered enough of a reputation of his own.

I followed him outside and into the parking lot. I wasn't sure what I was expecting him to drive, but definitely not the shiny black Tesla in the spot marked Chief of Police.

"Damn, civil service pays better than I thought," I murmured. He shot me a look of irritation, and I smiled stiffly. "Right. Too much talking."

Malcolm just rolled his eyes before climbing in and starting the engine. I hopped into the passenger's seat and buckled in. I was glad I had when he started driving fast enough to break the sound barrier.

To be fair, it wasn't like he had to worry about getting pulled over. I was used to a world of double standards, and it looked like the other side of the law was the same.

I looked down at my hands, and when I realized they were still shaking, I quickly shoved them under my thighs. That wasn't pathetic at all. I didn't know why, but I didn't want to look weak in front of this guy. I figured it was just because he was Silas's brother. That was certainly reason enough.

It was bad enough everyone already saw me as Enzo and Luca's soft, weak little brother. Even worse, they were right. The last few days had taught me that, if nothing else.

I could feel myself being watched, and when I looked over, sure enough, Malcolm was glancing at me. "You're lucky to be alive, you know."

"Yeah," I said. "Lucky."

He frowned. "Whose idea was it to let you go into medicine, anyway?"

I bristled at his remark, even if I was fucking terrified of him. "What do you mean, whose idea was it? You make it sound like I needed to ask my brother's permission."

"He is the don," he reasoned. "Isn't that kind of how it works?"

"Maybe in some families," I muttered. "Not ours."

"You sure about that?" he challenged. "Or do they just let you do whatever the hell you want to keep you out of the way?"

His words felt like a punch in the gut and hit a lot harder than I wanted to admit, even to myself. Especially considering the fact that I didn't even know this guy, so what the hell did it matter what he thought of me?

Maybe it was the fact that deep down, he was echoing what I had always thought myself. What I feared, and what I knew, even if I wanted to convince myself otherwise.

Malcolm sighed heavily. "Look, I'm sorry. It's been a rough day, and this isn't the way I wanted to end it."

"That makes two of us," I mumbled.

I realized we had missed the turn for Johnny's place, and I hadn't actually told him I wasn't staying at the house right now. Not at all, if I could help it.

"Actually, do you think you could drop me off at my cousin's?"

"Your cousin? Why? I'm taking you home."

"I'm not staying at the house," I answered, not wanting to get into it any further than that.

"Why?" he demanded.

I set my jaw. Great. Another interrogation. "Because I'm not, okay?"

"What, did you and your brother have a falling out?" he asked, his tone making it clear he thought I was just being a stubborn child.

"Yeah. Over your brother, actually," I said pointedly.

I expected him to make another smartass remark, but instead, he just snorted a laugh. "I'm surprised it took this long."

I sank back into the bucket seat. For an overpriced hunk of steel, at least it was comfortable.

"I just really don't feel like dealing with either of them right now."

"Sorry, but I'm under strict instructions to deliver you to your brother, and quite frankly, that's probably for the best."

"I'm not a fucking child!" I snapped.

He raised an eyebrow, like I had just proved his point. "If that were true, you wouldn't need to be told not to talk to the police."

"Says the police," I gritted out.

He just smirked and turned his full attention back to the road. If we weren't going a billion miles an hour, I might've been tempted to jump out of the car, just on principle.

"You know, this is basically kidnapping," I said.

"Oh, yeah? Call the cops."

I growled in frustration. Today just kept getting better.

I decided arguing with him any further was a moot point. I was just going to leave as soon as we arrived, and if Enzo gave me any shit for it, well, it wouldn't be the first time I'd snuck out and run off.

I was about to get out of the car when we finally pulled into the driveway, but Sergeant Douchebag switched on the childproof locks before I could open the door.

"Don't even think about running," he said. "I'll have every badge in the county after your ass."

I shot him a venomous glare. "Yeah, seems like a great use of taxpayer money."

He ignored me, but he unlocked the door. I got out, resisting the urge to prove him right by slamming it behind me. It was tempting, though. Petty, but tempting.

Before we could even reach the front door, it flew open and, unsurprisingly, Enzo was waiting on the other side to yank me past the threshold.

"Thank God," he whispered, looking me over and taking my face in his hands like a fretting mother. "Are you hurt?"

"No," I said, shrugging him off. "I'm fine."

I could tell he didn't believe it from the frown on his face, but he glanced up as Malcolm came up behind me.

"Thank you for bringing him home," he said, stiffening enough that I wondered if they had gotten into it before or something. Over what, I couldn't imagine. They were certainly a united front when it came to pissing me off.

"You don't need to thank me," said Malcolm. "Just remember your end of the deal."

Enzo grunted in acknowledgement, stepping back to let the other man inside.

"What deal?" I asked, reluctant to venture in any farther than the landing. I didn't want to be here. I was nursing the migraine of the century, my ears were still ringing from the damn gunshots, and I kept feeling like I was going to black out. I wasn't sure if it was from the surge of adrenaline, exhaustion from the interrogation, or shock. Hell, I wasn't even sure I'd fully recovered from the shock of Robbie's death, for that matter.

So much had happened in such a short period of time, and all of it felt enough for one lifetime and then some. I couldn't even keep my thoughts straight. I felt like I was on the brink of a meltdown at any minute, and even if I didn't know what form that meltdown would take, I certainly didn't want to be around them when it happened.

Neither Enzo nor Malcolm said a word, but Silas walked in right then, having us all outdressed in one of his obnoxiously stylish white suits. I doubted he even bought them off the rack. Probably had them custom made from magic silkworms or some shit. That seemed like exactly the kind of smug, ostentatious thing he would do.

No, I wasn't bitter at all.

"Look what the cat dragged in," Silas remarked, because he always had to have some smug, cool one-liner in his back pocket. "I hope you know you're not going out unsupervised until you're old enough to collect a pension."

"What, are you my father now?" I shot back.

"Of course not," he scoffed, his hands tucked into the pockets of his pants. "I'm alive."

I started to reply, but my jaw just kind of hung open. "Wow. You're a cunt, but I'll hand it to you, that was a good one."

"Silas!" Enzo scolded.

"What?" Silas asked in an innocent tone. "Too soon?"

Enzo just rolled his eyes and turned his attention back to me. "He's right, incidentally. Do you have any idea how fucking worried we were when we heard about the shooting?"

"Yeah, I'm sure he was broken up about it," I said dryly, looking over at Silas.

"Believe it or not, I've actually grown quite fond of you, precocious little imp that you are," Silas remarked.

I frowned. "By far the most insulting part of that is the implication that you like me."

He chuckled. That was rare. At least, it was rare for anyone other than Enzo to make him laugh.

"Well?" Malcolm asked impatiently, like he clearly had better places to be. Not that I could blame him for that. This wasn't my idea of a fun time, either. The sooner he left, the sooner I could leave, even if my bike was still at the hospital.

"Here you are," Silas said, reaching out to drop something into Malcolm's waiting palm. I wasn't sure why I thought it would be cash. Like either of these assholes didn't have bottomless pockets from all the bullshit they got up to.

When I realized it was the microchip, I gaped in disbelief. "What the hell? First you take it, then you use it as a literal bargaining chip with your brother?" I cried, freshly enraged. "Are you fucking serious right now?"

"Valentine, calm down," Enzo pleaded. "I can explain."

"Explain what?" I spat. "This is clearly a game to all of you. Robbie is dead, and that chip is the only hope of finding the motherfucker who did it!"

"That's the idea," Malcolm remarked. "And if that's what you really want, be glad it's out of your hands. I'll take it from here."

"Fuck you," I growled.

"Val..." Enzo warned.

The cop just gave him a lopsided smirk. "It's fine. I don't take the tantrums of children personally."

"I'll fucking kill you," I seethed, finding myself blinded by rage and out of control for the second time in a matter of days. Judging from the way Malcolm's eyes widened in surprise just slightly enough to be noticeable as I flew toward him, he wasn't expecting it.

That made two of us.

I had barely made contact, shoving into Malcolm's chest with both hands, and the pain shooting through my forearms was already making me regret it.

What, was he made of actual bricks?

I took a swing at him anyway. Because I was apparently either suicidal—and a little bit homicidal—or I had lost my mind. Maybe a little of both.

The punch didn't connect like it had with Chris. Maybe I was getting cocky just because I had managed to sucker punch a guy twice as big as me, but when Malcolm gripped my fist tight and pinned me against the wall, I realized I wasn't just playing outside my league. I wasn't even playing the right sport.

His other hand closed around my throat, gripping it just tight enough that I had trouble breathing. Although that could've been the adrenaline kicking in late. I wasn't sure how I even had any left at this point.

His smug smirk split into a devious grin. In that instant, any mystery about why they called him "Devil" evaporated. I was pretty sure if you looked up "sinister" in the dictionary, his picture was right there next to the definition, and his brother was filed under every synonym.

"You know, under any other circumstances, I'd be more than happy to have let you get in that hit and take it as *carte blanche* to use you as a punching bag, but I don't need to hear bitching for the next decade, so I'm going to chalk it up to what you've been through and let it go."

"Hey, get off him," Enzo snarled, grabbing Malcolm's arm and yanking him away from me. I was pretty sure the only reason he succeeded was because Malcolm allowed it. He had already made his point, and successfully dominated and humiliated me at the same time.

"That's quite enough," said Silas. He gave me a scolding look. "That goes for both of you."

"Are you really good with this?" I demanded, looking at Enzo. I pointed at Malcolm and Silas. "Letting two complete psychos have control over the chip when innocent people's lives are at stake?"

"If the alternative is you getting yourself killed, then yeah," Enzo shot back. "I'm pretty damn okay with it, Val. Do you even see yourself? Running off, getting in fights... this isn't you. You're clearly not okay. You never should've gone back to the hospital, and I never should've let you leave."

"Let me?" I snapped. "What, you think you can just control everything because you're the head of the family now?"

"Yeah," he said pointedly. "That's exactly what I think, because that's how it is."

I gave a dry laugh, shaking my head. "Well, in that case, you can consider me no longer a part of it."

Enzo gave me a look of frustration, but I could tell he didn't take me seriously. "Don't say something you're going to regret in the morning."

"I'm not just saying it. I mean it. I'm done with you and everyone else treating me like some idiot fuck-up you're all burdened with," I said before I could stop myself. I wasn't sure I wanted to, anyway. Everything I'd buried for so long was finally bubbling to the surface.

"Who said that?" Enzo challenged. "Because I can guarantee it wasn't me or Luca."

"You didn't need to say it out loud. It's obvious enough," I answered. "It always has been, but especially lately. I don't know why you give a shit where I go or what I do when you'd clearly be better off without me."

Maybe everyone would.

My words seemed to take Enzo by surprise, and I was kind of surprised that I'd actually said them out loud myself. I wasn't usually so blunt, not even in my own mind.

For a few moments, he just stood there staring at me, and it was long enough for me to resent the hell out of myself for saying anything at all.

"Is that really what you think?" Enzo asked. He sounded like I had just punched him in the gut, for reasons beyond my ability to fathom.

I shrugged, my arms folded over my chest because I felt vulnerable, and not for the first time that day. "Are you really going to tell me that's not the truth?"

"Of course it's not true," he said in a gruff tone. "You're my brother. And the fact that you're even thinking like that is just proof you shouldn't be out there on your own."

"I'm not by myself. I was staying at Johnny's," I muttered.

"Yeah, I know," Enzo said pointedly. "Why do you think I didn't have your ass hauled back here immediately? Johnny is worried about you, too."

I felt an immediate twinge of betrayal. "Johnny ratted me out?"

"He's worried," Enzo countered, as if that made it better. "We all are. You're not okay after what happened, and trust me, I get it. I wouldn't be, either, but it's my responsibility to look out for everyone in this family, and sometimes that means knowing when to take someone off the roster. The fact that you work on the outside doesn't change that."

"What are you talking about?" I asked. The way he was talking was scaring me. Yeah, sometimes I resented feeling like an afterthought to my brothers. I wanted them to take me seriously. I wanted them to include me, at least in the ways they could, but that didn't mean I wanted them making decisions for me. Or micromanaging my life, which was more what Enzo seemed to be leaning toward.

"You're not going back to the hospital," Silas answered. "Need I remind you, this time, they were explicitly after *you*."

"How did you know that?" I asked warily.

He raised an eyebrow. "What, did you think the nice lady was just a vigilante who happened to be in the neighborhood to save your ass?"

Of course she was one of his. Looking back, it was kind of hard to see how I hadn't put that together before. In fairness to myself, I hadn't really had a whole lot of time to think about much of anything, and I was obviously still very much in fight-or-flight mode. Fight wasn't really working, so I had hoped flight would pan out better.

"Come on, Valentine," Enzo said. "You can't go back, at least not right now. Not when you're being literally fucking hunted. This Demon guy obviously knows Robbie gave you that chip, or at least suspected enough to shoot up the hospital. How are you supposed to treat people if you just being there is a risk to you and them?"

I winced, but he wasn't saying anything that wasn't true. Logically, I knew he was right. I couldn't go back, not now. Not until Demon was dead or in a deep enough hole.

It was already my fault those people were dead. How many more? Hell, I probably wouldn't even have a job to go back to, and Chris would be a thousand percent in the right. Knowing something logically and being ready to come to terms with it were two completely different things, though. For me, at least.

"I know," I said. "But that's just all the more reason for me not to be here. If he knows where I work, he knows where I was, and this will be his next stop."

That was another realization that probably should've been obvious, but it had only just occurred to my chaos-addled brain.

Enzo frowned, and I could tell he was about to argue. Before he had the chance, Silas chimed in, "He's right about that."

Well, it wasn't a good sign if *he* was agreeing with me. Now I was second-guessing myself.

"About what?" Enzo demanded.

"Him being here is a risk—to you, to him, and to everyone else in the family," Silas explained. I was sure he could tell Enzo was about to argue because he added, "I'm not suggesting we send him out into the wilds, pet. Just that he should be in protective custody. Like any other witness."

"Witness?" I echoed warily. "What the hell is that supposed to mean?"

"You're the one who spoke with Demon's victim directly," Silas reasoned. "You're also his primary target at the moment. If I know my brother, he's not just going to be satisfied with torturing Demon for a couple of hours and then putting a bullet in his skull. He's going to want him to rot in prison for the rest of his life, or at least until he gets bored of making him suffer and arranges a hit from the inside."

I glanced over at Malcolm, who had been notably silent, watching his reaction to everything Silas had just said. Judging from the fact that he seemed unaffected, it was an accurate enough assessment.

"In that case," Silas continued, "you'll be a literal witness. And the fact that you're only useful to Malcolm if you're alive should be a comfort."

"Touching," Enzo quipped. "But he has a point."

"So what are you saying?" I asked, not loving the fact that my fate was presently up to the person I liked even less than his more sadistic brother.

"I'm saying you're going to be staying with Malcolm for the foreseeable future."

"Is he now?" Malcolm challenged.

"It's the only reasonable thing to do," said Silas. He had clearly made up his mind for everyone.

All I could do was hope that Malcolm would find the idea as odious as I did. He actually stood a chance of being listened to, as much as that pissed me off.

Instead, he just grunted in acknowledgment. "Sure. It's not like I have a city to watch over or anything."

"Wonderful. It's settled, then," Silas said, completely sidestepping his brother's sarcasm. Judging from the fact that Malcolm looked irritated, it was a good strategy. Good to know Silas could get under even his own brother's skin.

"I don't know," Enzo said. I knew better than to get my hopes up that he was on my side for once, though.

Silas put a hand on his shoulder. "Malcolm won't let any harm come to him, love."

Enzo didn't look convinced. "Normally, I'd ask for your word, but I don't think that's something you really concern yourself with," he said to Malcolm.

Malcolm snorted. "If you don't want to take my word, I guess you'll just have to take his," he said, nodding toward his brother.

Enzo sighed in resignation. Not a good sign for me. "Fine."

"Enzo!" I cried.

"Enough," he said in a stern tone, his eyes piercing. "This isn't up for debate. You're going with Malcolm until we can get this thing figured out. I came close enough to losing you already, and I'm not going to let that happen again."

I gritted my teeth in frustration, but I knew that look. Once it was there, there was no convincing him otherwise. "Sure. Why not? Why don't you send me to my room while you're at it?"

"Don't tempt me," said Enzo. "It's not forever. I'll bring your things over later."

I stalked back toward the door, too pissed to stick around and say any goodbyes. I could try to run, but between the three of them, I knew that was destined to go as spectacularly as everything else lately. Instead, I went straight to the car to wait for Malcolm, which didn't take long.

He seemed like he hadn't expected not to have to hunt me down, but I knew when I had been bested, and I knew there was no point in pretending otherwise. Not right now. Either way, I was no longer going to be under the watchful eyes of Enzo and his personal enforcer. I could regroup and figure out the rest later.

I was silent on the ride to Malcolm's place, which seemed to suit him fine. Eventually, we pulled up to the swankiest apartment building I had ever seen in my life. I wasn't sure why I was surprised. Malcolm clearly had a taste for the finer things in life, and he certainly wasn't working on a civil servant's budget. Probably kickbacks from politicians and anyone else who could afford to pay him off. Dad used to love paying off law enforcement, and Malcolm would've been a dream come true.

I followed him into the building and up a glass elevator that led to the very top floor.

"Penthouse suite," I remarked. "A bit ritzy for a guy with a government salary, isn't it?"

He just gave me a look, like he wasn't going to dignify that with a response.

When we made it to his apartment, it was as unnecessarily large as I had anticipated. It was a wide open, modern layout, with stainless steel appliances and furniture that looked like it cost a fortune. Not a small one, either.

"It's a one bedroom, so you can sleep on the couch," he announced. "There's a bathroom on the left, and I'll try to find something for you to wear until Enzo brings your shit."

I looked down at my clothes, noticing the blood spatter on my shirt for the first time. The sooner I got out of these clothes, the better.

Of all the things, that was what felt like it might push me over the edge. I felt nauseous and lightheaded, but passing out almost would've been a relief. At least then I might get some sleep.

I just nodded and walked into the bathroom to turn on the shower. I stripped out of my clothes as swiftly as possible and stuffed them into the wastebasket. I could probably get the blood out if I tried, but I didn't want to look at it again.

I climbed into the stall, letting the scalding barrage of water cascade down over my body. I felt like I was in danger of passing out, so I pressed one hand against the shower wall and the other over my mouth just in time to muffle the strangled sound that escaped my throat.

I wasn't sure if it was a sob or a laugh, but either way, I was pretty sure I was on the verge of hysterical. It was the first time since the shooting that I had been alone, and it was like the floodgates just unleashed.

Even as the tears cascaded down my face, I resented them. I resented my weakness. I resented the fact that I couldn't do anything. I couldn't stop what had happened at the hospital. I couldn't help Robbie, so what made me think I stood a chance at avenging him? I couldn't even protect myself.

I sank to my knees, doubling over as I tried hard to keep myself from making any sound. There was a scream inside me that had been threatening to come out for longer than I cared to admit, and I knew everything—including my sanity—depended on keeping it there. Stuffing it down and pushing it into the furthest, darkest corners of myself, along with all the other things I couldn't bear to deal with.

Robbie.

Dad.

The hole in my chest that just kept getting bigger and bigger, until I wasn't sure there would be anything left that it hadn't claimed eventually. And I couldn't help but think maybe that was a good thing. I couldn't run away from my problems because a good number of them were inside me, threatening to hollow me out until there was nothing left, and maybe the next best thing was just... letting them.

6

MALCOLM

Valentine had been staying with me for the better part of a week, and despite my initial reservations, he hadn't been half the nightmare roommate I'd expected. I had the place bugged, obviously, with a camera set up in the living room to send an alert the second he went within two feet of the front door, and I'd wired the security cameras on the rest of the floor as well.

That last part wasn't exactly legal—hell, neither was filming a guy twenty-four seven without his knowledge or consent—but after the way the little fucker had behaved, he was lucky there weren't cameras in the bathroom, too.

Besides, if he didn't try to run off, there wouldn't be any reason for me to check the footage more often than the occasional random audit. So far, he'd obeyed my orders to stick to the apartment and the pool I shared with a handful of the other penthouse suites. There was already a gym inside my apartment, but despite the fact that he had to be going stir crazy, he hadn't made any use of that.

The kid was soft in every possible regard. I assumed he had at least some tolerance for actual work if he'd made his way through med school, but then again, he was a DiFiore. Enzo might easily have paid them off. I wouldn't put it past him, either. They all treated Valentine like the spoiled brat he was. Even their dead father had used kid gloves on him, from all I could gather from what Silas had told me.

It was easy to see why. If Enzo was a lost puppy, Valentine was a neurotic kitten, ready to hiss at every junkyard dog who could wipe him from existence with a single bite. The kind of foolhardy little morsel who was a beacon to every predator within a hundred-mile radius.

I would know, considering the fact that I'd wanted to devour him from the moment I first laid eyes on him, still wide-eyed and trembling from his dear daddy's gruesome death at the hand of my brother.

It was a problem.

Especially now that the kitten was my responsibility to keep alive. Keeping him out of Demon's reach was only half the battle, and I was half certain Valentine posed even more of a threat to himself. But neither of them had anything on all the filthy, bloodthirsty impulses the boy had stirred within me.

Because what could possibly go wrong when you put the wolf in charge of the lamb?

That evening, I came home early since the majority of the neverending work I still had to take care of could more efficiently be managed on my couch from a laptop with a fifth of scotch in hand. My prisoner-slash-houseguest's brother was bitching about me watching him more closely, which meant Silas was bitching at me, so I figured I might as well appease them in the process.

It had nothing to do with the fact that I wanted to be near Valentine. It wasn't like I had even made any attempt to speak to him in the six days he'd been with me. He was more like a caged bird than anything, really. Observation was enough.

For now.

When I walked into my apartment and didn't see him occupying any of his typical spots, from the living room sectional to the kitchen where he was usually eating and drinking me out of house and home, I felt a twinge of uncertainty.

I checked the gym and he wasn't there, either, so I glanced at my phone to make sure I hadn't missed any motion alerts. Nothing.

Then, I noticed the light under my bedroom door was on.

He wouldn't dare...

Who was I kidding? He'd thrown a punch at me and actually thought he could get away with it, so why would snooping be past him?

It wasn't like he'd find anything of any use. I wasn't keeping the chip in my sock drawer, but if he did go looking there, he was bound to find some other things he'd come to regret.

Things I might actually have an excuse to use on him now. The thought alone was a thrilling prospect.

I flung the door open and walked in, expecting to find him rummaging through my things, but I wasn't prepared to find him at my bathroom sink, clad only in the small white towel wrapped low around his waist and drying off his long, pretty boy hair with a hand towel.

Holy fucking shit.

It was the first time I had ever seen Valentine anything other than fully clothed, and in his scrubs and street clothes, he just looked like a lean guy in his mid-twenties. It turned out, beneath the baggy sweatshirts and ripped skinny jeans, he was hiding a toned, muscular physique fit for a fucking runway.

He was still lean, in a willowy, almost elegant kind of way, but there was far more definition to his biceps and his chest than I had anticipated. He had perfectly sculpted abs tapering down to the cut of his Apollo's belt, luring the eye to travel down to the base of his cock, just visible above the folded towel. Droplets of water and steam gave his pale skin an iridescent sheen, and the way his honey-colored eyes grew wide with alarm as he turned to face me ignited a flurry of lust and hunger the likes of which I hadn't felt in years.

Maybe never.

"Malcolm?" My name came out as a croak as he dropped the smaller towel, backing up against the sink. My mind was already working overtime conjuring up images of bending him over the counter and tearing off the towel to reveal the perfectly round ass I knew to be waiting underneath. Those tight jeans were good for something, after all.

The fear in his voice told me I had let the filter slip for an instant. Just long enough to give him a glimpse of the predator waiting beneath.

My heart was hammering in my chest as loudly as his had to be, for very different reasons. I knew the look in his eyes as soon as it lit them. Fear. The primal instinct of prey in the presence of a hunter. A monster.

He might not have recognized it consciously, but his instinct was telling him a different story. I could tell from the way he jolted as I walked forward, a soft gasp parting his lips as I pinned him between my body and the sink.

"You want to tell me what you're doing in my room?" I demanded, my voice guttural and full of lust that sounded enough like rage for plausible deniability. Those two switches had always been a bit crossed for me.

He opened his mouth to respond, but as his eyes traveled down my face, all that came out was a strangled sound. Like a mouse squeaking under the paw of a cat. It was all I could do not to sink my claws into him then and there, and I was losing sight of why I had to restrain myself with each second that passed. With each barely visible flutter of his jugular vein beneath the column of his neck, stretched back as if to put as much distance between us as possible.

"Th-the other shower is broken," he stammered, like he was trying to get the words out as fast as possible. "I didn't think it was a big deal."

"Broken?" I echoed, disappointed he had an excuse, however flimsy it was.

"It's not draining," he eked out. "See for yourself."

I narrowed my eyes, reluctantly taking a step back from him. There was a void where the heat of his body had recently been, and my elation was already turning to disappointment as I realized I couldn't exactly justify punishing him for something so mundane.

Could I?

I'd justified worse to myself before. For far less reward, at that.

"It's probably not draining because it's full of your fucking hair," I said pointedly, taking the opportunity to reach out and draw a thick section of it through my thumb and forefinger. Even wet, it was as soft and silky as I'd anticipated.

God, how I wanted to dig my fingers into it, yank his head back from behind, and pound him into fucking oblivion.

"What's wrong with my hair?" he asked, combing his fingers through the tresses I had just touched and looking at them warily.

It's too hard to resist pulling, I thought. What I said was, "Stay out of my room. And don't touch my fucking things unless you ask permission first."

He swallowed audibly. "Okay. Jeez, I'm sorry. It won't happen again."

I paused to consider whether his apology was good enough. Unfortunately, I determined it was. He'd have to fuck up a lot more brazenly than that for me to be able to justify turning him over my knee and whipping his perfect ass red and raw the way I wanted to. It wasn't the kind of self-restraint I usually would've bothered with, but he wasn't just some twink I had procured for the weekend's entertainment, he was Enzo's precocious little brother. He was the one man I couldn't take my fill of, because the consequences of that couldn't be paid off and swept under the rug.

"You can use my shower until I can get someone up here to have the other one fixed," I finally said, keeping my voice stern and authoritative, relatively free of the scathing hunger lurking beneath. "Just don't touch anything else, and I'll know if you do."

"How?" he asked doubtfully.

I gave him a hard look and it took all of two seconds for him to melt under it.

"Never mind," he mumbled. "I won't. Um. Can I go now, or…?"

He pointed to the door, and I realized I was still crowding him against the sink. Not half as much as I wanted to, but I was definitely too close for his comfort.

Not that a full room's distance between us would have been enough under any other circumstances.

I stepped aside to let him pass, and the sight of him walking past my bed was enough to reignite the impulse of the chase. I had never been a particularly imaginative person, but my mind's eye was running wild with the thought of throwing him onto the bed and having my way with him. From that first startled cry to the subsequent moans of pleasure and pain I could draw from him in such perfect symphony, if given the chance.

Before he could slip from the room entirely, I called after him, "Wait."

He froze in his tracks, looking at me over his shoulder in nervous anticipation. "Yeah?" he asked, his voice quivering.

I could all but taste his fear. "Your brother called today to check on you. He wants to visit, and he says you haven't been returning his calls."

A hard edge came into the boy's gaze. "There's a reason for that," he muttered.

"He's looking out for you," I told him. A fact he should be grateful for, considering it was the only thing standing between him and me.

"He's trying to control me," Valentine said.

"There's not always a difference," I shot back.

He frowned, and I could tell he wanted to argue. Maybe he was learning, because he asked instead, "Has there been any progress on the case?"

It took me a second to realize what he was talking about. Demon should have been the foremost if not the only thought in my mind, but for the time being, he had taken a backseat to more prurient subjects.

"No," I answered. "Not yet."

His brow furrowed deeper in disappointment. "Did you at least figure out what's on the microchip?"

His question grated on my nerves, namely the fact that he felt he had the right to question me at all, but I pushed it aside. "I'm still working on it. It's heavily encrypted, and I can't exactly put cryptography on the case."

"Silas can't do it?" he challenged. "He's a mastermind at everything else."

"Once upon a time, before he had a whole outfit, I'm the one Silas went to for this kind of shit," I informed him. "What, you think I got where I am on charisma?"

"Definitely not that," Valentine muttered under his breath. He seemed to immediately regret it, because he added, "Why do you even want this guy so bad, anyway? I'm pretty sure you don't give a fuck about some dead mobster."

"You're right," I said. "I don't. You don't need to worry about my reasons, all you need to do is what you're told.

You want the guy who killed your friend to pay? That's how."

"That's bullshit," he said, growing bolder. "You can't expect me to trust you when I don't even know what your motivation is."

"My motivation?" I chuckled. "Frankly, kid, I don't give a shit what you think about my motivation, or whether you trust me or not. If I wanted to, I could keep you in a dog crate until this thing goes to trial, and it'd be the same difference to me. Keep being a pain in my ass, and that can be arranged. Your call."

His eyes lit up with anger that just made him all the more appealing, and I found myself hoping he was going to snap again. That his childish temper and impulsiveness were going to give me another excuse to do what I'd wanted to do to him from the beginning, and this time, his brother—and mine—wouldn't be there to stop me.

Instead, he set his lips into a pouty little scowl and turned to stalk out of my bedroom.

Good choice, little lamb. Run away before the wolf can sink his teeth in.

There was always next time, and given what I had seen of Valentine's nature thus far, there *would* be a next time.

I was counting on it.

7

VALENTINE

It had been a few days since I'd gotten caught in Malcolm's room, and even though he had technically given me permission, I still waited until I was sure he was gone and wouldn't be coming back for hours to use the shower.

That afternoon, boredom had finally overcome me enough to use the state-of-the-art gym he had all to himself. It was just one of the many absurdly luxurious aspects of the apartment, from the fancy kitchen appliances–most of which I didn't even know the purpose of–to the skylight in the sunroom overlooking the city below.

If nothing else, the guy had good taste. He made the Mafia look frugal in comparison.

Working out wasn't exactly my idea of a good time, but it beat reorganizing the spice rack in the kitchen. Why he even had one was beyond me, considering he ordered in every night of the week. Malcolm's place was a bachelor pad on steroids.

I had always toyed with the idea of moving into my own place one day, or maybe rooming with Chuck or Johnny. The truth was, though, I actually liked living at home–or at least, I had. Multigenerational households were one of the few aspects of Mafia life I found appealing, but in the wake of Silas, all that had changed.

I knew it wasn't entirely his fault, and there had been cracks in our family bliss that ran deeper than I could have imagined long before he'd ever reared his head, but he was an easy target. It was easier to blame him than to admit everything about my childhood had been a lie.

It was a harder pill to swallow since I didn't even have hope that the future would be any better. In the week and change I'd been gone, I had already come to regret my words about leaving the family, but it wasn't the first time I had run my mouth without thinking about the consequences. If there was one silver lining to the fact that no one took me seriously, it was that Enzo probably hadn't believed that, either.

I still couldn't bring myself to take it back, though. Not yet, not when my pride was already in the shitter. I was on hiatus from work for obvious reasons, and without even a distant ETA for that to change, my future felt wide open and directionless once again. It reminded me of the time me, Johnny, and Robbie had all stolen a canoe for a joyride out on the lake, and Johnny being his usual dumbass self had lost the oars in the water, so we just ended up paddling aimlessly for like a solid hour until I finally dove into the water and found the oars. And got sucked on by half a dozen leeches in the process.

My adult life wasn't faring much better, if I was being honest with myself.

Now even Johnny had his shit together. Relative to me, at any rate. Enzo and Luca were both married and running the family business while I was stuck on some guy's couch I barely even knew, living for the prospect of revenge that seemed to dwindle with each day that passed.

For all I knew, Malcolm and the others were just pacifying me by pretending like they actually planned to hunt this Demon down. I didn't want to believe Enzo would go along with that, but who the hell knew with him anymore?

I'd hoped a good workout would help purge some of the pent-up energy and frustration that had been festering inside me like an open wound, but as it turned out, walking around the ER all day was not as decent a substitute for a regular cardio routine as I had hoped, and lifting weights just fucking sucked. There's only so far you can run on a strip of moving rubber before you remember why humans happily traded being endurance predators for McDonald's in the first place.

Now, I was just sweaty *and* pissed off. I checked to make sure there was no sign that Malcolm had come home early before I went into his bedroom, tiptoeing into the bathroom because I felt like I was trespassing on sacred ground and a mummy was going to pop out of a sarcophagus in the closet to violate me at any second.

Pretty sure that was how booby traps worked, anyway.

I turned the hot water on and got undressed as the bathroom filled up with steam. The endless hot water heater was one reason to be glad Malcolm was a spendthrift with money I was ninety-nine percent sure he hadn't gained by any legitimate means.

I let out a deep breath as the hot water hit my skin and put the showerhead on a pulse setting that painfully worked out the tension in my aching muscles. It felt good, but it wasn't doing much about the frenetic energy still surging beneath my skin.

If I didn't get out of this place soon, I was going to go crazy. And that was if Malcolm didn't kill me first.

My thoughts started drifting back to that day he'd caught me in here, and the look in his eyes as he'd had me pinned against the counter. I couldn't help but compare it to the way he'd looked when I'd tried to hit him. Then, he'd just been pissed, but last time was... different.

Why was it different?

At first, I'd thought that look in his eyes was anger, but on closer consideration, I'd decided that wasn't it. Even when I'd hit him, Malcolm hadn't seemed legitimately pissed, which I only knew because of the way he'd gone all alpha silverback on the lady cop down at the station.

That was rage, and everything else seemed like a pale approximation in comparison.

He was as hard to read as his brother, and just as soulless, even if his human disguise was a bit more sophisticated. They were both cold, hard machines, and if anything, Silas seemed to be the one with more potential for humanity. Over the last few years, I had grudgingly come to acknowledge that he did love my brother in his own way. It was a strange, animalistic, fucked-as-hell kind of love, but it somehow seemed to run even deeper than the normal kind.

I wasn't even sure Carol and Luca's romance was as fairy-tale perfect as I'd once believed. Sure, all couples fought, and having a kid had to compound the list of stressors, but I couldn't help but feel like there was more going on below the surface.

Of course, I was just Luca's dumb kid brother, so all my attempts to hint he could open up to me if he needed to had fallen flat.

All I really knew was that if even they couldn't make it work, a schmuck like me didn't stand a damn chance at finding anything more lasting than a one-night tinder hookup.

Lately, even that wasn't an option. It wasn't like I could invite some chick over to fuck on someone else's couch. Even I wasn't that shameless.

Not yet. One more week of being this horny and pent-up, though, and that might change.

The thought of what Malcolm would do if I even tried was kind of funny, though. Until it wasn't. Until the thought of him pinning me against the wall, his hand wrapped around my throat, became something else entirely, and...

Fuck, I really was desperate. What the hell was wrong with me?

I was *not* getting turned on by the thought of being choked out by another guy.

Especially not that guy.

My cock had other ideas, though. I told myself it was just the fact that it was fucked up and I was already so tightly wound that made it exciting. Taboo and forbidden. That was normal enough, right?

It wasn't Malcolm, it was the situation itself. I'd always been into the kinkier shit. Whips, chains, handcuffs... hell, I'd once let a girl put me in chastity gear and fuck me with a strap-on just because she was hot and I was horny. I tried to guide my thoughts back to more innocuous forms of perversion and caved to the temptation to start stroking myself off, figuring maybe that would get it out of my system.

Unfortunately, my thoughts kept drifting back to Malcolm. To his hand around my throat, squeezing tighter. The feeling of his body pressed against mine, his thigh pressed against my hardening cock and his own erection pushing into my lower abdomen, because the motherfucker had a good six inches on me in height.

I didn't even want to think about how many inches he was packing below, so of course, that just drove my thoughts headlong in that direction.

Fuck!

I slapped the stone tile of the shower wall in frustration and released my grip on my own cock. What the hell was wrong with me?

Okay, chill, I coached myself. *You're just giving yourself a complex because it's taboo.*

That seemed reasonable enough, even though my handful of psych classes from the first year of med school were hazy at best. I'd been high during most of them. Still, it made sense. It was an explanation I could live with, and if that was it, it should be easy enough to resolve. If I couldn't get Malcolm out of my head, and trying to repress it clearly wasn't working, then I just needed to try the opposite. To get it out of my system and shrug it off. It wasn't like anyone else would know.

My breath faltered on my lips as I closed my eyes and swept my fingers over the swollen head of my cock, my flesh so heated even the water felt lukewarm in comparison. I forced myself to relax and this time, when the thoughts came, I let them, instead of trying to fight it.

I let myself imagine that weird little encounter that had somehow tweaked my brain just sufficiently to spark an obsession. And once I let it happen, my imagination took full rein.

Fantasy Malcolm grabbed me and hoisted me up onto the counter like it was nothing, because that was exactly the kind of infuriating thing he'd do just to humiliate me, and his hand wrapped around my throat once more, strong and huge and warm. I could feel the callus formed along the pad of his trigger finger pressed against my throbbing jugular, my pulse fluttering like a hummingbird's wings in his grasp.

He squeezed tighter, gradually constricting more and more until I could barely breathe, and slammed me into the mirror hard enough that I blacked out a little. Just for a second. Just long enough that when I came to, his other hand was traveling up my thigh, tearing off the towel that was all that was standing between his hands and my bare flesh.

But he wasn't naked himself. No, that would be giving up too much control. Too much vulnerability. He had to be partially clothed, even as he used his free hand to take off his belt and free his cock from the confines of his slacks and boxer briefs–because he was definitely a boxer briefs kind of guy–fully in control and dominant while I was exposed and vulnerable.

His cock was stupidly thick, obviously, heavy enough that even though it was rock hard, it wasn't standing all the way. The sheer size would weigh it down, and he'd give it a few long, languid strokes all while making eye contact, just to give me a second to contemplate exactly how much it was going to hurt when he...

A strangled groan escaped me, and I bit my lip so hard I tasted the metallic tang of blood on my tongue as I sank down to my knees. My lips parted in a gasp as I stroked faster, harder, all the while imagining it was his rough hand drawing the faint sounds of mingled pleasure and resistance from my crushed throat.

And when I couldn't bear it anymore, he'd turn me over and bend me over the counter, his fingers penetrating my ass without warning or preparation. A cry would tear from my throat, because I was now free to breathe and scream for him, but he wouldn't care. Of course he wouldn't. He'd just give that rough, bestial chuckle and tell me I should be grateful he was using his fingers first instead of his cock.

And then that would change, and he'd clamp a hand over my mouth to muffle the cries of pain and conflicted protest, because a man like him would definitely know how to straddle the line between pain and pleasure, torture and tenderness. He'd fuck me ruthlessly, relentlessly, until I was broken and bloody, but even as I cursed his name, I'd be moaning it, because ecstasy and torment would not be mutually exclusive concepts in Malcolm Whitlock's hands. The one would stir the other, and they'd feed off each other like some twisted ouroboros, until I was crying and begging him for release, and...

Another cry tore from my throat, this one audible enough that if anyone else was home, they would undoubtedly have heard. I couldn't stop it, though, any more than I could stop the surge of pleasure that had started between my thighs and worked its way up to my core and down my shaft. I came with his name on my lips, still stroking myself furiously and imagining it was him fucking me senseless. I came harder than I ever had, and even as the orgasm subsided, I was left trembling with fear and shame and need. I was left in awe of my own pathetic depravity, and hungering for more debasement all the same, wishing it was more than just a fucked-up fantasy.

Wishing it was real.

I'd started out wondering what the hell was wrong with me, but now, I had a dangerous suspicion that I already knew.

The water was still hot, so I spent the next ten minutes hastily scrubbing my skin raw in an ill-fated attempt to wash the shame of what I had done down the drain with the evidence of my degeneracy. I'd indulged in plenty of postcoital self-loathing before, but this was a whole new low.

Once I got out and realized the apartment was as empty as I left it, I felt a surge of relief that my shame would remain mine alone. I got dressed and reached for my phone only to find I'd missed a series of text messages. Most of them were from Enzo, who I was ignoring, and Luca, who kept apologizing for not checking in more often. I really didn't have the emotional bandwidth to respond to either of them right now, and I doubted I could have focused on a conversation, anyway, but when I saw that one of the messages was from Chris, I did a double take.

The existing thread with him in my messages consisted of a whopping seven texts, spread out over the last year or so, all one-sentence proclamations about my work schedule, the most recent one being the only exception.

Just wanted to check in and see how you're doing. I think we should talk in person. Let me know when you're free.

Not "let me know if you can," just "let me know when." Typical of him, really. But I could use a dose of normalcy, if nothing else.

I chewed on my bottom lip, contemplating my options for a moment. I was under strict instructions not to leave the building, or even the floor, for that matter, but I had also been assured that house arrest wasn't going to be a permanent thing. So far, there was no sign of an end anywhere in sight, and while I couldn't exactly show up to work, that didn't mean I had to live under a rock for the rest of my life. Besides, Malcolm never got back before eight during the midweek, even when he was home from work early, so I should have plenty of time.

Sure. I have some time now, if that works for you, I replied.

Almost as soon as I sent the reply, I saw dots appear on the screen to let me know he was typing a response.

Perfect. Where are you?

I hesitated, not sure it was a good idea to narrow it down, considering the less he knew, the better for him and everyone else.

I'm near Main Street, downtown. There's a coffee shop across the street from the library, if that's not too far.

More typing, then, *I'll be there in fifteen.*

Never let it be said the man was indecisive. I sighed, grabbing my sneakers and a hooded black denim jacket from the bag of clothes and things Enzo had sent over. It was a pretty normal jacket, aside from the embroidered cat peeking out of the chest pocket. I hadn't worn it in years, but of course that was the jacket Enzo sent. Probably just his way of getting back at me for being a bitch.

Oh, well. With any luck, Chris wouldn't notice, and it wasn't like he saw me as a sophisticated, mature, cosmopolitan individual to begin with.

I told myself the only reason I even cared was that he was my boss. Or at least, he had been. I still didn't know where I stood in that regard, and trauma leave wasn't exactly something I had enough knowledge of to know what to expect from this point on. I figured that was probably what Chris wanted to talk to me about. Even he wasn't enough of a curt dick to fire someone over text, it seemed.

Under any other circumstances, I probably would have preferred that over the alternative, but I was glad for the excuse to leave. And it was easier than I expected. When there was no magic forcefield keeping me from getting on the elevator, I relaxed a little. I made it past the doorman without a fuss, keeping the hood of my jacket up in hopes it would be harder for him to identify me just in case Malcolm had told him to keep an eye out for me.

Once I made it outside of the building and the fresh evening air hit my lungs, I felt a million times better than I had. And I felt like a fool for not trying this sooner. Just because Malcolm acted like he was omniscient and omnipresent didn't mean he actually was. There was only so far he could observe and control me. I was still an adult. DiFiore or not, I had rights and freedoms, and he needed me a hell of a lot more than I needed him. He couldn't kill his star witness.

I hoped.

At the very least, he seemed to care enough about Silas–and only Silas–that he wouldn't want to jeopardize his relationship with Enzo over me.

Again, I hoped.

It wasn't a bad walk to the library, and Malcolm definitely lived on the swankier side of town, so the view wasn't bad, either. Other than all the hipsters, and the overpriced Americanized versions of Italian restaurants.

I ordered a frothy, sugary mocha drink along with a sandwich since I hadn't eaten yet and settled in at a table near a window in the back. I was still slightly paranoid I was being followed, either by Silas's goons or Demon.

Not long after I arrived, Chris showed up, and I realized it was the first time I had actually seen him outside of work. The first time I had seen him in anything other than scrubs and a lab coat, for that matter. He was wearing nice dark wash jeans, a relatively casual button-down, a gray blazer that had those professor patches on the elbows, and a big wool scarf. He was also wearing dark-rimmed glasses, which was another first.

I waved until he spotted me, and I was pretty sure I looked like a dweeb, judging from the way he was smirking at me.

"There you are," he said as he came over. "I was afraid you wouldn't show."

I blinked. "Why is that?"

"After what happened, I just assumed your brother would have you under lock and key."

"Oh, right," I said with an awkward laugh. "My brother doesn't get to tell me what to do."

He didn't look convinced by my words, which was kind of annoying, but considering he was right, I wasn't going to push it too much.

"How are you holding up?" he asked, his voice uncharacteristically soft with concern.

"Me?" I asked, surprised by the question. "I'm fine."

He didn't look convinced by that, either. "Really?" he asked. "I suppose that makes one of us."

I immediately regretted my words, but I'd spent my entire life trying to convince everyone I didn't possess the emotions I had been raised to see as signs of weakness. Even though Enzo and the others didn't call me "crybaby Val" anymore, I still carried the knowledge with me that I was the weakest link. For whatever reason, our father had never been as hard on me as he was on Luca and Enzo, so maybe that was why I had turned out so pathetic.

From an outside perspective, it probably would've looked like I was the favorite. Hell, even Enzo and Luca seemed to think that. In reality, I was pretty sure it was just that Dad had never bothered to be as overbearing with me as them because he knew it was a waste of his time to try to mold me into a carbon copy of him. He'd managed with relative success when it came to Enzo and Luca. Enzo was the oldest and a guaranteed success, and he had Luca as a backup. Me... I was just the third son. Extra. Unnecessary.

At first, I had tried to follow in his footsteps regardless. I'd used my brothers as a roadmap, making every clumsy, inadequate attempt to do what they did. To be like them.

Eventually, I'd realized it was a lost cause. I'd realized I was never going to be more than a pale substitute for any of the strong, unflinching men around me, so I might as well try to differentiate myself in some other regard.

Despite what everyone thought, I had been good at school. Math and science came easily to me, and I was naturally curious, preferring to spend my time indoors reading and fooling around with the science kits Mom had always bought for me on my birthdays and Christmas, despite Dad thinking it was a waste of time. The traits that made me an outsider in my own family had made me a favorite among my teachers and the adults who existed outside the strangely brutal cloister of the family.

I had spent so long trying to compensate for the weak, human part of me–and when that failed, trying to hide it —that sometimes I forgot the outside world was the opposite. It was acceptable, even expected, to be shaken after something like that. Normal people weren't just expected to roll with the punches and get over it a few days later.

As different as Enzo had actually turned out to be from our father, even he didn't seem to fully understand why Robbie's death had affected me the way it had. Or that of the strangers whose names I didn't even know, because I couldn't stomach reading any of the news articles to find out. And that made me feel like shit, too.

I was a tangle of raw nerves and crossed switches, and here I was, sitting across from the one person who probably would've understood—to a degree at least—pretending I was a machine, because that was what I had always been raised to do. It was the only thing I knew how to do.

"You know, it's okay not to be okay after something that fucked up," Chris said at length. "No one is going to judge you for that." He paused as if he was considering it. "At least, I'm not."

I forced a smile, but it felt so stiff it was in danger of cracking, so I gave up. "Yeah, I guess it's just force of habit." My throat grew tight as I braced myself to ask the question that had been plaguing me for longer than I cared to admit. If I didn't, I was going to chicken out. "How is everyone? The ones who were injured, are they—"

"They're alive," he answered, kind enough not to leave me in suspense. "It was touch-and-go with Matthew for a while, but he's expected to make a full recovery."

Matthew. That name hit like a punch in the gut. He was one of the new orderlies, and we had always been on friendly terms during the short time we had known each other. Here I was, bitching about not having freedom, while he was in the hospital fighting for his life. Because of me.

Just when I thought I couldn't hate myself anymore than I already did.

"I'm glad he's okay," I said. "If there's anything I can do, anything that his family needs, please just let me know."

"I think your anonymous donation to cover everyone's hospital bills was generous enough," he replied. When I found myself gaping at him, he smiled a little. "It wasn't very hard to figure out, and your face just confirmed it."

I breathed a sigh, looking away. "Trust me, that's the least I can do, considering it's my fault."

Chris tilted his head. "How do you figure that?"

I froze, cursing myself, but it was far from the first time my mouth had gotten me in trouble, and I knew better than to think it would be the last.

He hadn't been there when the assassin had asked for me in particular, but I had just assumed the police would've filled him in. Apparently not.

"How much did they tell you?" I asked. As tempted as I was not to incriminate myself any further, I was the reason Chris and the others had almost lost their lives. The reason they had experienced something that would change them forever, as I knew all too well. I owed him the truth, at least.

"Not much," he said. "I'd rather hear it from you, anyway."

"They were after me," I told him. "Robbie, the guy who came in that day... well, the people who killed him are after me now, and that's why they showed up at the hospital."

"I see," he said thoughtfully. His voice was devoid of any tone, anything that might give away what he was actually thinking. I'd always thought he and Silas would get along, and that was just one of the reasons. "Well, I figured that might've been the case, truth be told. The police were quite hush-hush on the matter, so I assumed your brother-in-law had something to do with covering up whatever did happen."

I grimaced. Leave it to Malcolm to be conspicuously inconspicuous.

To be fair, it probably wasn't a connection most people would have made, but Chris was sharp. He had an edge to him, and he probably would've been a hell of a lot better of a mob boss than I would be, if our places were reversed.

"Listen, I know this sounds sketchy as fuck, but trust me when I say, the less you know, the better."

"You're right," he said in a dry tone. "It does sound sketchy, but I've never been in the business of shying away from the truth just because it's inconvenient. Or dangerous."

"First time for everything," I said. When I could tell he wasn't buying it, I sighed and realized I was picking apart my napkin, so I clenched it in my fist and tried to be less of a nervous wreck. "There's not all that much more I can tell you, anyway."

"Can't or won't?"

"Both," I admitted. "Look, you said when I first started, you were worried about having a DiFiore working for you. You thought I would be a liability. Well, you were right."

Chris listened intently, frowning once I was finished. "What changed?" he asked. "Your friend told you something, didn't he? Something that made you the target of whoever killed him."

I stared at him in shock. "You know, if you get tired of being a doctor, you could make a killing as a private investigator."

The corner of his mouth lilted up at one end. "Deductive reasoning isn't just for the MCATs. But if that's the case, and the killer is still out there, that means you're still in danger."

"And so is everyone associated with me," I said pointedly. "So if you came here to fire me, you don't need to bother. I'm not coming back."

His brow furrowed. "Actually, I was hoping to do the opposite."

"You were?" I asked doubtfully. "A little more than a week ago, you were trying to convince me to quit."

"Yes, because I believed that was what's best for you," he countered. "And I still do. But there's a difference between quitting on your terms and quitting out of fear."

"A guy had a gun aimed at my head, and he killed people," I said. "Fear seems pretty warranted in this case."

"Maybe so," he conceded. "I'm not saying I know what the answer is, but I would hate to see you throw everything away for good. When it's safe, and they've apprehended who's responsible, I hope you'll consider coming back."

His words took me by surprise, mostly because I'd been convinced he would be relieved he didn't have to deal with me any longer. I wasn't sure what to make of it now that I knew that wasn't the case.

"I will," I said, since considering it didn't seem like such a commitment. "I don't know when that will be, though."

And the truth was, my heart ached at the thought of leaving it all behind. Maybe I had started out wanting to go into medicine to prove something. To my father. To my brothers. To myself. To prove that I wasn't just the airheaded brat who couldn't take anything seriously that they all thought I was. It had become something more, though. Maybe a calling was a bit dramatic, but medicine had given me something I'd never really had—a sense of purpose. A sense that I belonged somewhere, and I could do something of value. Something that mattered.

"Hopefully not too long," he remarked. "It's rare for anything that happens in the city to still be in the news cycle a week later, but I would imagine if nothing else, your brother-in-law is eager enough to wrap things up before the next election."

"Election?" I echoed. "Oh, yeah, the chief of police is appointed by the mayor."

"Yes," he said. "Which is why there's going to be pressure on him to find a replacement chief of police, assuming Malcolm is incapable of doing his job."

"Oh," I murmured. "Right."

There was a faint glimmer in Chris's eyes. I had a bad feeling it was amusement. "For a mobster, you're a bit naïve about the political machinations of this sort of thing, aren't you?"

For some reason, my face grew warm. "It's never been my forte, no."

"I think that's what it is," Chris mused.

I looked up, convinced I had missed something. I definitely wasn't in optimal condition, mentally or otherwise. I had been having a harder time sleeping than usual, and there was no need to guess why that might be. "That's what what is?"

"What makes you so intriguing," he answered without missing a beat.

I opened my mouth to reply, but nothing would come out. My brain just kind of short-circuited. I didn't know what to make of his words, let alone what to say to them. And there was no way in hell he meant them the way they sounded, but I was having a hard time figuring out another explanation.

"Sorry," he said with an equally apologetic smile. "Probably the worst time I could've dropped that on you, but I guess the shooting made me want to be more forthcoming."

"You know, you could've just let me convince myself that you didn't mean it that way," I said.

He laughed. "I probably could have. You're not very certain of yourself most of the time, so it would be easy enough to convince you you're just imagining things. But I find I respect you too much for that."

Now that caught me off-guard more than if he had just flat out said he wanted to dick me down right there on the table in front of all the hipsters. It somehow felt more intimate, too.

"That... means a lot, especially coming from you," I admitted. "And I'm flattered. Really, I just..."

"You're not into guys," he said in a knowing tone.

I hesitated. A day ago–hell, a few hours ago–I would've agreed without a second thought, but considering the fact that I had just jerked off to a fantasy about the man I hated, I wasn't so confident about that anymore. Or much of anything else. He was right about that, too.

"At the risk of sounding like a sixteen-year-old on Facebook, it's complicated," I admitted.

"I get it," he assured me. "I hope I didn't make you uncomfortable."

"No," I said, probably a bit too quickly. "No, not at all. Honestly, this is the first time I've really talked to anyone normal since Robbie, and it's nice."

"Normal?" he asked wryly. "Is that what I am?"

"Trust me, it's a compliment," I said emphatically.

He chuckled. "Well, that's good. Because I'd like you to know I'm here for you, regardless."

"I appreciate that," I said quietly.

"I mean it," he insisted. "I want you to know you can talk to me. Any time, day or night."

Anyone else saying that would've come off way too strong, but with him, it was different. I felt... safe. That unnerved me even more than getting turned on by Malcolm had. Somehow, finding comfort in another man felt gayer than jerking off to the thought of being rawed by him.

Before I could respond, a look of realization crossed his face and he reached into his pocket for something. "I almost forgot. I actually came here to bring you these," he said, dangling my keys from his fingertips. I recognized them immediately from the gaudy fuzzy dice hanging off them. The dice had been a gag gift from Johnny a few years back, based on an old inside joke, but I hadn't taken them off for some reason. Now I was seriously regretting that.

"My keys," I said with an awkward laugh, taking them. "Thanks. I kind of forgot about my bike in all the bullshit."

"That's a surprise, considering how well cared for she is," he remarked. "The hospital director was bitching about having it towed, so I figured I might as well bring it. I hope you don't mind."

"God, no. Thank you, I appreciate it," I said, slipping the keys into my jacket pocket. I appreciated it now more than ever, considering it might be my only option of getting any sufficient distance from Malcolm if and when the opportunity presented itself. "My brothers always said I'd lose my head if it wasn't attached."

"Don't mention it," he said, frowning. "How are you getting around, anyway?"

"Oh, uh... I'm actually staying with Malcolm for a while, and he lives downtown, so everything's within walking distance."

"I see," he said, and I could see the wheels turning behind his eyes.

I was still processing what I'd said to raise his suspicion when Chris looked up and a look of irritation came over his face. I knew it well, considering I was usually the one who put it there.

"Speak of the devil," he muttered.

I turned around to find Malcolm standing in the door to the coffee shop, and at the same exact moment, his eyes locked on mine like a velociraptor that had just spotted its furry, skittering prey in a jungle.

Shit.

His gaze drifted over to Chris, and the indignation behind his rage turned to confusion. He stalked over to us, and I found myself frozen, just like I had been that day in the crosshairs of that asshole's gun. It wasn't exactly the most efficient response to stress, but if I ever needed confirmation that being a mafioso just wasn't in the cards for me, there it was spelled out in neon lights.

I was so screwed. And not in a fun way.

MALCOLM

"There you are," I gritted out. I wanted to add a whole string of epithets onto the end of that sentence, but we were in a public place, and we had an audience. But if Valentine thought that was going to save him for any longer than it took to haul his scrawny ass out to my car, he was sorely mistaken.

As a matter of fact, he was about to be sore in more than one way. The boy was clearly lacking in discipline, so I was going to make up for it where his father had failed him. A few swats on the ass, and maybe he wouldn't be so quick to disobey me again.

If he was, even better.

Valentine had left the apartment, and I should've checked my phone like usual, but he had been on relatively good behavior for long enough that I had grown complacent and assumed he'd finally decided to check out the pool. I'd assumed he had finally come to accept the fact that he wasn't going anywhere and decided to behave like a reasonable adult.

That was my second mistake. One that was absolutely and completely unforgivable, considering who we were talking about.

Not a mistake I would be making again.

"Malcolm," Valentine said in the same wary tone he had used when I found him in my room without permission. I was already regretting my decision to go easy on him then, since that had clearly taught him an unfortunate lesson. One that was going to be a very painful process for him to unlearn. "What are you doing here?"

"I could ask you the same thing," I said tersely. I glanced over at the guy next to him, still not sure what the fuck they were doing together. I knew every member of the DiFiore family because it had become my business to know, and even under constant supervision, they found plentiful ways to cause me problems. "And who are you, exactly?"

"This is Dr. Adams," Valentine answered, looking appropriately wary. He wasn't nearly as frightened as he was going to be, and it was a shame that he lacked the foresight to be scared enough of me to think better of his bullshit, but that would change. Starting tonight. He added pointedly, "My boss."

As if he thought that was going to moderate my behavior. Such a naïve assumption. Precious, really.

"You mean your former boss," I said slowly, for emphasis. "Because you don't work at the hospital anymore. Remember?"

Valentine swallowed audibly, watching me with a delicious mixture of hatred and fear. The concoction was almost as alluring as the scent left on the white T-shirt I had let him borrow, the one I hadn't had the willpower to launder.

Yes, I was sick, but what else was new?

Besides, that was about to become the most innocuous thing I had ever done concerning him. Just as soon as I got him home.

"Chief Whitlock. What an honor," the prick said, his voice dripping with sarcastic condescension. He held out his hand. "Please, call me Chris."

"Malcolm," I said through my teeth, returning his handshake. He was exactly the kind of pretentious, yuppie scumbag I hated, even more than I hated most people, and that was saying something.

"So, you're his brother-in-law?" he asked doubtfully, even though he knew the answer to that question as well as I did. Considering who worked for him, I was sure he had done his research on Valentine's family. That much was public knowledge, even if I didn't exactly go around publicizing it when I could help it. The media was more than happy to do that for me.

"Yeah, and?" I asked, not in the mood to play nice. Especially not when he wasn't bothering to hide his smart-assery.

"I see," he said, making no attempt to hide his judgment, either.

The implication was clear. Storming into a restaurant and tracking down your brother-in-law when he was meeting with someone wasn't exactly socially appropriate behavior, or even explicable behavior outside of our present circumstances, but I wasn't interested in explaining myself to some nerd who'd let a modicum of authority go to his head. And I was certainly not interested in preserving Valentine's ego in front of him.

"I think it's time we got going," I said pointedly, turning back to Valentine.

He frowned, but he was already starting to get up when Chris put a hand on his arm to keep him there.

The sight was enough to send me into a blind rage, and even though I told myself it was just possessiveness by virtue of being the one who was responsible for this idiot now, it was far from convincing even to me.

"Just a moment," Chris said, staring me down. "We were in the middle of a conversation."

"Conversation's over," I said, no longer bothering to keep up the thin pretense of civility—or normalcy, for that matter. I really didn't give a shit what this asshole thought about our relationship dynamic. I wasn't even sure why I was bothering to pretend Valentine had any autonomy in the matter at all. If I humiliated him in front of his boss, him trying to sneak back to work was one less of his harebrained schemes I had to worry about thwarting.

I turned back to Valentine, and for the first time in memory, I repeated myself. "It's time to go."

He frowned, looking between us like he was actually thinking about whether he was going to continue to defy me. He really was dumber than he looked, and with a face like that, it was clear he'd inherited his mother's beauty and none of his father's cunning.

The nerve, though. He sure as fuck had that.

"Can you give me a minute?" he asked through his teeth.

"No," I said immediately, pointing out the window to my car waiting at the curb. "Car. Now."

Chris craned his neck to look out the window. "Parked in front of a fire hydrant." He clicked his tongue. "My, Chief. That's not setting a very good example to the average civilian, is it?"

I snorted a laugh. This guy was rich. "Feel free to write a complaint to the city," I said, grabbing Valentine by the arm since he'd already burned through my meager patience. I hauled him to his feet, and he stumbled into me, grimacing in humiliation, but this was nothing compared to what he had coming.

The shift that came over Chris's expression was instantaneous and extreme enough that for a second, I thought the guy was actually going to try to intervene. Instead, he set his jaw and gave me a look that left little room to imagine exactly how he felt about me.

It's mutual, prick.

"Okay, fine, I'm coming," Valentine muttered, shirking out of my grasp. I let him, if only because we were drawing an audience, and the last thing I needed was another bullshit scandal going up on the town page. He glanced back at Chris, but his head was bent down and he wasn't willing to look directly at him. "Sorry."

"Don't be," Chris said, lowering his voice. "Just remember what I said. Any time."

Valentine gave a shaky nod, flinching when I put a hand on his shoulder to lead him out of the cafe. I wasn't sure if he was intentionally acting like an abused puppy to make me look bad, or if it just came naturally. Either way, he was in for a rude awakening if he thought this was harsh.

"What the fuck was that about?" I demanded, keeping a tight grip as I led him out of the restaurant and over to my car waiting at the curb.

"Nothing," he mumbled.

I narrowed my eyes, debating for a moment about whether I wanted to call him on his bullshit here and now. I ultimately decided it wasn't worth the public scrutiny, considering the mayor was already up my ass about catching the one who'd orchestrated the hospital incident. I opened the passenger door instead, pushing Valentine in like a perp in the back of my squad car.

Ever since my days in vice, I'd garnered a reputation for being a violent, brutal son of a bitch, and most of it was warranted. I'd never raised a hand against someone truly innocent, but those were few and far between in my world. The boy in my passenger seat was as close as it came, but he had just forfeited his right to whatever gentleness and mercy I might have shown him before.

"I hope you enjoyed that," I said once we'd been on the road for a few moments. I wasn't sure if Valentine had the sense to keep quiet or if he was giving me the silent treatment. Probably the latter.

"Enjoyed what?" he asked.

"Your last outing for the indefinite future," I answered. "Because from now on, you're not going to be able to so much as breathe without me up your ass."

"Sounds kinky," he muttered under his breath.

I sneered, gripping the wheel tighter. This little smartass elevated temptation to an art form. "Keep talking, kid. Just another nail in your coffin."

I didn't even mean it as a mortal threat, but that certainly got his attention. "You can't do anything to me," he said, even though his voice wavered with uncertainty. "Silas—"

"Silas gave you to me," I interrupted. It was time to disabuse him of every self-destructive notion of autonomy he had. It was for his own good. And if it happened to appeal to my sadistic pleasure, that was just icing on the cake. "Just like the chip, you're mine. Mine to protect, and mine to punish as I see fit. So far, I've been very generous, but if you don't like your gilded cage, fine. You get an iron one. And if you still haven't learned your lesson, it'll be barbed wire, because if there's one thing you need to get through your solid concrete skull, it's that it can always get worse. And tonight? You just earned yourself a whole fucking downgrade."

Valentine fell silent for long enough that I looked over to find he was staring at me like I was a madman he found himself captive to. And fair enough. "What do you mean, punish?"

Hunger coiled in my gut like a serpent ready to strike at the wariness in his tone.

"Oh, you're going to find out," I assured him. The truth was, I hadn't even settled on one yet. Just when I finally thought I had, another prospect would raise its head, even more tantalizing than the last. He was a muse to my inner sadist, and I was going to turn his body and his soul into a canvas for every depraved fantasy that happened to cross my mind.

He swallowed audibly. God, he was too much. And I couldn't fucking get enough.

When I'd first come home and realized he was nowhere to be found, I was pissed. It didn't take long to track him by his phone, though, and on the short drive to collect my little runaway, I'd come to see it a different way. This was it. This was the excuse I had been looking for, and he had so unwittingly given me carte blanche.

"I didn't do anything wrong," he gritted out. Already moving into the denial phase. Just as well. That meant bargaining was soon to follow, and I'd been longing to hear him beg from the day we'd met. "I'm not a fucking prisoner."

"You are now," I shot back, taking a sharp turn toward the street my building was on. "And from now on, you're going to be tethered to my side."

"Literally or figuratively?" he asked warily.

"That's up to you."

He made a sound dangerously close to a whimper. "Please don't."

My knuckles were white on the wheel and a shiver was crawling its way up my spine. My cock was already painfully stiff. At this rate, I wasn't going to have the willpower to wait until we left the parking garage.

I said nothing at the risk of discouraging the begging. Better to let him think he stood a chance. He'd find out soon enough that I didn't have any heartstrings for him to pull.

"What about work?" he asked suddenly, like he'd just come up with his own salvation. Cute.

"You're coming with me," I answered.

"You can't be serious. You know how that's going to look? Pretty sure there's no such thing as 'take your prisoner to work' day."

"You should've thought of that before you disobeyed me," I said, getting out of the car and keeping it locked so he couldn't get out without me. I came around to open his door and took him by the arm to pull him out.

"Get off me," he snarled, trying to pull his wrist out of my grasp.

I tightened my grip, not enough to do any damage, but enough that he winced and stopped struggling long enough for me to lean in and whisper, "Rule number two–don't ever embarrass me in public again or I'll make sure you regret it tenfold when we're inside."

To anyone else, it might have looked like an intimate embrace, and it wouldn't be the first time I'd brought a pretty boy like him up to my penthouse. The neighbors wouldn't think twice.

This time, there was no mistaking the whimper as he leaned away from me, but he'd given up on fighting. He was learning. Slowly, but that was fine by me. All that really mattered was that he did learn.

"What was rule number one?" he muttered.

"Don't fucking disobey me," I answered. "You already broke that one, but don't worry. I'll make sure you don't forget it again."

I stepped back, keeping his wrist firmly in my grasp. My hand could wrap around it two times over and then some. Compared to most people, he was on the tall side of average, but compared to me, he was small. Fragile. And not just physically. It would be so easy to break him, and there was a part of me that was eager to do just that. I couldn't go all out, if only because I didn't trust myself to pull back, but that didn't mean I had to go easy on him. Not by a long shot.

As Valentine was about to learn, my version of kid gloves was a little bit different from what he was used to.

9

VALENTINE

I had fucked up countless times in my life, and in countless ways. I was something of an artist at it, but never had I crafted a masterpiece of fuckery as fine as the one I was in now.

We had only been back at Malcolm's apartment for a matter of minutes, and I already found myself dreading whatever he had in store.

Judging from everything he had said in the car, and outside of it, it was nothing good. I wasn't sure exactly how far he was willing to go, but my attempts to call his bluff before had ended so disastrously, I didn't dare to make that mistake again.

Malcolm had just come in from whatever the hell he had been doing in his bedroom for the last minute or so, and my body went frigid as he approached me, walking a slow, deliberate circle around me as he studied me like a predator assessing his prey. That was exactly what I was to him.

This wasn't too far from how that sordid little fantasy had started, but all of a sudden, it was less of a novelty.

I had always considered Enzo to be the prideful one out of the three of us, but standing there with Malcolm stalking around me like a shark, the fact that I was still having such a hard time swallowing my pride was proof it was a vice I possessed in at least equal measure.

"Look, I'm sorry, okay?" I began. The words were bitter on my tongue, but apologizing was preferable to whatever he had planned.

"You're sorry," he echoed, an all-too-familiar smirk playing on his lips. I was getting déjà vu in the worst way, and while I would've loved to be able to say I didn't have a thing for smug, domineering psychos like my brother did, recent events made that lie even more difficult to swallow than contrition.

"You know, you say that a lot, but words don't really mean much without actions to back them up," he said, coming to a stop directly in front of me. There was a gleam in his eyes that had me on edge even more than his words. "I take it you never learned that from your father, so I'll just have to be the one who teaches you."

I bristled, and all of a sudden, the idea of swallowing my pride went out the window. "You don't know shit about me," I spat. Because apparently, I was a glutton for punishment. "And keep my family out of your mouth."

He gave a low, menacing chuckle. That, too, was uncannily familiar. If anything, he made Silas seem almost agreeable in comparison. "That's cute. You want to be a tough guy like your brothers, huh? Defending the honor of your famiglia when you can't even defend yourself."

I clenched my jaw, trying to see through the red. Fear and loathing were the two polarities I was always being pushed and pulled between where Malcolm was concerned. Right now, I was smack dab in the middle.

"What the hell is your problem?" I asked incredulously. "A week ago, we were practically strangers. You didn't give a shit about me, and now, you act like you own me."

"Oh, little bird," he murmured, cupping my face in his hand. It was as warm and rough as it was in my fantasy, and my heart responded the same way to his touch, beating furiously. "I do."

When I tried to turn my head away, his grip tightened, but in reality, my response wasn't arousal. It was rage.

At least some part of me was in working order.

I took another swing at him, as suicidal as that impulse was, and he caught my fist in his palm as easily as he had the first time. Unlike the first time, he didn't just pin me against the wall. He yanked my arm behind my back fast enough to spin me around, and before I could even get my bearings, his knee swept into my back hard enough to send me to the ground. He was right on top of me, landing with his knee pressed into the small of my back.

The impact was hard enough to knock the breath from my lungs with a wheeze, and with him on top of me, I couldn't replace it with another full breath. He arched his body over mine, gripping a handful of my hair with his other hand and tugging it back so I could feel the scrape of his stubbly jaw along my exposed throat.

"Thank you for that," he purred next to my ear, the heat of his breath tickling my earlobe.

"For what?" I gritted out, trying in vain to break free of his vice grip.

He had to be at least two-hundred and fifty pounds of solid muscle, and it was hard just to breathe with him on top of me, even though I knew the fact that I could breathe at all meant he was intentionally not crushing me. I had gone up against plenty of guys who were bigger and stronger in my life, but the difference in size and strength between us was so extreme as to be comical. No amount of scrappy determination or fighting dirty was going to get me out of this one, but I wasn't going down without a fight all the same.

Call it pride. Call it stupidity. If this day had taught me nothing else, it was that I possessed an abundance of both.

"For what? For giving me a reason," he answered in a voice that sounded like rubbing velvet against the grain, smooth and rough at once. The response it stirred within me was equally contradictory, and just when I'd found reason to hope that the harsh reality of Malcolm was enough to kill whatever sick hunger I had been nursing for him, it came back with a vengeance.

I was grateful I was flush against the carpet, because at least he couldn't tell I was hard. And shit, I wasn't even sure if it was from fear or lust. Maybe both.

Before I could ask what the fuck he meant by that, he lifted off me without letting go of my arm and the sound of metal scraping metal made me flinch. I twisted to look over my shoulder, but while I couldn't see what he was doing, the sensation of handcuffs snapping around my right wrist soon answered my question.

"Hey!" I cried as another surge of panic and adrenaline washed through me. I thrashed and squirmed until I managed to get up on one knee, but Malcolm planted a hand between my shoulder blades and pushed me back down like it was nothing, fastening the other cuff around my left wrist.

He tugged the restraints to check that they were secure before he hauled me to my feet like it was nothing. I barely had time to stagger before he wrapped his hand around my shoulder and pushed me forward with enough momentum that I couldn't even trip.

Once I realized he was leading me to his bedroom, I put on the brakes. "Let me go!" I seethed, somehow managing to turn partially to face him. He ignored my cries of protest, and when my struggle proved enough of an irritation, he grabbed me by the waist and flung me over his shoulder.

A strangled gasp of alarm escaped me, followed by a grunt as he unceremoniously tossed me onto the bed.

I wriggled and thrashed like a worm on a hook, managing only to get onto my side in time to see him taking off his belt. What the hell? Before I could fully process what was happening, he rolled me over all the way, and when he started unfastening my belt, I felt another surge of adrenaline, this time tinged with horror.

This was actually happening. This wasn't a dream or some fucked-up fantasy, it was real. My shock lasted only for a moment before I started struggling, managing to get in a kick to his abdomen that didn't even seem to phase him.

"Get off me!" I hissed, thrashing hard enough that I was pretty sure I had popped my shoulder out of its socket.

He ignored me, tugging my jeans down to my knees before he grabbed the back of my neck like I was a feral kitten and tossed me over his lap. Confusion made my head spin as one nightmare scenario gave way to another that was less horrible but just as mortifying.

"I told you I'd make you pay tenfold for every time you defied me," he said in a voice so perfectly calm and composed, it stood in stark contrast to the brutality of his actions, making them all the more terrifying in comparison. "So far, that's three times. The day you trespassed in my room without permission, your decision to leave after I explicitly told you not to, and just now, when you tried to hit me. The first time was free, but I won't be so merciful in the future."

"You can't be serious," I said through my teeth, straining to get a look at him over my shoulder even though he had me stretched horizontally over his lap, my feet dangling off the floor since the bed was elevated. His were solidly on the floor, of course. "You can't fucking spank me!"

"I can do whatever I want with you. The sooner you grasp that, the easier your life will be," he said in that infuriatingly calm, pedantic tone, like he was talking to a child. And considering our current circumstances, I was pretty sure that was how he saw me. "It's clear your father didn't provide you the proper discipline when he had the chance, so it falls to me. But don't you worry, boy. I'll teach you to be good yet. We've got all the time in the world."

His words made me shudder violently enough that my teeth clacked together, and I wished I could say it was all revulsion. There was plenty of that, but far more concerning impulses were capable of coexisting alongside it. Even now, I was painfully hard, and with my cock pressed into his lap, separated only by his clothes and my boxers, it had to be just as painfully obvious.

"All right, I get it," I cried hoarsely. "You've made your point, okay? I won't disobey you again."

"That would be in your best interest," he mused. "But it has no bearing on tonight's punishment. You pay for your sins in retrospect, Valentine. Not in advance."

Before I could ask what the hell that was supposed to mean, I felt him giving my boxers a tug and tried to bite him.

He swatted the outside of my thigh hard enough that I jolted. It didn't hurt so much as the impact jarred me.

"Don't struggle or I'll add ten more," he said in a gruff, scolding tone.

I went rigid, save for my shuddering breath and trembling. I wasn't sure if it was fear anymore or just rage, but either way, I held still while he tugged my boxers down just far enough for the air to hit my bare ass.

My face was burning up with humiliation, and the worst was yet to come. I flinched at the sound of leather snapping against leather, and try as I might to prepare myself, nothing could prepare me for the first strike of that belt against my bare ass. That stung like a motherfucker.

A startled cry escaped me, and with each subsequent hit, I felt the breath knocked from my lungs anew as my body lurched forward on his lap. I gave up trying to get a full breath at all and settled for gritting my teeth. By number four, my flesh was whipped raw, and just when I thought it couldn't hurt any more, the next strike proved me wrong.

Hot tears streamed down my cheeks and a strangled moan welled up in my throat. Five. Five blows was all it had taken to strip me of my pride, but it hurt too bad to formulate the plea being crushed out by the pathetic, sniveling sounds. For some reason, that cry stopped him even though he was only on number five, but I knew better than to even entertain the idea that it was mercy.

It was an opportunity, either way. A chance to gulp in a breath and plead, "Please! Please, stop, I won't do it again. I swear, please."

Malcolm remained silent, but every second he paused in contemplation was a second of reprieve. My ass still stung like someone had lit it on fire, but it was bearable. That was more than I could say for the humiliation.

"Begging already?" He sounded disappointed, but there was no telling with him. He was so far removed from human reason or emotion that it might as well have been delight.

"Yes," I gritted out, barely able to see through the tears soaking into his comforter. I knew I looked exactly how I was. Weak. Pathetic. Childish. "Please."

He paused another moment in contemplation before he finally set the belt down, and only then did I let myself take in a full breath. "I take it you've learned your lesson?"

"Yes," I said in earnest.

It was the truth. I had learned my lesson. I wasn't sure if it was the lesson he'd planned on teaching me, but either way, it was etched into my mind like ink, indelible. Malcolm Whitlock truly lived up to his moniker, Devil, wearing a suit of human skin and the thin veneer of civility. The truth underneath was raw and ugly and utterly twisted.

"And what might that be?" he asked, lifting me up so I was sitting on his lap, my pants still around my knees. I couldn't bring myself to look into his eyes, which were burning with tears, but he cupped my chin between his thumb and forefinger with unexpected tenderness and turned my head so I had no choice but to look at him. "Humor me."

I was shaking so badly I couldn't speak, having to grit my teeth together just to keep them from chattering. "Obey."

That answer seemed to satisfy him, judging from the change that came over his face. It wasn't that his expression softened, but rather that the burning silver of his eyes smoldered with a different kind of malice. And that, too, taught me a lesson. That his cruelty could be appeased one of two ways–punishment or submission. One way or another, the latter would be the final result. He would break me, and it had taken shamefully little. It was just a matter of how much of the former I had to endure before he succeeded.

"Good boy," he said in a voice that sounded like the collective frequency of every dark and depraved sin mankind had ever committed. "I think that's enough for tonight."

With that, he pulled me off his lap and kept his hands on my hips to steady me until I could get my own footing again. Humiliation seared through my soul like burning coals as he grabbed the waistband of my boxers and pulled them back up before urging me to step out of my jeans the rest of the way.

I was still handcuffed with no way to defend myself, as futile as I now knew that would have been. When Malcolm took my arm and gently turned me around so my back was facing him, unlocking the cuff around my left wrist, I couldn't believe my luck.

And I shouldn't have, because the next moment, he pushed down on my shoulder, forcing me down on my knees so he could fasten the other cuff to the bottom of the metal post at the foot of the bed.

I looked up at him in confusion only to find him staring down at me, a placid look on his fiendishly handsome features. "You're going to sleep there tonight. It's clear you can't be trusted with even a modicum of freedom, so you're going to have to earn everything from this point out. Trust. Comfort. Dignity. I have to keep you alive, but don't think for a minute that means I can't make you wish you were dead."

With that, he walked over to the door and turned out the light. A moment later, I heard clothing hit the floor and the bed creak under his weight. Long after the sound of his steady breathing told me he was asleep, I lay curled up on my side, contemplating everything that had just happened and everything that was yet to come.

Of all the fucking men I could have picked to get the hots for, it had to be him.

At least now I knew his aesthetic appeal to be just another ploy he used to lure in his unsuspecting victims.

A dazzling display, meant to seduce stupid little creatures into coming close enough that he could sink his claws in deep. By the time they realized the truth, it would be too late.

It already was for me.

MALCOLM

Valentine had been sulking ever since I'd found him huddled against my footboard with his knees drawn up to his chest that morning. I'd given him a simple choice, because that was by far the most effective way to retrain a mind.

Pure force was efficient, but it didn't produce any lasting change. Like water straining against a dam, the moment the structure crumbled, it would all just cascade in the direction it had been pushing toward all along. If you really wanted to control the way the water flowed, you had to direct it through carefully planned channels and streams.

With a stubborn boy in possession of inverse quantities of book smarts and common sense, the process was going to be a gradual one. Delicate and complicated, just like him.

I had given him the choice between staying cuffed to my bed, naked and alone while I went to work, and he could piss himself on the floor for all I cared. Or, he could behave himself and get dressed to accompany me.

He had chosen the latter. In his mind, it probably wasn't a choice at all, but that didn't matter. It gave him the illusion of control. Something to work toward.

In time, he'd come to see pleasing me was a reward in itself, but for now, his obedience in the interest of survival would do.

He was silent the entire ride to the station, which was fine by me. He prattled on entirely too much, anyway, about the most inane shit. The fact that I usually found it charming was cause for concern.

I knew Miller and the others were going to be up my ass even more than usual for bringing a hostage to work, but what choice did I really have? I wouldn't have left him alone even if he had chosen that. Not that he needed to know that.

If he had been sent along with any remotely professional clothing, I might have been able to pass him off to anyone who didn't recognize him already as an intern, but Enzo seemed to think not sending anything other than sweatshirts and jeans was going to keep him out of trouble.

It didn't really matter, though. I planned on getting him a new wardrobe anyway, since he was going to be accompanying me everywhere. If he was going to be a royal pain in the ass, he might as well be eye candy tailored to my preferences.

As for when we were home, well, I planned for him to be wearing so little it didn't matter.

"Morning, Chief," one of the rookies said as soon as I walked through the front door. I didn't remember her name, but I waved on my way past her.

"Stay close," I muttered to Valentine, low enough so that only he would hear me.

His only response was a glare, but I hadn't yet laid down any expectations for how he was to respond properly. I was keeping it remarkably simple, and so far, that proved to be a necessity.

I went straight to my office, wanting to give him as little time to be noticed as possible. With my luck, he was going to start blinking out an SOS in Morse code.

I opened the door and waited for Valentine to walk in, watching as he looked around and studied my office.

"Fancy," he muttered, dropping into the chair across from my desk.

"You stay here, and make no mistake, this is a test," I said pointedly, cuffing his left wrist to the chair for good measure. "If you try to run, you won't even make it to the front lobby. Do I make myself clear?"

"Crystal," he said bitterly.

"Good," I said, leaving the office. It was still early for a test, no matter how minor, and my expectations of him weren't high to begin with, but he had to start somewhere. And if I was going to get through an entire day of work with Valentine tethered to my hip, caffeine was a necessity.

I hadn't been in the break room for two full minutes before I felt someone approach and turned to find Miller standing near the coffee maker, her arms folded as she leaned against the counter. "So you brought your boy toy —sorry, *brother-in-law*—to work today."

"You pay a lot of attention to what your superiors are doing for someone with a full caseload," I replied, pouring myself a cup of coffee and one for Valentine, even though he was already wired enough. A cranky mob brat was enough to deal with without throwing caffeine withdrawal into the mix.

She just smirked. "What can I say? I have a curious mind."

"I've noticed," I said. "A dangerous trait to have in this city, don't you think?"

She scoffed, but I could tell from the way her gaze darkened she knew it was no idle threat. "What do you think the mayor's going to say about your pet DiFiore?"

"Not as much as he would have to say about you meeting his daughter at the Bellagio last month," I replied. I sneered at the look of dismay on her face. "What, you think you're the only one who's curious?

Anger burned in her eyes, and she clenched her jaw. "Really? Blackmail?" she asked flatly. "Carmen is twenty-three. She's old enough to make her own decisions."

"Sure. I bet if you put it like that to her daddy, he'd be more than happy to give you his blessing."

While she was still simmering with rage, I continued, "You're a good cop, Miller. Tough, but principled. Damn near incorruptible. That's a rare combination these days, and that's more than reason enough for you to make some very powerful enemies. A few of them have suggested I get rid of you over the years."

"So why haven't you?" she asked through her teeth.

I smiled. "Plausible deniability. You don't like me, and I don't like you, and everyone knows it. If I keep you around—maybe even promote you to deputy chief in a couple of years–it makes me look fair and reasonable, and it's a feather in your cap. A win-win situation."

"You're trying to bribe me with a promotion," she said flatly.

"Oh, it's not a bribe," I assured her. "I don't need to bribe you. Make no mistake, the second you cease to be more convenient as a shield than you are a pain in my ass, all bets are off. Now, knowing you, you might be willing to take that risk, for the sake of principle, but I wonder if that nobility extends to the people you love? That kid brother of yours, what's his name?" I asked, scratching the stubble on my jaw. "Ivan, right? He just got promoted to vice, didn't he?"

She didn't answer, but she didn't need to. The look on her face was more than explicit enough.

"Of course he did, now I remember," I said, snapping my fingers. "I actually put a word in for him."

Miller frowned in confusion. "Why would you do that?"

"Because he's a good kid, and we could use more of those out on the street," I said with a shrug. "But it's a dangerous job. Puts you in the right position to make all the wrong kinds of acquaintances. And shit happens. But don't you worry, I've still got plenty of friends from my own days on the beat. They'll keep a close eye on him, if I give the word. Just to make sure nothing... *unfortunate* happens. You catch my drift?"

Rage and the first tinge of fear I've ever seen in her flickered across her face. "You son of a bitch," she seethed. "You're fucking scum, you know that? You're everything that's wrong with this profession."

Her hand twitched at her side, and I wouldn't have been surprised if she went for her gun right there. I had seen better cops snap over less. You didn't really know someone until you knew what they were capable of under pressure, and as I had learned over the years, everyone was capable of just about anything, given just the right amount of it. Just the right little nudge in the wrong direction.

I hadn't exactly expected to have this conversation today, but it had been a long time coming. I had just been waiting for the right opportunity to find out exactly where her limit was.

"You may be right about that," I agreed. "But the next time you think about threatening me, think about this first: I was here a long time before you, and I'll be here a long time after you're gone if you keep going in the direction you are now. Because that's the thing about scum, Miller. It sticks."

I leaned in, patting her on the shoulder. "I'm glad we had this little talk."

With that, I left her to marinate in her righteous indignation. Only time would tell if my words sank in, or if she was a problem that needed to be dealt with sooner than later–but for now, I had shit to do.

When I went back to my office and found that Valentine was right where I left him, I was pleasantly surprised he hadn't tried to escape. Of course, I knew better than to attribute to obedience what I could attribute to incompetence when it came to him. If his brothers hadn't taught him how to steer clear of men like me, they probably hadn't taught him that basic skill, either.

That was something I would have to change in the future. Granted, him being helpless was conducive to my interests right now, but that wouldn't always be the case. Eventually, once he had been sufficiently broken down, I could begin the process of molding him into what I wanted. If not into a suitable pet, then at least into the kind of person who wasn't going to get himself killed the second I wasn't in charge of keeping him alive anymore.

I wasn't even sure why I gave a shit. Or if I did, in any meaningful sense of the word.

I told myself it was just the fact that once I had taken responsibility for something, as rare as that was, that made it mine. And I didn't take kindly to people touching my things.

Valentine had curled up with his knees to his chest in the chair by my desk, after turning it so it was facing the window. He looked up from the view of the city below, a familiar wariness entering those big brown eyes.

I set the cup of coffee on the window ledge in front of him. "I assume you take it with cream and copious amounts of sugar."

"No," he mumbled, even though he brought the cup to his lips eagerly enough.

I snorted, taking a seat behind my desk to begin my work. I managed to get all of twenty minutes' worth of work done before I heard a pained groan across the room and found Valentine sinking down, half out of his chair.

"This is torture," he whined. "You can't seriously expect me to just sit here for eight hours while you work with nothing to do."

It looked like the night before hadn't rendered him quite as broken and listless as he had seemed. Maybe he had a bit more mettle than I had given him credit for.

Good. That meant there was plenty of fun left to be had.

"It's usually more like ten," I informed him.

He gave a mournful howl of dismay. "That's not fair. If you're going to treat me like a child, you could at least get me an activity book or something."

I snorted a laugh. "That can be arranged."

"I'm serious. I have ADHD. This is a Geneva-Convention-breaking level of inhumanity."

I raised an eyebrow. "Are you really bitching more about being bored than you did about having your ass whipped red?"

His face turned a rather appealing shade of pink, and he leaned away from me. "I don't need to be reminded, thanks. Come on, at least give me a phone or something."

"What, so you can call and cry to your brother about how cruel I am?" I asked.

His silence was proof enough that was a valid concern. And really, it didn't truly matter what Enzo thought, because it wasn't up to him. Not anymore. He had given Valentine over to my care, and it wasn't my problem that Silas hadn't sufficiently warned him exactly what that might entail. Still, the less bitching I had to deal with, the better.

"I'll tell you what," I said, pushing up from my chair. "I have a few errands to run downtown, anyway. If you can manage to stay here and behave yourself for the next hour, then we'll see about getting you something to read."

He clearly wasn't happy with it, but he knew better than to argue. Or at least, he was learning to choose his battles. "What if I have to piss while you're gone?" he demanded.

I nodded to the coffee cup in his hand. "I suggest you finish that, then."

I heard him mutter "asshole" under his breath as I went to the door and got my jacket. I chose to pretend like I hadn't heard it for the moment, because I couldn't punish him as effectively as I wanted in here without drawing unwanted attention. I was already going to be keeping a running tally for when we got home, anyway, and I was certain of one thing.

By the end of the day, there would be others.

I locked the door to my office and stopped by the desk just around the corner on my way out. It was occupied by Dallas, a young guy in his mid-twenties who had just earned his way out of rookie status. He was a college boy, eager to prove himself as more than a spoiled academic, so while trust was not a luxury I had, if nothing else, I trusted his brown-nosing ambition.

"I need you to do me a favor," I said, waiting on the edge of his cubicle.

He looked up, taking out his earbuds. "Sure, Chief. What is it?"

"That guy in my office," I said, "Make sure he doesn't go anywhere. And make sure no one tries to go in. If anyone knocks, tell them I took an early lunch."

"You got it," he said, a knowing glimmer in his eye. "A little young, isn't he?"

I wasn't sure what gave him the impression I was looking to shoot the shit about my personal life, but I gave him a blank stare, planning on disabusing him of that notion immediately.

He cleared his throat awkwardly. "Right. I'll keep an eye on him."

"I appreciate it," I said before leaving the station. I glanced at my watch, figuring I had just enough time to catch my contact down at MIT before his next class started. As annoying as it was to admit, I didn't have many options if I wanted to find out what was on that damn chip, and I had already exhausted the limits of my abilities.

The more I worked on the damn thing, the more convinced I became that it was, impossible as it seemed, really Demon we were dealing with. And if that was the case, it raised more questions than answers. Chief among them was whether Silas was lying to me.

After Owen's death, I'd had my trepidations about Silas being the one to take Demon out, and those doubts had been exacerbated when he had decided to more or less go MIA for the next five years.

The fact that there had been no further encounters with Demon after that was proof enough to me that he really was gone, and Silas had kept his word.

Now...

No, trust was not a luxury I had. Not even for my own brother.

When I arrived on campus, the parking lot outside the main computer science building was packed. The place was the ideal hunting ground to scout new talent, and considering how many of these brilliant young minds were drowning in student debt, it had always been easy enough to procure their cooperation. Money was a decent enough substitute for loyalty, in most cases, and that was another fairy tale I had ceased to believe in a long damn time ago.

I got a few looks as I parked the car and walked into the building, but I doubted I was the only asshole with a Tesla around this place. Pretentiousness was practically a requirement for tenure.

I walked down the hall, past a throng of trust fund babies and eager nerds. This was the kind of place where everyone had an app in development, and half of them were going on about bullshit like "disrupting the market" because they had an idea for a new dating site. The other half were diehard, too smart for their own good, and too precocious to realize that no matter how brilliant they were, and no matter how much they wanted to change the world, they would never be permitted to change it for the better. Because that just wasn't how shit worked. The only thing all their ingenious inventions would ever succeed in accomplishing was making some rich asshole even richer.

When I reached my destination, the door was closed and I could hear voices behind it. I glanced at the sign papered to the door with cheesy '90s clipart of binary code and microchips that read: *Prof. Rosenfield's Office Hours: 9 AM to 11:30 AM Tuesday and Thursday.*

Looked like I was right on time.

I waited a few moments until the door opened, revealing a young woman in a hoodie with the university letters printed on the front, smiling stiffly and nodding in poorly feigned enthusiasm as the man behind the door prattled on about some shit that went over even my head.

She did a double take when she saw me before scurrying out of the room as quickly as possible.

"Oh, and don't forget the quiz next Wednesday," he called after her, freezing and turning a few shades paler when he finally noticed me. His voice went up an octave and cracked as he said, "Oh. Chief Whitlock, what a pleasant surprise. I wasn't expecting you again so soon."

"You're as bad at lying as that kid is at pretending like you're not boring her to death, Elijah," I informed him, walking into his office.

He looked flustered as he closed the door. "I'm sorry, but I don't have any new developments on the... project... you gave me. But I can assure you, you'll be the first to know when I do."

"Yes, I can see you're really burning the candle at both ends working on it."

He pursed his lips together and pushed his clear, perfectly round glasses further up his nose. It was a nervous tic I had picked up on the first time I'd met him while consulting on a homicide that happened to cross over into the cyber crimes division. Elijah was pretty much the poster boy for MIT faculty, inside and out. He was on the shorter side of average, with a pudgy build he seemed to think his structured vests were hiding, and even though I knew he was in his late thirties, he was clean-shaven with a baby face framed by golden brown hair in a tousled style that made him look even more boyish.

He was also flighty, neurotic, and a verifiable genius with the credentials and IQ scores to match. He'd worked for the NSA for a few years before securing tenure and a cushy corner office, in part thanks to my recommendation. To say he owed me would not have been an exaggeration.

"I have class," he protested. "I can assure you, I stayed late every night this week working on it. If you don't believe me, you can check the logs in the computer lab."

"I just might," I said, leaning on the edge of his desk. His office was cluttered with papers and books the entire wall of shelves behind his desk couldn't fully accommodate. He might've been a computer nerd, but his love of Chaucer and Proust was proof enough he wasn't entirely one-dimensional, like most of his colleagues. That was part of the reason I had chosen him as an asset. He was the soft, romantic type, literally and figuratively, and it had been easy enough to convince him of the nobility behind the cause in the beginning.

We were the better part of a decade into our working relationship, and I was sure he had been properly disabused of that notion. He was a genius, after all. But he was in too deep to turn back now.

"You know, it might help if you told me what's on this thing," he said, wringing his hands as he walked over to the window, not so subtly trying to put as much distance between us as he could. "Or who encrypted it in the first place. If I could just narrow down what kind of cipher they might've used, that would go a long way."

"You know everything you need to know," I said firmly.

He didn't usually push back, so when he turned to face me, his brow furrowed in frustration rather than the quiet deference I was used to, I was surprised. "You know, I've been involved in enough of your illicit dealings through all these years that if I were going to flip on you, I'd be going down with the ship, too."

"True," I said, drumming my fingertips on the edge of the desk. "I'm sure you're smart enough to know only one of us can swim in waters that choppy. Plenty of sharks who'd just love to munch on a tasty little seal like you."

He scowled, pulling his vest down over his rounded stomach. "So what's the harm in giving me the information I need to do my job? Since you aren't happy with the current timeline."

It was a fair question. I wasn't accustomed to changing my mind, but I wasn't opposed to it within reason. "The name 'Demon.' Does it ring any bells for you?"

Judging from the way he went from pale to sheet white, it did. "I... I thought he was dead."

"That makes two of us," I said, folding my arms. "You can imagine my surprise when a satellite of the DiFiore family turned up on death's door, saying that thing is the key to figuring out where he's been hiding all these years."

He swallowed audibly, sinking back against the wall. "So that chip... It belongs to... And I've been... Oh, God."

There it was. The reason I didn't want to tell him. Self-preservation was a hell of a hurdle to overcome. "Does that narrow it down any, Prof?"

He paused a moment before nodding shakily. "It gives me a better idea, yes. Do you have anything else from him? Encrypted correspondences he sent in the past, old files...?"

I hesitated. "I don't. But I know someone who might."

"Get them to me as soon as you can," he said, shrinking in on himself a little. "Please."

I pushed off his desk, walking over to the door. "I'll be in touch shortly." I paused at the door, my hand lingering on the knob. "And Elijah? Just so we're clear, anything Demon might do to you in the highly unlikely event he manages to connect you to the chip and hunt you down is going to be an absolute treat compared to what *I* do to you–and everyone you care about, including that perky little undergraduate–in the extremely unfortunate event that you survive it. Do we have an understanding?"

He was trembling visibly, but there was still an impressive amount of fire in his gaze. "Yes," he said stiffly. "We do."

"Smart man," I said before leaving the office. Sometimes an asset just needed a little reminder to prevent him from becoming a liability. That was why I took time out of my busy schedule for house calls every now and then.

I slipped back into my car and put on my sunglasses before pulling out onto the highway. I was headed back to the station when I got a call through the radio. An explosion on the side of the highway, not far from my exit. There was no mention of an accident, which was strange enough, but it was the description of the car that really got my attention. A dark red 1951 Pegaso Z-102. Considering the fact that there were fewer than fifty of them left on the road, something made me doubt that was a coincidence.

I put on the lights on my dash and sped up, but by the time I made it to the scene, the bomb squad was already there, and I could see the car. It was a shelled-out hunk of metal, but it was nonetheless unmistakable.

A staggering wave of déjà vu hit me as I got out of the car and walked over to the team. Some were setting up a barricade of yellow tape around the scene while others stood around, looking at the wreckage.

"What's going on?" I asked, even though I had a sinking feeling I already knew. Probably even better than they did.

The nearest cop looked surprised to see me, glancing back at the accident. "Beats me, Chief," he said, rubbing the back of his head. "No driver to be found, and no one in the area reports noticing any suspicious activity. No one was around, so no one got hurt."

I nodded absently, because that was far from the first thought on my mind. "Engine malfunction?" I asked hopefully, even though I already knew what the answer would be.

He shook his head. "No, too clean for that. And too powerful. This one was some asshole's science project. Looks like a remote detonation."

My throat grew tight, but I couldn't take my eyes off the wreckage. I could understand why the man next to me was looking at me the way he was. I had come upon truly gruesome scenes without so much as flinching. Hell, I had to remind myself not to eat at a crime scene half the time, but this...

This was something else. And as I stared at the wreckage, I found myself frozen in shock and dragged back to the darkest day of my life. There were plenty to choose from, but none of them held a candle to this one. Not a single one.

And it was, undoubtedly, a message. A message meant for me that only one person could have sent.

I jolted out of my stunned state with another realization.

"Valentine," I seethed, stalking back toward my car. I drove back to the station like a bat out of hell, because the wreck wasn't just a message. It was a distraction.

II

VALENTINE

I had spent the better part of an hour trying to pick the lock on the handcuff securing my wrist to the chair, and I was really starting to regret zoning out during all the times Enzo and Luca had tried to teach me that kind of shit.

"Never leave the house without at least two lockpicks," was pretty much Luca's mantra as I grew up. I'd been annoyed they thought I was a prime candidate for a kidnapping, but here I was.

Come to think of it, they had put a lot of focus on trying to decrease the likelihood that I would be kidnapped in general. Looking back, I was pretty sure I should be insulted by that. Guess I just seemed like the kind of kid that would get into a stranger's van on the promise of puppies and candy.

Who was I fucking kidding? If there was a puppy and candy van, I'd get in it now. No questions asked.

I was pretty sure Malcolm had either forgotten about me or something else had come up. That, or he had just completely ditched me. Probably that.

I had thought I would be better off going to work with him, considering there was only so much he could do to me in a building teeming with police.

I hoped. That, or he would have an audience.

In any case, I was wrong. I was actually starting to wish he would just take me home—to his place, anyway.

He still wasn't back when I heard some commotion outside the door, other than the usual hum of chatter and the bustle of the busy office. If nothing else, at least I was able to take consolation in the fact that Malcolm's job was boring as fuck most of the time. And I thought Enzo had it bad.

Not working was driving me crazy, though, and it had only been a little over a week. I didn't do downtime. The only way I could even force myself to relax once in a while, just to avoid the inevitable crash and burn, was if I got wasted.

Now that was something else I missed. Something told me Malcolm was going to be weirdly restrictive about that, too. It had become clear to me that the closest thing he possessed to a moral compass was the firm and unwavering belief that it was his responsibility to make sure I didn't have anything resembling a good time.

The sound of gunfire jolted me out of my pity party. I sat up at attention, trying not to freak the fuck out, for the two seconds it took for the screams of alarm to precipitate more gunfire. In the span of a single moment, a full-on gunfight had broken out on the other side of the door.

What the actual fuck?

When the gunfire drew closer and something hit the wall of Malcolm's office, I gasped sharply and fell back on instinct, toppling over the back of the chair. I hit the ground hard, my arm twisting enough that I felt a hard pop followed by a sickening burning sensation that radiated from my shoulder all the way down to my elbow.

Okay, *now* it was out of its socket.

I was still trying to get up when I realized someone was literally battering in the door. Holy fucking shit.

I gave up on trying to escape and instead ducked and covered behind the chair, at least as much as I could with my wrist still cuffed to the damn thing. For all the good that would do me. With another resounding thud, the door exploded inward, pieces of wood and plaster from the door frame spraying the floor.

Through the smoke, I could see the vague outline of a man with a grotesquely twisted face holding a police-issued battering ram that had definitely been commandeered. Judging from the silence outside the office, this was not a battle the good guys had won.

As the smoke cleared and the figure stepped into the room, I realized why his face looked so weird. It was a mask. Shiny, paper white plastic, if not something more durable, printed with the 3D design of a demon's face, its unnaturally wide mouth stretched into a crooked grin complete with two rows of razor sharp teeth. The eyes were cut out, but all I could see behind them was black shadow and the faint hint of light from pupils.

I coughed, because even though the dust had mostly settled, the smell of gunpowder and smoke in the air was tickling my throat. I moved as far back as I could until my back hit the wall, dragging the chair with me in the process, but I couldn't even focus on the pain in my shoulder. It was like it belonged to someone else. All I could do was stare up at the man who was now standing right in front of me, a mere few feet away.

The masked man tilted his head to one side at an unnatural angle, or maybe it only seemed that way because of the mask.

"Valentine DiFiore," he said in a voice garbled by some kind of distortion device. A good one, too, not just the kind any kid could buy online as a gag gift. "We meet at last."

"That's a pretty clichéd villain line, you know," I said, my voice strained but not quite as weak sounding as I had expected, especially considering the fact that I was pretty sure I was two seconds away from pissing myself.

He chuckled, and even his laugh was robotic and wrong. "I assume you know who I am, then."

"Yeah, you're the motherfucker who killed Robbie. The mask kind of gives it away," I said flatly. "If you're hoping for a big, dramatic reveal, you might want to go with something a bit more subtle next time."

"Sarcastic, even in the face of death," he mused. "Now that brings back memories. I can see why Malcolm is so fond of you."

"What the hell is that supposed to mean?" I asked, figuring as long as I kept this freak talking, that was another second for the cops to arrive. Assuming there were any left in the damn city.

"You remind me of his lover," he answered, like it should be obvious. "The one I killed."

What the fuck? Silas had left out that little detail.

The Demon raised a double-barreled pistol, and while going to the range wasn't exactly a hobby for me like it was for Enzo and Luca, I knew enough about guns to know it was not one you could just buy on the regular market. That shit was custom. "And that's something else you'll have in common besides sarcasm."

Everyone says your life flashes before your eyes right before you're about to die, but I didn't have that experience. I wasn't sure if it was because that wasn't really what happened to anyone, or because I just hadn't actually lived enough of my life for there to be a highlight reel.

That was kind of a depressing thought, but it was far from the most prominent realization that happened in the span of that eternal moment. The most pressing realization was what I felt most keenly. Fear, regret, longing, and guilt over the fact that here I was, face-to-face with the guy who'd killed Robbie, and I could do fuck all about it... those things were all there, sure, but in such small quantities relative to another emotion so intense and deep that it threatened to sweep them all up into itself, like a tornado collecting debris in its path.

Relief.

Maybe it was just shock, but I was pretty fucking sure that wasn't what you were supposed to feel right before you were about to be violently murdered.

It wasn't even like it was just adrenaline that had crossed the wires in my brain, considering the fact that I could think of not one, but several reasons why that perplexing feeling was there.

For one thing, it was the realization that had been forming for a long time–and finally crystallized in that very moment–that my brothers and the rest of my family, Johnny and Chuck included, would be better off. They would feel like shit for a while, sure, and I felt guilty for that, too, but they would be down one burden, and I was a better memory than I was a brother.

This whole recent escapade was proof that I just really didn't have anything to offer in the way of a meaningful contribution to the family. Enzo was their brave, noble leader, the scion of the DiFiore line, and Johnny was his right-hand man now. Luca was the calm, level-headed one, the one everyone went to when they needed advice.

Chuck was the muscle, and even Silas had come to fit into the family better in a handful of years than I had in my entire lifetime.

What the hell was I even good for? Comedic relief? I was the joker and the punchline, and not much else.

Despite the fact that I had always kind of been a romantic and hoped that I'd have a wife and kids one day, I had never had any romantic connection more meaningful than a short-term relationship or one-night stand. Hell, the closest I had ever come was the boss who had hated me until a month or two ago, and a man I hated more than anything even if he did make me feel things that made me hate myself even more than I loathed him.

And even that was probably just some weird side effect of Stockholm syndrome.

Yeah, I was a mess. And not the fun kind of mess, like after hosting a house party that's totally worth having to clean stale popcorn out of the sofa cushions for the next three weeks. The pathetic train wreck of a life kind of mess. A life poorly lived, ended prematurely in one sense and not soon enough in another. Not even with a bang, but a whimper.

That sounded about right, actually.

His finger closed around the trigger, and I took a deep breath, closing my eyes to meet my fate. Because if I couldn't go down fighting, I was at least going to be a fucking drama whore about it.

A shot fired, but I didn't feel anything. That, too, seemed to line up with what I knew from my brothers.

Except I didn't feel anything. No cold, no hot, no pain. When I opened my eyes and saw Demon stagger forward, I realized he wasn't the one who'd fired first.

"Get down!" Malcolm snarled. I heard him before I saw him coming into the room with guns blazing. One in each hand, like a fucking action hero. He looked the part, too, and that was the biggest joke of all, because no matter what the guy in front of me had done, Malcolm was still the villain.

I had barely ducked before he fired three shots into the man who hadn't fully recovered from the first. Demon's body lurched violently, but when I realized there was no blood, I knew something was wrong.

There was always blood. So fucking much of it.

He was wearing a bulletproof vest. Of course he was.

The chair tumbled after me as I dove for the side of Malcolm's desk, the closest thing to shelter the open room could provide, covering my ears even though I was pretty sure the crossfire had already at least partially deafened me.

When there was finally a reprieve from the gunfire, I looked up to see Demon shoving past Malcolm, who turned and fired another round of shots before he emptied his clip.

"Shit," he hissed, taking a step to follow only to stagger, leaning heavily to one side. There was blood soaking through the side of his shirt and jacket as well as his upper left shoulder, and he had definitely been shot at least once, but somehow, he was still standing.

"Malcolm!" I cried.

He hesitated at the door, but whether it was because he realized there was no hope of catching up with Demon–at least not without getting killed–or in response to my plea, he muttered something that was almost certainly profane and probably blasphemous under his breath before he came over to me.

He knelt down, reaching into his pocket for a set of keys linked to his belt. He hastily unlocked the cuff tethering me to the arm of the chair. His hands were shaking, but I was pretty sure it was adrenaline and rage rather than fear.

"Are you hurt?" he asked.

"I'm fine," I said, trying to get a better look at where he had been shot. "I'm not the one who's Swiss cheese."

He ignored me, pulling me to my feet. I reached out, but he brushed my hand aside. "I'm fine. There are survivors. Go check on them."

I hesitated a second, maybe a fraction of one, but it was long enough for him to bark, "Go!"

It was enough to jolt me into action and I ran out into the bullpen, looking around for any sign of life among the fallen bodies. There were five that I could see, but judging from the sounds of the gunfire, there had been a hell of a lot more than that.

"Over here," a familiar voice cried. I followed the sound of it to the detective who had been grilling me when they brought me in from the shooting at the hospital.

Her left arm was bleeding, but she had already fashioned a tourniquet out of ripped cloth. The man next to her wasn't doing so hot. He looked barely conscious, sitting up against the wall and leaning on her. There was a huge spot of blood soaked into his shirt where the bullet had struck his lower right abdomen. Not a great spot. Too many important things it could've hit. He looked like he was around my age, his light hair and features similar enough to hers that I wondered if they were related.

"I'm fine, just help him," she said, her voice breaking.

I nodded, dropping down beside the man. "Where's the first aid kit?"

"Down the hall, I'll get it," she said, already on her feet even though I could tell she was reluctant to leave his side.

While she was gone, I decided I had to do something about my shoulder. I grabbed my upper arm near the elbow, took a deep breath, and forced it back into the socket. A strangled cry escaped me, but it wasn't as bad as what Malcolm had done to me earlier.

The detective was gone all of thirty seconds before she returned with what looked like a heavy-duty kit. Definitely more than the kind most people kept in the bathroom cabinet.

"What's his name?" I asked, opening the kit to take an assessment of its contents.

She hesitated before answering, "Ivan."

"Okay, Ivan, stay with me," I said, opening his shirt. There was blood gushing from the wound, so I carefully got down on the floor and shrugged out of my shirt, since the cloth she had been holding against it was soaked clean through. "You're gonna be okay."

His eyes were glazed, and I had seen that look often enough, and recently, to know it wasn't good. "I'm going to fucking die," he groaned.

"Don't say that," the detective hissed, grabbing his wrist. "You're gonna be fine."

"What's your badge number, Ivan?" I asked. They both gave me a strange look. "Humor me."

He hesitated, staring up at the ceiling. "Two one six... eight... eight, uh..."

"Eight what?" I pressed, grabbing a pack of coagulant powder and tearing it open with my teeth before I started packing the wound.

He winced before continuing, "six three four."

"Great, now give it to me backwards," I said, reapplying pressure.

The detective looked up, frowning. "Exactly what is the point of this?"

"Keeping him awake," I answered. "Put your hands here, and hold pressure on the wound, like you're trying to keep him from getting up. And keep him talking. Gotta check on the others."

She nodded reluctantly, and as I left, I could hear her urging him to recite the number backwards.

In the next room, I could see Malcolm kneeling next to the outstretched body of the kid from reception, and judging from the look on his face, it wasn't good. He looked up, shaking his head somberly.

I went over to the body closest to me, checking for a pulse, and repeated the same for another six, minus the first group I had seen outside Malcolm's office.

There were only four survivors, including the two of us.

Four out of over a dozen.

Since there was no one else left, I turned to my other patient. Probably the most difficult one I had ever had.

"Sit down," I said, trying to push Malcolm toward the nearest chair.

His eyes narrowed, and he planted his feet, making it clear I wasn't going to push him anywhere he didn't want to go.

I gave him a disbelieving look. "Seriously? This is the one time you might want to defer to my expertise."

He clenched his jaw, but he sat—or more or less collapsed—in the chair and tore his shirt open the rest of the way, peeling it off with a faint grimace. I could hear ambulance sirens in the distance, not a second too soon.

Malcolm had been hit in the left shoulder, a few inches from his heart, and the side of his lower abdomen had two wounds that didn't look bad. The one in his shoulder was worrying me the most. There was a major artery there, so I grabbed his shirt and tried to rip it, but he made it look a lot easier than it was. Instead, I just settled for wrapping it around his shoulder to make a tourniquet as best I could. It wasn't ideal, given the location, but it was better than nothing.

"The bullet is still in there, probably fragmented," I said. "Try not to move. I don't think it hit the artery, but that could change if one of the fragments gets dislodged."

Malcolm nodded as I tore open another pack of coagulant powder.

"This is going to sting," I warned.

He gave me a withering look.

I shrugged and started packing the wound, and he let out a furious hiss through his teeth. "Son of a bitch."

"I warned you," I muttered, taking a little more pleasure in this than I wanted to admit. The Hippocratic oath was a promise to do no harm, but it said nothing about a little schadenfreude when harm was already being done.

I must not have done quite as good a job of hiding it as I had thought, though, because he said, "You know, you could pretend like you're not enjoying this."

"I probably could," I agreed.

He blew a snort through his nostrils. "I'll be okay. Go check on the kid."

I hesitated again, for some reason reluctant to leave his side.

"Go," he snapped.

I frowned, but turned on my heel and went back to check on Ivan. He was still reciting that number, awkwardly and with long pauses in between, but he was conscious.

The detective looked up, relief lighting her eyes. "The bleeding has slowed down a lot. That's good, right?"

"It is," I said, even though I was more encouraged by the fact that he was still conscious than anything. He had lost a lot of blood, and I didn't have the equipment to tell just how much damage had been done.

A moment later, the paramedics rushed in, and after filling them in on what I knew about my patient's injuries, I went to check on Malcolm. He was where I had left him, angrily fending off the advances of the two paramedics who were desperately trying to treat him.

"Would you stop being a martyr?" I groaned. "Bleeding out because you're too fucking stubborn to accept help from literal medical professionals is not going to win you any macho points, I promise."

He shot me a withering glare, and I was sure I would be paying for that the moment we were alone as thanks for my assistance, but if it got his ass to the hospital, fine. Why I gave a shit, I still wasn't sure.

Instead, he gave a grudging sound of acknowledgment and stomped past the medics, probably intent on going out to the ambulance on his own. Of course he was. I decided to wait to roll my eyes all the way back into my head until I was at least reasonably sure he was going to live.

All of five minutes later, we were at the emergency room, and the fact that my hospital was the closest was an unfortunate reality. They took Malcolm and Ivan back immediately, and while I could tell everyone was confused and more than a bit wary to see me, they let me go back with him for everything except the x-rays. Guess I was family, in the most technical sense of the word.

A moment after they got Malcolm a bed, which he insisted on sitting up in, Chris came in, still wearing his outdoor coat and slightly out of breath like he had just run in.

"Valentine?" he cried, rushing over to my side. He stopped, putting a hand on my shoulder as he looked me over, genuine fear and concern in his gaze. "What happened? Are you hurt?"

"I'm fine, I'm not hurt," I assured him, nodding to Malcolm. "He's the one who got shot."

Chris turned to face his actual patient, frowning. He wasn't the kind to let his personal feelings get in the way of his job, but I could tell he wasn't happy about it all the same as he went over to the other man.

"Hey, Doc," Malcolm said with his usual malicious sneer, even though there wasn't quite as much bite to it as usual. "Long time, no see."

Chris just frowned harder, looking over his wounds. I was surprised Malcolm was even letting him.

"We got the blood loss under control, but he lost a lot of it," I remarked. "He's A negative, and don't let the bluster fool you, he'd be an asshole on his literal deathbed."

Malcolm shot me the filthiest look yet. "I'm not a fucking dog at a vet."

"You're right," Chris said in a bored tone, prodding at one of the wounds in Malcolm's side unnecessarily, just to make him grimace. "Most dogs are better behaved, and not as much of a rabies risk."

"You wanna go, Doc? Because I can bleed out a few more minutes to make it a fair fight if you want."

Chris scoffed a laugh. "Yes, by all means, do threaten the man who's going to do emergency surgery on you." He pulled his stethoscope off from around his neck and put the earpieces in before placing the chestpiece over Malcolm's heart.

"Surgery?" Malcolm asked warily. "I don't have time for that shit, I need to go after him."

"After who?" Chris asked, frowning. "You're not going anywhere, regardless."

"Want to bet?"

I walked over to put a hand on Malcolm's shoulder, even though I didn't know why I thought that would have any remotely positive effects, considering how he felt about me. If nothing else, it seemed to stun him into momentary compliance.

"Demon is already long gone by now," I reasoned. "And you will be, too, if you don't let him operate. I trust him wholeheartedly."

"You know why that's not exactly a ringing endorsement, right?" Malcolm asked gruffly.

I rolled my eyes. "Okay, I guess you could always let me do it here without anesthesia."

"Fine," Malcolm muttered, which was a shock in and of itself. "But this had better not take long."

"Yes, I'll be sure to let the OR staff know you're in a hurry," Chris said, his voice dripping with sarcasm. He rolled his eyes as soon as Malcolm's back was turned. "The pre-op team will be in to get you in a minute."

As soon as we were alone, I expected Malcolm to bitch me out for daring to defy him in front of others. Especially Chris, since he had some weird grudge against the guy.

"Before you say anything, I know," I said, preempting him.

He frowned in confusion. "Before I say what?"

"That I'm in trouble for mouthing off to you and you're going to punish me for it later," I answered.

He snorted. "Oh, you are, and I am. But I was going to thank you."

I stared at him for a moment. "Maybe you are dying. If you see a light, don't go into it."

He rolled his eyes. "I'm serious, and it's not something I say often. Or ever, so just take it," he said in his usual gruff tone.

I smiled a little, but I was more worried than I was letting on. Maybe there was something to that whole Stockholm syndrome theory, after all. That was fast. "Yeah, well, Demon was about to pull that trigger when you came in, so we'll call it even."

Malcolm was back to his usual serious, bordering on menacing, self in an instant. "Silas is on his way to get you. If I go in there before he gets here, I want you to promise me you're going to stay put. Demon has already come after you twice now, and he doesn't leave anything unfinished."

"Considering the fact that he's back from the dead, I guess not," I mumbled. A memory resurfaced from all the chaos just then. "Hey, he said something earlier I was wondering about."

"Who, Demon?" Malcolm asked, frowning.

"Yeah. He said he killed your lover. Is that true?"

His gaze turned even darker, if that were possible. "Yeah. It is."

I wasn't sure why that took me by surprise as much as it did. Guess part of me was expecting him to deny it, if only because it was an admission that he had been vulnerable enough to love another person, at least once in his life.

"Oh," I said awkwardly. Now that I had my answer, I wasn't really sure what to do with it. "I guess you really are invested in taking him down, then."

"No shit," he said. "Why do you sound so surprised about that?"

"I'm not," I answered. "I'm surprised you stayed with me rather than going after him."

He didn't seem to know what to do with that. It was rare that I had him at a loss for words, and I decided I would take it. The others came in to prep him, anyway, and after grudgingly leaving his phone and personal items in my care, Malcolm left with them.

I had been in the OR plenty of times, and the last time, it had gone about as disastrously as it could have. I wasn't used to being on this side of it, though—waiting helplessly while someone I cared about was in surgery.

It fucking sucked.

It occurred to me then that I did actually care about Malcolm, if only for one reason. Thanks to Demon, our fates were now inextricably intertwined. And we had at least one thing in common.

We both wanted him dead more than anything.

VALENTINE

As soon as Enzo and Silas got me back to the house and Luca showed up, Silas, who was totally not worried about his brother at all, went back to the hospital. Just in case Demon showed up there or something. Again, not because he was worried. Nope. Not that.

One thing that had changed since I'd left was the fact that there were now four armed guards stationed around the property, and those were just the ones I could see. Knowing Silas, he had an army of fucking ninjas lurking in the shadows watching the place.

And that would be pretty fuckin' sweet, I had to admit.

The fact that he wouldn't leave until Luca arrived, though, was proof he didn't want to leave Enzo alone. I could tell my brother knew, too, and was kind of pissy about it, but he didn't complain. Probably because Silas was Very Not Worried and he was going easy on him, because that was definitely the kind of shit he'd normally bitch about.

"Val?" Luca asked, a worried crease in his brow as he strode down the hall. "Shit, I came as soon as I got Enzo's text. You okay?"

"I'm fine," I said, for what felt like the thousandth time. He really wasn't the huggy feely type, so I didn't take it personally that he didn't run to squeeze the life out of me like Enzo had. My shoulder was grateful, too. I could tell from the look on his face he was freaked out, though, which made me feel like shit for thinking he wouldn't have been all that affected by my death. I still thought it, but I felt bad about it.

I could tell he didn't believe me, but he didn't push it, which I was also thankful for.

"I just saw Silas drive out of here like a bat out of hell, so I assume he's going back to the hospital," said Luca.

"Yeah, he went to check on Malcolm," Enzo said with a sigh. "He thinks Demon would be more likely to show up at the hospital."

"What's his condition?" Luca asked him, like the guy with the medical degree who'd been literally treating the patient in question an hour ago wasn't standing right there.

"He's in surgery," Enzo answered before I had the chance. "They said it could be a few hours before we know anything, but it was just his shoulder."

Luca nodded.

"That's not actually a good thing," I said.

They both turned to look at me.

"What do you mean?" asked Enzo.

"The shoulder's one of the worst places you could get shot," I answered. "I mean, there are four major arteries in that area alone. The bullet nicks any one of them and you're in trouble. That's why Silas got so fucked up when Dad shot him. And he got shot in the side, too, but I'm not as worried about those, all things considered."

"Oh. Right," Enzo said dismissively. "Anyway, this Demon asshole got away and now he's loose, so I've got Johnny mounting a search party across the city, for all the good that's probably gonna do."

Luca grunted in acknowledgment. "Probably not much. This guy stayed hidden for what, five years? Ten?"

"Something like that," Enzo said. "Silas has gone full-on 'the less you know, the better' with this bullshit."

"That's convenient," I mumbled.

They both turned to look at me again, and Enzo frowned. "Why were you even at the station, anyway? You were supposed to be staying at Malcolm's place."

Like that was the safe haven he seemed to think it was. I bristled at the tone in his voice, like I was a stupid kid who couldn't stay put. "Well, it was 'take your prisoner to work day,' and he couldn't find a sitter, so it just seemed like the most reasonable thing to do."

"For God's sake, Valentine, you're not a prisoner," Enzo shot back. "He's looking out for you."

"You sure? You might wanna run that by him, then, because I'm pretty sure he thinks you sold me to him as an exotic pet," I shot back.

He frowned. "What are you talking about?"

Luca was watching me intently, too, waiting. This was my chance. My opportunity to finally tell Enzo exactly what Malcolm had done, because if anyone could save me from the devil, it was the devil's brother—and if anyone could save me from him, it was mine.

Except by admitting what had happened, I would basically be proving them right about everything. That I was a helpless kid who couldn't stand up for himself. That I was weak. That I'd let another man literally beat my ass into submission, and then some.

Then there was that old fear that if I did tell my brothers what was going on, they would come to the rescue, because that was just what they did, because they weren't pathetic. Because they stood up not only for themselves, but everyone around them, too. Hell, Enzo had almost gotten himself put away for life, if not killed, because he'd murdered a guy in defense of a complete stranger. And there was no doubt in my mind that he would definitely go to bat for me, no matter what the consequences were. To his life. To his relationship.

I clenched my jaw and shook my head. "Nothing. Just forget it," I muttered.

His brow furrowed even harder. "I'm not gonna forget it. What do you mean, he's treating you like a pet?"

"Just being my usual dramatic self," I said in a dry tone. I knew that was what he and Luca always said behind my back, anyway. "He's a dick, but I'll live."

"That's the point," said Enzo. "Look, I can't stand the guy personally, but he's good at what he does, and he's got the kind of connections we can't afford to lose. Especially not right now. Not until Demon is either dead or locked up. Like I said, it's not forever, but I need you to be patient just a little while longer, and at least try to be on good behavior, okay? For me."

"Yeah, sure," I sighed, already walking past them. "While I'm here, I'm gonna grab some things. You're shit at packing."

I didn't need to turn around to know he was flipping me off. Once I got up to my room, I grabbed the duffel bag under my bed that I'd had since the last time I'd tried to run away as a teenager. That had lasted all of five hours, until I got hungry.

I was still throwing clothes into the bag along with my tablet and some backup chargers just in case when I felt I wasn't alone. I turned to find Luca leaning in the doorway, watching me in silence with this weird nostalgic look on his face.

"Well, that's not creepy at all," I said, turning to face him.

He blew a puff of air through his nostrils. "Just been a while since I've been in here, that's all. Reminds me of all those times you used to come into my room in the middle of the night begging me to check your closet because you were convinced there was a goblin living in there."

"Yeah, well, *Troll 2* did a number on my prepubescent psyche," I muttered. "No actual trolls in that, by the way. Total ripoff."

"He's just worried about you, y'know. He doesn't handle not being able to fix things very well."

"Yeah, I've noticed," I said, folding my arms. "He's been trying to fix me for years."

"That's not true, Val."

"No?" I challenged. "You sure about that? That's not why I heard you guys talking about what to do about 'the Val problem' after Dad died?"

His face went blank, and while I thought it would feel good to finally call him out on it, it didn't. It just made me feel even shittier. "Valentine, you—"

"Weren't supposed to hear that, yeah, I know," I said. "But I did."

"You don't understand the context of that," he insisted. "Like you said, it was right after Dad died. We were all scrambling to get our alibis straight, and the whole thing was delicate. Like a house of cards, and all it would've taken is one little mistake for the whole thing to come down."

"Sure. And I'm always the weakest link."

He gave me a look. "You're not weak, you're just... Look, until that DA's prick son, we were practically the fucking Waltons of the crime world. Even Enzo was fucked up over that shit, and as much bad blood as there was between him and Dad, he was still our father. None of us had ever dealt with anything worse than him out there, and all of a sudden, we were knee-deep in the highest profile clusterfuck this city's known in the last twenty years. We didn't know if you could handle it. Shit, some days, I wasn't sure if I could."

"What, you think I'd crack and betray my own brothers because I'm upset?" I demanded.

"Of course not. That's not what I said. It's not that it would be intentional, but you have to admit, you've always been... sensitive," he said after a long pause.

"Sensitive," I echoed with a bitter laugh. "What, because I have emotions and unlike everyone else around here, I'm not constantly jacking off to the fantasy of being some inhuman robot who feels nothing? Just because I'm not as pent up as the rest of you doesn't mean I'm some unstable little bitch."

"Again, I never said that. But you don't always react to things in the most measured way, this being case in point."

I clenched my fist at my side hard enough my nails dug into my palms. "Right. Because it's so much better to be like you guys. Maybe I should lie to myself and everyone else for a quarter of a fucking century like Enzo. Or pretend like I have my shit together when everything's falling apart. That's much healthier."

Luca narrowed his eyes in suspicion, and I immediately regretted the words, but it was too late. They were already out. "What the hell is that supposed to mean?"

"Nothing."

"Fuck that," he said, stalking into the room. "You said it, so you might as well be a man and fucking own it."

I gritted my teeth, trying not to cave to the frustration. "I know you and Carol aren't exactly living the little slice of domestic bliss you want everyone else to see. And I know you've been fucked up about Geo ever since your bromance broke up, but you think not talking about it is somehow going to make it all go away, and it's fucking not."

He just stared at me for a few seconds, his expression completely blank.

I let out a deep breath. "I'm sorry. I shouldn't have—"

I broke off as he took a swing at me, and I barely ducked in time for his fist to hit the wall rather than my chin.

"What the fuck?" I cried.

"You little bitch," he seethed, lunging at me again. This time, he succeeded at pinning me against the wall, but I tried in vain to shove him back, my hands around his throat, and the struggle sent us both to the floor.

"Yeah, you're right. This is real calm and measured," I choked out, pushing him away from me as he fisted my shirt in one hand, gripping a handful of my hair with the other since that was the closest thing to my throat he could reach.

"Oh, shut up, you fucking brat," Luca snapped. I brought my knee up into his stomach and threw him off me with a wheeze.

Before I could get to my knees, he was back on his. He grabbed my ankle, yanking me back until I fell forward. He grabbed my arm next and twisted it behind my back, moving close enough behind me I could smell the alcohol on his breath.

"Day drinking again, brother?" I taunted, throwing my head back until it hit something. Probably teeth, judging from how bad it hurt and the fact that I could feel something hot and sticky trickling down my scalp.

"Fuck off," he spat, twisting my arm even harder. "Take it back. Now."

"What, the part about you having a shit marriage, or the part about you being a functioning alcoholic?" I shot back.

He grabbed another fistful of hair to slam my head into the hardwood floor, covered only by a thin rug. "Like the guy who's made a drunken fool out of himself at every family gathering in the last ten years has room to talk."

"At least I know I'm a mess," I yelled, elbowing him hard enough with my injured arm to send him flying off me and onto his side with a thud. I staggered to my feet. "You act like you're Mr. Fucking Perfect who pisses gold and has never fucked up in his life!"

"Is that what you think?" he demanded, getting back on his feet, still panting with exertion. "You think I don't live in Enzo's shadow? You think I never felt like a colossal fucking disappointment? Enzo's the firstborn and you were always Dad's favorite. The one who could do no fucking wrong. So don't give me that shit!"

"Me?" I gave a dry laugh. "Favorite? Try invisible. I don't even need a whole hand to count the number of times he ever even acknowledged me by name."

"Aww, poor Valentine," he said in a mocking tone. "That must've been so hard. You think his attention was some father-son bonding moment? Like he didn't call me a faggot for crying at our mother's funeral, or beat the shit out of me every time he got drunk."

"Yeah, because he was a fucked-up son of a bitch, and that was how he showed he gave a shit," I cried, even though I knew it was bullshit. That just didn't stop the words from coming out. "At least he cared how you turned out."

"What the fuck would you know?" he demanded, shoving me back. "He never even hit you, for Christ's sake."

"Oh, please," I said with a bitter laugh, shoving him back harder. Hard enough to stagger him. "You don't know shit."

"No?" he challenged, taking a step closer. "Because I'm pretty fucking sure I do. He treated you like a princess, probably because he knew you'd shatter like glass if he ever touched you."

Something snapped in me, and I took another swing. This time, it hit, and blood sprayed from his split lip, but a second later, he tackled me again, sending us both into my desk. One of the wooden legs splintered and I landed hard on my back with Luca on top of me, his hands wrapped around my throat tight enough that there was no room to doubt he was trying to choke me out.

The fear and rage I should have felt when Malcolm had me in this position kicked into overdrive, and I clawed at his face, going for his eyes even though I should have been focused on getting his hands off me.

"Name one fucking thing you ever did that he punished you for even a fraction as bad as he punished me and Enzo for just existing," he demanded.

I grimaced, straining in vain to push him off, and he had my legs pinned, too, so it wasn't like I could just kick him off me again. "Go... to hell... Luca," I gritted out.

"Not until you answer," he growled. "One fucking time, Val. Just one, and I'll never say it again, but you can't, can you? You can't, because it never happened."

"Fourth of July," I choked, starting to see black at the edges of my vision as my brain was starved of oxygen and panic took over.

"What? What the hell is that supposed to mean?"

"You asked when Dad ever punished me the way he punished you," I said through my teeth. "Fourth of July, two-thousand six. That's when."

I could tell he didn't believe me, but his grip loosened just enough to let me speak. I still couldn't take a full breath, though. "So you pulled a random date out of your ass, that doesn't mean shit."

"How do you think I got that broken arm I had when you and Enzo got back from camp?" I demanded.

He frowned. "You were always getting into shit, and he never raised a hand against you for it. What the hell did you do that he broke your fucking arm over it?"

"Fuck off."

His grip loosened, but he replaced it with his forearm instead, a far more effective method of keeping me pinned and compressing my jugular enough that I started to feel lightheaded again. "I'm not letting you up until you say it."

I felt another surge of panic-fueled adrenaline and tried to throw him off, but it didn't work. No matter how I thrashed, I couldn't push him away and frustration and exasperation overcame me as I hissed, "Mr. Hoffman!"

Luca froze, his eyes filling with confusion. "Who, the gym teacher? What does he have to do with anything?"

"Get off me," I cried, feeling tears of frustration spring to my eyes at the worst possible time. All the adrenaline and terror and sheer fuckery of the day came crashing down on me all at once, along with Luca's weight, and it wasn't just my throat that was tight, it was my whole chest.

"What happened, Valentine?" Luca demanded, concern and wariness edging into the anger in his voice. Something flashed in his eyes that was dangerously close to realization, and his voice grew even rougher. "What did he do?"

My teeth ground together so hard my jaw hurt, like that was going to keep me from betraying the most humiliating, fucked up memory of all. The one I'd dug a hole so deep and dark for, and drowned in so much booze and meaningless sex and pointless fights to bury, and it still wasn't enough. It was still there, watching me in the background, like some intruder inside my own mind.

"Get off," I choked out, barely able to see through the tears in my eyes, even though it came out more as a plea than a demand this time. All the fight left me at once, and even though Luca's hold on me had weakened, I still couldn't have pushed him off if I tried.

The look of horror and understanding on his features had left nothing more than an ember of the rage and indignation that had been there before, but it was a thousand times worse. He opened his mouth like he was about to say something when Enzo's voice echoed through the room.

"Hey!" he bellowed, followed by the sound of thunderous footsteps. A second later, he grabbed the back of Luca's shirt and hauled him off me before shoving him. "What the fuck is wrong with you?"

Luca could've stood his ground normally, but he still seemed dazed, and he didn't take his eyes off me even when his back hit the wall.

I rolled onto my stomach and started to get back on my feet even though the room was still spinning. When I felt a hand on my shoulder and realized it was Silas trying to help me up, I shoved him off and staggered to my feet on my own.

"I'm fine," I said, pinching the bridge of my nose and tilting my head back to stop the blood flow. I didn't know when I'd gotten a nosebleed, but I was still a little unsteady on my feet and that was making it worse, so I decided to just let it stop on its own.

"You're not fine!" Enzo cried, gesturing to me. "Look at you!"

"I started it," I lied. "I hit him first."

Enzo narrowed his eyes like he didn't believe it and turned to Luca. "Is that true?"

"Given recent events, it does seem likely," Silas said in a dry tone, looking me up and down. "I have to say, he did more of a number on you than Demon."

"Well, something happened, and someone's gonna tell me what the hell it was," Enzo demanded, looking between me and Luca. "Now."

"Nothing happened," I insisted. "Luca was trying to tell me you were just looking out for me, it pissed me off, and I snapped and threw the first punch, okay? You're right.

You're both right. I'm immature, and I lost my temper, so I had it coming."

Enzo frowned as he listened, but Silas was giving me a weird look, like he knew it was bullshit. And as good of a liar as I was, he was better, so he probably did.

"Is that true?" Enzo demanded of Luca. "Did he hit you first?"

Luca started to answer, but I shot him a pleading look. He hesitated a moment before he grudgingly said, "I shouldn't have hit him back, especially with everything he just went through. It was both of us."

Enzo paused to contemplate for a moment before he said, "I'm disappointed. In both of you. We've got enough to worry about right now without being at each other's throats."

"God, you sound like Mom," Luca muttered.

I snorted a laugh before I could stop myself, and even though Enzo glared at me in return, Luca's mouth tilted slightly at one corner. It didn't quite meet his eyes.

"Care to change your mind, love?" Silas asked in a knowing tone.

"Change your mind about what?" I asked warily, eyeing him and Enzo.

Enzo just heaved a sigh of exasperation. "Silas wants to send you and Malcolm both to a safe house while we clean all this up. Not this," he said pointedly, gesturing to the wreckage of my room. We had really done a number on it. "But the Demon situation. And I agree with him."

"That's bullshit," I cried. "I'm not going to go into hiding any more than I already am."

"It's not up to you to call the shots," Enzo said firmly. "Not anymore."

I turned my attention to Silas, trying to make his head burst into flames with my mind. Now would be a really great time for those pyrokinetic superpowers I'd always wished for as a kid to kick in.

"Malcolm is out of surgery, and he's going to be out of commission for a while," Silas said. "We need somewhere for him to recover physically, and you from your nervous breakdown."

"Fuck off, Budget Moriarty," I hissed.

Silas chuckled, to add insult to injury. "I've always considered myself more of a Hannibal Lector type, but touché."

"How long is it going to take you to get them out of the country?" Enzo asked.

"I've already made arrangements, and there's a jet waiting on the landing strip as soon as Malcolm is out of the hospital," Silas answered. When he saw the incredulous look Enzo was giving him, he added, "I figured you'd change your mind."

Enzo rolled his eyes, but he didn't argue.

"Great," I said, grabbing my duffel bag and slinging it over my shoulder. "I'll wait downstairs. What would I do if it weren't for the Whitlock brothers deciding the course of my life?"

"Valentine," Enzo pleaded.

I ignored him, stalking out of the room. Before I could make it to the stairs, Luca called, "Val, wait."

I turned to see him walking toward me. He stopped a few feet away, looking guilty when I shifted the bag on my shoulder, just in case he decided to deck me again.

"I'm sorry," he said quietly. "About... everything. I know this isn't the best time, but if you want to talk about—"

"I don't," I said, softening my tone. "I really... really don't. If you want to help, just keep this between us. Better yet, forget it completely. Okay?"

He hesitated, giving me that worried look I preferred infinitely less than a solid uppercut to the jaw. At least that was invigorating in a fucked up kind of way. He finally sighed, his shoulders slumping. "If that's really what you want."

"It is," I assured him. When I saw Silas over his shoulder, I frowned. "See you whenever, I guess. Give Carol and Timmy a hug for me."

"Yeah," he said stiffly. "I will."

It occurred to me that for the first time, Luca and I had something in common. We both had skeletons in our closet we didn't want to acknowledge. Not even to ourselves.

13

MALCOLM

When I came out of anesthesia to find the last person I wanted to see staring down at me, I was out of it enough that my first response was blind, unadulterated rage. I grabbed the mask around my face and yanked it off along with the tubes sticking out of my arms and sat up sharply, ready to tear into anyone who tried to stop me.

"Easy, Kong," the doctor said in a dry, condescending tone that really didn't make me want to strangle him any less once I remembered who he was and why I was there. The room was small but comfortable, and more private than most recovery suites. "I see you're one of the twenty-two percent who experience emergence agitation as a result of being under. What a shock."

"I have to say, I'm kind of surprised I woke up," I said, my voice still raw, I assumed from the tube they'd had down my throat. "Thought you'd see your opportunity to take out the competition."

Chris gave me a tight, crooked smile, but he didn't bother to deny it. "What can I say? I prefer to do things the old-fashioned way. Especially where such delicate matters are concerned."

I scoffed, sitting up on the edge of the bed to look down at my recently bandaged wound. I peeled at the corner of the bandage and examined the thick black stitches. "Not a bad job. You teach him that handiwork, or you just spend all day ogling his ass like a perv?"

"It takes one to know one, Chief," he shot back. "But for the record, Valentine was one of my most promising residents. I patched you up because that's the oath I took when I became a physician, and some of us actually care to adhere to the ethical standards of our profession, but I'd be lying if I said I had no ulterior motives."

"Of course you do," I sneered. He was better at hiding it than most, but it all had to come out sometime. If anything, I actually respected him more for admitting it. "Well? What is it? A malpractice suit you want to have hand-waved away? Or do you prefer cold, hard cash so you can buy yourself some more of those nice soap opera glasses?"

He set his mouth into a firm line in agitation. "I want him back," he answered. "When all this is said and done, I want him to be able to return to his old life. To his family, his friends, his calling."

"To you, more specifically," I accused.

That tight-lipped smile crept back onto his face. The one that was only a faint echo of the hardness in his eyes. This guy talked a big game about being a noble healer, but he was a snake. It took one to know one. Like the inverse of the same innate instinct that led monsters like me to our prey, one monster recognized another.

"That, too," he conceded. "I don't like you, Malcolm. As a matter of fact, I detest you and every other corrupt, power-drunk, arrogant predator you stand as a perfect exemplar for and carbon copy of. The names change, and you wear a more appealing mask than most, but I've met you a thousand times before, and I know you. Hell, I've even loved you, and intimately enough to know that there's one thing a sick fuck like you can't resist. Would you like to know what that is, Chief Whitlock?"

"Can't fuckin' wait, Doc," I growled.

"Innocence," he answered, his tone growing as cold and hard as those eyes. "Men like you always crave the one thing you can't have, because by virtue of merely touching it, you eat away at it like a cancer. Like a disease. Because in the end, all you really are is a virus, and all you're ever really good for is taking something good and pure and whole and leaving it a broken, festering mound of decay. Am I wrong? About any of it?"

I stared at him for a few moments, contemplating just how easy it would be to snap his fucking neck here and now. Just a tight grip, and a little pressure, and... pop. Off like a bottle cap.

"No," I said. "You're not."

"Points for self-awareness, I suppose," he sneered. "Like I said. I hate you, and I'm quite sure the feeling is mutual, but I also believe you're the one monster who's probably capable of keeping him safe from the one who's after him. And I have no doubt you'll succeed at taking the threat out eventually, because that's the other thing viruses are good for. Taking out any threat to their own existence. The only question is, when that happens, who's going to keep Valentine safe from you?"

I narrowed my eyes, filled with indignation even I didn't quite fully understand the cause of. It wasn't his words. For one thing, I didn't give a shit what he thought. For another, he wasn't saying anything I didn't already know. None of it had ever bothered me before. The only explanation I could think of, really, was possessiveness. It was the fact that he or anyone else thought they were entitled to touch what was mine.

And Valentine was mine. Mine to protect, mine to punish, and mine to keep as long as I damn well pleased. "Sorry, Doc, but if that was your aim, you really should've let me die on the table. Once I've made something mine, I don't let it go. Ever."

He stared me down for a moment before giving me a deceptively pleasant smile. I wasn't the only one who wore a mask, apparently. "That's quite all right," he replied. "I'm not worried. I expect in the time between now and then, he will have come to realize exactly who and what you are, and the choice will be clear enough."

He was probably right about that. Which was exactly why I didn't plan on giving Valentine a choice at all.

"Well, I'll let you recover," he remarked, turning to leave. "The desk says your brother is here."

"Is he now?" I asked, annoyed by that revelation almost as much as the doctor's existence. He just chuckled on his way out.

When Silas walked in a minute later, a cup of coffee in hand like he'd been here for a while, I was even more pissed.

"You're supposed to be watching Valentine," I snapped.

"Good to see you, too, brother," he said, kicking out the chair next to the bed before he sank into it, one leg draped over the other. "I hear you were a model patient."

"Fuck off. Where is he?"

"At home, with Enzo and a small army of heavily armed men," he answered. "But don't worry, it's a temporary state of affairs. I've already got a jet waiting to whisk you two away to a lovely little villa nestled in the picturesque mountains of central Romania."

"Yeah, you really missed your calling as a tour guide. What the fuck are you talking about?" I sat up, ignoring the sting as my stitches pulled. "I'm not going anywhere. In case you haven't noticed, half my fucking force just got wiped out by your ex."

"It was barely five percent," he countered. When he saw the rage on my face, he added, "Which is absolutely tragic. But that's all the more reason you can't be here right now. If only because you're a bullseye for Demon to aim for."

Annoyed as I was by his reasoning, he was right. Until I put a bullet in Demon's skull, my existence was a liability. So was Valentine's.

"You still want Valentine alive," he challenged. "He's not going to make a very efficient witness from the grave, and it's pretty clear even you can't protect him here."

I narrowed my eyes. Even though he probably didn't mean those words as a challenge, I certainly took them as one.

He was right, though, as much as I didn't want to admit it —even to myself. Staying in the city, it was only a matter of time before Demon got to one of us. And if he didn't, he would tear the whole damn city apart trying.

"Fine," I said through my teeth. "But there's something else we need to discuss."

"Oh?" he asked.

"My people were killed," I began. "And you want me to go to the other side of the world because this freak isn't going to stop until we're all dead. I think you owe me an honest fucking answer."

Silas listened patiently, and even though his expression betrayed no trace of his thoughts, that was nothing new. "And that would be about what, exactly?"

"What do you think?"

He sighed. "You still don't believe I killed James."

"I know you didn't," I said pointedly. The mention of his name was enough to set me off. I didn't care what he'd been to Silas once. To me, he always had been and always would be a demon. "We wouldn't be in this situation if you had. But what I'm not sure about is if you even tried."

Silas sighed, as if he had grown weary of the subject. Well, that made two of us.

"I did. But it doesn't matter what I say, does it?" he challenged. "You're not going to take my word for it."

I paused for a moment to consider it. "No," I agreed. "I guess I'm not."

Silas was my brother. I loved him, at least as much as I was capable of loving anyone. But I didn't trust him. Less now than ever.

When I arrived at the landing strip, the jet was waiting for me, and Valentine was already there, curled up in one of the large, plush leather seats. By the window, of course. He had his phone in his hands, and he was focused enough he didn't notice me right away, not until I was right up on him.

"Holy shit," he muttered. "How can someone so huge be so quiet?"

"I could ask the same of you in reverse," I said, walking over to him. I held my hand out. "Let me see your phone. I want to check something. And any other electronics you brought."

He looked at me warily. "What for?"

"Now," I ordered.

He rolled his eyes, but reached down to rummage through his duffel bag at his feet for a tablet. I checked the bag, ignoring his protests, just to make sure there was nothing else. Satisfied, I took the phone and tablet and tossed them both onto the tarmac.

"Hey!" he shouted. "What the hell?"

"We're running from a genius who wants to kill us both," I said. "You really think carrying two glorified tracking devices around on you is a good idea? I'll get you a flip phone when we get to Romania."

He sank back into his chair, glaring daggers at me. "You could've just told me to leave them here."

"I could have," I agreed. "But I didn't have my phone."

He flipped me off as I took the seat in front of him.

He looked pointedly around the empty cabin. "It's a private jet. You could sit literally anywhere else."

"I could," I agreed, leaning back with my hands on the armrests.

He rolled his eyes. "You shouldn't even be out of the hospital."

"It's a hell of a lot safer than being in Boston at the moment."

He grunted in acknowledgment. "Yeah, whatever. Did they at least give you warfarin or rivaroxaban?"

"What?"

He sighed. "Anticoagulants. You're at a heightened risk for blood clots after surgery. Especially on a long plane trip."

"Guess I just have to take my chances, then."

He gave me a look. "Just walk around every hour and you'll be fine. I've got aspirin in my bag."

"My own private physician," I said flatly. "How nice."

"You know, most people would be grateful to the guy who saved their life."

"Considering I'm keeping you alive, I'd say we're even," I countered. "I am curious about something, though."

"What?" he asked warily, still sulking. He was cute when he pouted, I had to admit.

"Why didn't you rat me out to your brother?" I asked.

Valentine frowned. "About what, the belt, or you treating me like a prisoner of war?"

"Both," I answered.

He blew a puff of air through his nostrils. "Well, for one thing, it would kind of put a damper on family harmony if Enzo tried to kill you."

I chuckled. "And for another?"

He didn't answer, but the look in his eyes made it clear enough.

"Oh," I said in a knowing tone. "You're embarrassed."

The way his face lit up with further humiliation just confirmed it. "Oh, fuck off."

I just leaned back in my chair, smirking. "It was a wise decision, either way," I told him. "One that might earn you a modicum of freedom when we reach our destination, if you play your cards right."

He frowned, as if he wasn't sure what to make of that. I liked keeping him on edge. And while I detested the idea of hiding from anything, especially Demon, the idea of spending some time alone with Valentine in a secluded setting had its appeal.

More than I wanted to admit.

14

VALENTINE

To say it had been the week from hell since our arrival would be at once an understatement and an overstatement. At least hell would've been interesting. This was more like purgatory, and while Malcolm came and went as he pleased—even though it was anyone's guess what he was doing other than when he occasionally brought home food—I was stuck on the property. It wasn't only because he had boarded and locked all the doors, but also because there was a fucking electric fence surrounding the property as well.

That afternoon, I decided fuck it. I was getting some fresh air, whether he liked it or not, and I used the chair from the kitchen to break open a window on the second floor since it was bolted shut rather than being boarded up like all the ones on the first floor. And of course, Malcolm had cleared the house of everything that might possibly be used, either as a weapon, tool, or a way to escape my miserable existence.

I tossed a thick tablecloth over the broken glass I wasn't able to clean up and climbed out. I knew I was going to be in a world of trouble later, but I didn't really care all that much. I was bored as shit, and it had been long enough since the first punishment that I'd had time to convince myself it wasn't really that bad. At least not in comparison to the alternative, which was staying put and slowly but surely losing my sanity.

Not all that slowly lately.

The fresh air was nice, and I had to admit, the view was second to none. Assuming you liked mountains, and... more mountains. That was pretty much what life on the outskirts of a village that barely even qualified as a village had to offer.

With any luck, I would have a few hours to myself before Malcolm came back. There was no way I could fix the window, so I didn't really see a point in scrambling inside.

The rooftop ledge was wide enough to be comfortable, and while I never would've imagined sitting and watching sheep graze on the hillside was a pastime that would offer me any meaningful entertainment, beggars couldn't be choosers.

As midafternoon turned to twilight, and the sky grew darker, I began to grow a bit more apprehensive. Malcolm would be back at any moment, and while I was enjoying the fresh air, I really wasn't sure this was the right hill to die on.

Maybe I could tell him I fell out the window. I doubted he would believe it, but his opinion of my intelligence was so low that he just might. I swallowed hard when I noticed the bike he had either rented, purchased, or commandeered from some unsuspecting soul come rumbling down the path.

That son of a bitch just had to look cool doing everything. I loved my bike, but somehow the fact that we shared that mode of transportation made me like it a little less.

I was about to get up to go inside when I saw him pause at the front door, keys in hand, like he sensed a disturbance in the force.

Freak.

I held my breath and didn't dare move at all, but it was all for nothing when he looked up, his eyes locking on mine. In an instant, they went from their usual stony gray to burning agitation.

"What the fuck are you doing up there?" he demanded.

I swallowed hard, trying to displace the fear in my voice. I knew contrition was pointless, and the damage was already done.

"Counting sheep?"

His eyes narrowed, and he walked over to the low slope of the ledge. The motherfucker was so tall, his head almost came up to it. "Down," he said, pointing to the ground at his feet. "Now."

There was something about how chilled his tone was that had me immediately on edge, even more than usual.

"Yeah, okay," I muttered, standing to brush off the knees of my jeans. "I'll come in."

"Not in," he said firmly. "Down."

I blinked at him. "You've gotta be kidding," I said with a dry laugh. "You want me to jump?"

His expression didn't change or waver.

"No," I said, trying to make my tone sound firm and not like a petulant child. I didn't really succeed, unfortunately.

Malcolm walked closer and I started to move back, convinced he was actually going to haul himself up to kick my ass. And he probably could, if he wanted to. I definitely wasn't expecting him to grab me by the ankle instead. He yanked me unceremoniously off the ledge and held me up by the back of my shirt like I was a stray kitten, and I thrashed and struggled, but all my attempts to escape fell flat. He didn't even seem to give a shit that I was clawing at his arm hard enough to draw blood, or that he hadn't come out of surgery all that long ago.

"I have to admit, I'm surprised. I didn't think you were going to make it this long without fucking up. I was getting bored."

I shot him a filthy glare, which he ignored as he promptly slung me over his shoulder, keeping me there with only a hand on the back of my thigh, dangerously close to my ass.

"Put me down," I hissed, clawing at his back now as he unlocked the door, oblivious to all of it, and carried me inside. He went straight past the living room and upstairs into the bedroom, where he tossed me onto the bed hard enough that I bounced.

I felt another twinge of panic and backed away from him as far as I could, but he simply grabbed my ankle again and yanked so I was flat on my back.

My heart started hammering in a familiar concoction of rage and fear and excitement. Too much of the latter for comfort, really.

I sure as hell wasn't bored anymore. And I could tell from the glint of malice that bordered on glee in his eye, neither was he. "You should be happy," he taunted. "Your little cry for attention has been heard loud and clear."

"It's not a cry for attention," I snapped as he climbed onto the bed on top of me. "I just wanted some fucking fresh air. I've been stuck in here for a week while you go wherever the fuck you want."

"And do you know why that is, Valentine?" he asked calmly. I would've preferred it if he were pissed off. The fact that he seemed amused, if not downright excited, was far more unnerving.

"What?" I asked, grimacing as his knee pressed against the mattress between my thighs, dangerously close to brushing my cock.

Heat filled his gaze as he studied me for a moment, gripping a handful of my hair and pulling my head back before answering, "Because I'm in charge. Since you've somehow failed to grasp that simple fact, I guess I'm just going to have to make it even clearer."

I swallowed hard, staring up at him with my heart going at a rapid-fire pace, barely able to take a breath. "What are you going to do?" I asked, my voice trembling in spite of myself. "Are you going to..." I trailed off, afraid to put the thought into his head in case it wasn't already there.

He tilted his head slightly, as if he found it a strange question for some reason. "Why?" he asked, his knee pressing into my crotch, which was uncomfortable considering it was already rock fucking hard. He leaned in, his breath a whisper against my throat. "Does the thought excite you, Kitten? Is that what you think about when you touch yourself?"

His words sent a bolt of lightning down my spine, mortification and horror in electric form, outweighing the fear and arousal that always seemed to exist in equal measure when he was around.

"What the fuck?" I seethed as rage momentarily overtook all of it. Then, the answer occurred to me and it went into a spiral. "You've been filming me?"

"Of course," he said without a hint of shame. "But that was actually just a guess. Thank you for confirming it."

My eyes widened as I realized I'd walked right into his goddamn trap and outed my most shameful secret in the process. One of them, at any rate. "You son of a bitch," I snarled, moving to attack him only for him to pin my hands effortlessly to the mattress.

Should've seen that coming, really.

"That's a naughty little kitten," he purred, his gaze darkening with some primal hunger I recognized on a deep, instinctive level. The same instinct that told me I was prey. "Now, how should I punish such petulant behavior? Especially when it's clear punishment is just a reward in disguise."

I grimaced, turning my head away from him and keeping my body still, because it was taking all my willpower not to grind against his fucking leg like an animal in heat. "Fuck off."

He leaned in closer, and when his tongue dragged up over the stubble along the side of my throat, something else inside me snapped, only this time, it wasn't my temper giving way. It was something else entirely. A far more dangerous kind of control to give up. My entire body went rigid as a result, and I lost the ability to breathe or even blink as I stared up at the ceiling in shock. Both because of what he was doing and because of my own response.

"Is that really what you want?" he taunted, his tongue flicking against my earlobe. "Or do you want me to fuck you?"

A sound too close to a whimper for comfort escaped me, and I realized only then I was trembling beneath him. The only reason my hands weren't was the tight grip he had on my wrists, keeping them pinned and immobile. "Does it matter? You're just gonna do whatever you want anyway."

"I could," he said thoughtfully, his voice rough with hunger, like he was savoring the idea. "There's a first time for everything, and if ever I had reason, you've given it to me a hundred times over. But I don't think I want to make it that easy for you. I think I want you to admit it. Or does that ruin the fun for you, if it's consensual?"

I gritted my teeth, trying to squirm into a less compromising position, until I realized that was just making it worse.

"I know," he continued, because he clearly didn't need this conversation to have two sides. My body was carrying enough of it, though. "We could always come to an agreement."

"What the fuck are you talking about?" I asked, finally daring to look back at him. Big mistake. The malevolent gleam in his eyes was back, brighter than ever.

He finally released his grip on me and got off me, much to my dismay rather than relief. As usual, his sudden shift in behavior left my head spinning. "We're both bored, and we both have certain... appetites that are more compatible than not."

Appetites. That was hilarious. The Big Bad Wolf had nothing on this guy. And I was pretty fucking sure he was about to swallow me whole.

"I'm straight," I said, reminding my cock as much as him.

"You like furry porn, from the way my brother tells it. Aren't those mutually exclusive?"

The heat between my legs seemed to shift direction and rush to my face. Some of it, at least. "Your brother is a fucking ass and he needs to mind his own business."

"Or you should clear your browser history every now and again," he said flatly. "I have a hard time believing you've never bottomed before."

How the hell did we even get on this subject, anyway? I had backed up against the headboard, putting as much distance between us as possible. "Getting pegged by a hot chick is different from getting fucked by..." I gestured up and down at him. "You."

He smirked, and that slanted little quirk of his lips did shit to me that made me second-guess everything.

"I'll take that as a compliment."

"It wasn't one."

"All the same."

I let out a growl of frustration, my head dropping back against the headboard. "I don't even know what you're suggesting. We pass time by hatefucking and then pretend like it never happened? What happens in Romania stays in Romania?"

"Something like that," he answered. "How does that sound?"

"It sounds fuckin' gay, that's how it sounds."

Malcolm chuckled. "Doesn't have to be. Not if you're not the one in charge."

I eyed him warily. "The fuck is that supposed to mean?"

"You want me to fuck you, but you don't want to want it," he said with a shrug. "But if it's not your idea, it doesn't really matter, does it?"

I hesitated, considering his words and the implication behind them. "Are you asking me to give you permission to do shit without permission?"

He smirked. "Now you're catching on. Think of it as blanket consent."

I gulped, more afraid of myself at the moment than him. Of the fact that I was actually considering or even taking any of this remotely seriously. Malcolm was dangerous, and I had no doubt the things he'd do to me if I said yes would be equally perilous, but not half as much as the fact that I wanted him to.

"Creative," I mumbled. "And if I change my mind?"

"You don't," he answered in a stern tone. "Not once you've made it up."

"That's not really consent, then, is it?"

He rolled his eyes. "Fine. We'll use a safe word. I assume you've used one of those before."

"Obviously," I muttered. "Aardvark."

"I'm sorry, is that your safe word or one of those deviant mascots you get fucked by?"

"The former!" I snapped. "I have standards, even I wouldn't fuck an aardvark."

"Huh. Well, I'm not going to be able to take any of this seriously if I know there's a possibility you're going to be crying out the name of a glorified pig."

"I said aardvark, not Malcolm."

Irritation flashed in his gaze.

"Okay, so what would you suggest?" I asked before he could decide keeping me alive was more trouble than it was worth.

He paused to consider it a moment. "Devil."

"Devil?" I echoed. "Your supervillain name? Seriously?"

"You'll be crying out my name one way or another. Take it or leave it."

My face turned hot again, right when my humiliation had started to cool off. "Whatever. It's a little megalomaniacal, but I guess that's to be expected."

"Then it's settled," he answered. "For the duration of our time here, you're mine. Mine to discipline, fuck, and torture however I see fit, with no exceptions and no release, unless and until you call me by that name. Does that sound amenable?"

I opened my mouth to respond, but he interrupted, "I suggest you give it a bit of consideration, because this is your last chance to back out."

I swallowed the lump in my throat.

He was right. This wasn't something I should be agreeing to lightly, and the fact that he was actually giving me a choice in the matter was almost as shocking as the fact that I had already made up my mind.

I had, though. I knew I had, even as I found myself sitting across from an incubus in wolf's clothing, staring me down like he was waiting for just one little word to eat me alive.

The word that was already dancing on the tip of my tongue.

"Yes."

It came out as more of a question, really, but my voice was too tight to offer any corrections. Not that he asked for any.

Instead, hellfire came into his eyes and a slow, malevolent smile tugged at his lips. One look in those eyes, and I knew exactly why they called this man Devil.

And I had just sold myself to him, body, soul, and all.

MALCOLM

"Yes."

That one little word got me harder than any dirty talk or moans of pleasure ever had. But to be fair, it wasn't just a word. It was the magic spell that broke the chains that bound me, like some demonic soul buried in an undiscovered tomb, just waiting for some poor, naive little fool to unleash him.

And he had. Even now, I wasn't sure he fully understood what he'd done, but he had done it, and my due diligence was over.

"Yes, what?" I asked, my voice tight and rough with hunger.

My thoughts were racing with possibilities of all the filthy, depraved, twisted things I'd been longing to do to this boy from the moment fate had thrown him at my altar, like a virgin sacrifice.

And he was, for all intents and purposes—mine, anyway—a virgin. No matter how many people he'd been with in the past, no one had ever done the things I was about to do to him, and no one ever would.

Even if his little fantasy of running back to a mundane, relatively normal life where he was the one in control played out exactly the way he expected, he would be ruined. He'd never be able to come again without thinking about me. I'd make sure of that.

He stared at me, confusion softening his innocent features. "What do you mean, yes, what?"

"Yes, Master," I clarified.

He blanched. "I'm not calling you Master, for fuck's sake."

"No," I mused, already changing my mind. "No, you're going to call me Daddy. I think I prefer that, spoiled brat in need of discipline that you are."

His jaw dropped, and the particularly pleasing hue of rose that came into his cheeks only confirmed my decision. "Okay, fine, Master," he mumbled.

"That's what I thought," I said, grabbing the front of his shirt to tear it open. He gave a startled cry as I yanked the fabric down his toned shoulders, revealing his perfectly smooth torso. "New rule. No clothes in the bedroom.

You're going to be ready and accessible for me at all times."

"You've got to be kidding," he muttered.

I ignored him, already unfastening his jeans. I had already seen him close to naked, but I hadn't gone all the way. My imagination was adept enough at filling in the gaps, but I wasn't content with just imagination any longer. He was mine now, and I'd have all of him, any way and anytime I pleased.

"I can undress myself," he said, reaching for his zipper.

I pushed his hands away, too eager to unwrap my prize to bother disciplining him properly. There was plenty of time for that later.

I hissed a breath through my teeth as I tugged his jeans off all the way, along with his boxers, revealing his half-stiff cock for my view. Long and slender, just like the boy himself, and perfect in every way, from the way it curved slightly up to the crown glistening with precome, partially obscured by foreskin just begging to be pierced.

My mouth watered at the sight of him revealed at last, but I resisted the urge to taste him just yet. I'd been staving off my baser instincts where he was concerned for long enough that another hour or so wasn't going to kill me, and he would have to earn that. Letting him know just how much I wanted his pleasure as well as mine this early would be a poorly calculated mistake.

Instead, I gripped the curve of his shaft and pushed the foreskin all the way back before running the tip of my finger over the swollen head. He was slumped back into a half-reclining position, staring down at me through his legs with an enticing combination of arousal and mortification in his eyes.

Just the way I wanted him.

"I think your cock likes me a little more than you do, Kitten."

His cheeks flamed even hotter and he looked away, mumbling, "Don't call me that."

Well, now I was going to call him little else. I gave the outside of his thigh a hard swat, enough to sting and make him jump. "You don't give orders. As a matter of fact, from now on, you don't speak unless you're spoken to. You already know the punishment for disobedience. Ten times over, and this time, I won't have mercy on you."

He looked like he wanted to protest, but he pursed his lips instead and let his eyes do the talking. Eventually, that would earn him a swift punishment, too, but that could wait. My little kitten was feral, and it was going to take some effort to get him to that level of obedience.

A challenge I was more than eager to accept.

Momentarily satisfied, I continued my exploration of his cock, tracing the jagged line of the vein running up along the underside all the way down to his balls before cupping them. They tightened so enticingly as I rolled them gently in my palm, so I steadily tightened my grip until he squirmed in panic.

"Hold still," I ordered, at once relieved and disappointed when he obeyed. His thighs were trembling, but that was hardly a punishable offense. I released my grip once he relented and traced his perineum down to the puckered hole below, spreading him open with my fingers so I could get a better look.

Tight and pink, clenching in anticipation as I ran my finger around it. I shifted on the bed and hooked my hands beneath his knees, pushing his legs up and apart. His cock flopped back against his abdomen, and when it bobbed back up, there was a trail of precome stretched from the tip to his navel.

I leaned over and spit on his hole, which wasn't difficult at the rate my mouth was watering. He muttered under his breath, "What the fuck?" but I pretended I hadn't heard, since I didn't want to be delayed any further.

I pressed two fingers against his hole and pushed them in, suddenly enough that he clenched down with a strangled cry.

"If you think that's rough..." I said with a dry laugh, using the makeshift lubricant to work my fingers in deeper. I angled them to press into his prostate and this time, the cry on his lips was one of pleasure, which seemed to bother him even more. "When was the last time anyone used your hole, Kitten?"

He shot me a murderous look that dissipated as I continued stroking his spot, and his eyes rolled back in his head. "F-fuck, I... I don't know."

"Long enough," I murmured, pulling my fingers out.

As tempted as I was to take him raw after the shit he'd pulled—and because I wanted to know if his cries of agony were half as sweet as his pleasured whimpers—there was no way I'd be getting more than the head of my cock inside him without lube, and even that was iffy. Not without tearing him too badly to use anymore for a week if not more. Besides, if I gave him the worst now, there'd be nothing to work up to.

I got off the bed and opened the drawer on the table next to it to pull out a bottle of lubricant. I coated my palm and slicked it down my shaft.

"Y-you're not gonna wear a condom?"

I gave him a look and smacked his flank with my left hand, harder this time. "No. I wrap it up for my sexual partners, which, for the record, I require to get tested. My pet, however, I come inside when and where I want."

Anger flashed in his eyes, turning them a brilliant shade of gold, and I waited for him to relent. If he was going to back out, it was probably going to be early on.

I just wasn't entirely sure I was going to be able to keep my end of the bargain if he did, any more than I'd be able to keep the implied promise that I'd let him go back to his old life when all was said and done.

Fortunately, I didn't have to make that decision. Not right now.

"Fine," he mumbled, partially covering his face with his hand. "Just do it."

"You don't get to call the shots," I reminded him, flipping him over onto his stomach. "On your hands and knees. I won't ask twice."

He obeyed hastily enough. He was learning. I took a moment to admire the view of him presenting his perfect ass to me. I wouldn't be able to see his face, which was the only downside, but I planned on taking him more than once tonight. Breaking him in.

I spread his cheeks open and positioned the head of my cock, throbbing already with need, between them. His breath hitched and his body grew tense as I settled my hands on his hips. He was quivering beneath me, and a decent man might have sensed the palpable fear coming from him and gone just a little bit easy. But I was no decent man.

I drove into him with enough force that his arms buckled, leaving his head down and his ass in the air. This time, the cry that tore from the boy's throat wasn't just laced with pain, it was agony in its purest form. My reward was the blinding pleasure of being enveloped in his tight hole from tip to base, but his punishment was only just beginning.

16

VALENTINE

"Fuck!" I cried, burying my face in the crook of my arm as Malcolm's fingertips bit into my hips and he started thrusting all of two seconds after he'd just sheathed himself inside my ass without warning.

I wasn't sure what I had expected, really. Not gentleness, but... not complete and utter brutality.

That was my mistake.

My first mistake was putting my body in the hands of a madman to begin with. But it was a mistake I had made willingly, and the thought of what I would have to do in order to revoke it was more trouble than it was worth.

Even now... even as each thrust sent a shock wave of pain through my lower body, to the point where I wasn't even sure how I was going to be able to walk in the morning, I didn't want to hit the nuclear button. I didn't want it to end.

If there had been any doubt I was completely and totally fucked in the head, it just went out that shattered window.

I moaned in quiet desperation, clutching the bedsheets in a futile attempt to brace myself, but the pain wasn't the only part of my fantasies the encounter was living up to. My cock was painfully stiff and already weeping precome as it struck my lower abdomen each time he thrust into me. He hadn't even touched me yet—and given how brutal his fucking style had been so far, I had reason to doubt he ever would—and I was already this close to coming?

I'd busted a nut to more humiliating things, to be sure, but this was definitely up there. Top five at least.

His nails dug into my hips hard enough that the sting momentarily eclipsed the abuse he was lavishing on my ass, like he was trying to keep me in place. It wasn't like I was going anywhere. More like he was in danger of railing us both through the damn floorboards, creaking bed and all.

Every time I thought of tapping out, he seemed to know somehow, and he slowed his rhythm just slightly enough that the pleasure of him pushing into my prostate outweighed the pain. Just by a hair. Then, the moment I let my guard down, he'd fuck me harder, just to make up for it.

The guy was a complete psycho in his everyday life, so I wasn't sure why it surprised me he'd be that way in bed, too. But the way he talked about the other men he'd fucked made me wonder...

Was he only this way with me? The thought was more appealing than it had any right to be. And the thought of him with anyone else was equally maddening.

And so, as I let my mortal enemy pound me into oblivion, I found myself repeating the same question that had occurred to me so often throughout my life, but never more than when I was in his presence.

What the fuck was wrong with me?

I'd figured if there was one silver lining to his roughness, it was that he couldn't last that long the way he was going. I was dead fucking wrong, of course. Maybe the pain just stretched out the time, but it seemed like he'd been going forever when his breathing grew shallow and his thrusts picked up speed. I'd been on the verge myself too many times to count without shaming myself even further, but he seemed to know that, too, and always kept me right on the edge before he'd make it hurt too badly to finish. He wanted complete, absolute control. He wanted to fuck me over, even while he was fucking me, and that shouldn't have come as a surprise, either, now that I was thinking about it.

When Malcolm reached around and palmed my cock, my entire body stiffened up along with it.

Fuck. Why did I have to respond to him so violently?

Even the pleasurable sensations he elicited from me came on the edge of a knife.

"You're going to come for me, Kitten," he said in a voice so rough and raw it sounded like a threat or a taunt rather than sexy banter. But that turned me on more, anyway.

A strangled whimper escaped me and my ass clenched down in response to the slight change in angle. Slight, but enough to make his next thrust more painful as he drove into me, even if he was still hitting my prostate dead on.

I shuddered, more overwhelmed by my own body's immediate submission to his command than his roughness itself. He only had to stroke me a few times before my cock pulsed hot streams of come onto the bed linens and my hips rocked violently into his hand, even though it made what he was doing to me all the more excruciating.

Malcolm growled as he came a moment later, and I wasn't sure if it was his come trickling down the insides of my thighs or blood. Probably both. Either way, I was still so high off the orgasm cutting through my body like a serrated blade that I couldn't bring myself to care.

I was sure I would care plenty come morning. I was sure all the shame and confusion would come crashing down on me along with a healthy heaping of regret, but as I collapsed, held up only by my knees wedged beneath me, I didn't care. There was only the dull, aching bliss of pleasure as its gentle melody faded, and the brutal rhythm of pain that lingered long after, pulsing into me with each beat of my heart.

His. Mine. I wasn't sure which was which anymore. I could feel his pulse throbbing deep within me. Deeper than it should have been possible, at least until he pulled out as roughly as he'd gone in.

I gave a pained cry, my hands fisting in the sweat-drenched sheets my face was buried in. "Could you at least have warned me?"

"No," was his simple, unapologetic answer as he lay back, his hands propped behind his head. He turned to face me, a devious look in his eyes. "Catch your breath. I'm not done with you yet."

I whimpered, but as much as I was questioning my own sanity, I still wasn't ready to tap out. Not by a long shot.

MALCOLM

It was rare that I spent an entire night with someone, let alone woke up with them in my arms. Rarer still that I wasn't bored, even if I had ravaged the sleeping man a few times the night before.

Somehow, I still wasn't satisfied. And yet, I was. More than I had been since... ever, if I was being honest.

Valentine groaned in his sleep, rolling into me with his face buried in my chest. For some strange reason, I didn't feel like pushing him away. Instead, I found myself staring down at him, taking in the configuration of his features. His straight nose, his full lips, the sharp angle of his jaw and the way the light streaming in through the slats in the blinds made the little golden highlights in his hair stand out.

And now I knew his body to be as perfect as his face. The perfect blend of hard muscle and smooth, sun-kissed skin.

The fact that I had explored every inch of him hadn't remotely sated my curiosity. It just left me wanting more.

"Awake already?" I asked as his eyes fluttered open, dazed and confused. "You practically hissed at me the last time I tried to wake you up before eight."

"Might have something to do with the pain," he mumbled, pushing back like he was the one who was horrified by our intimate position.

I snorted. "You'll live."

He shot me a half-hearted glare. "I don't know how I'm supposed to walk."

"You're not," I said pointedly. "That's one way to keep you put."

The second glare wasn't so half-hearted. "You're a dick, you know that?"

"So I've been told," I replied.

He sat up with a grimace and leaned against the headboard. "Shit. Could you go a little easier next time?"

"No," I answered. "Probably not."

Valentine scowled. He was cute when he was like that. Half irate and half asleep.

Hell, he was cute no matter what, and I could see how easily he might become a vice. How quickly eliciting all his various reactions and emotional states could become an addiction.

I found myself wondering what it was like to feel everything so strongly. To be so easy to manipulate, both to the heights of euphoria and the depths of despair. He was painting with colors I not only lacked in my own pallet of emotions and experiences, but ones I couldn't even see. And yet, through his eyes, they were a little clearer. Just tinges in the corner of my eye, but I could see how with more time, they might easily become more than that.

I found myself wondering if this was what my brother felt. Enzo had given him a lens through which he could view the world. Through which he could see and experience things that people like him and I just weren't meant to.

It was a strange thought. A dangerous one, I decided, so I dismissed it as quickly as it had occurred.

"I need a shower," he said pointedly.

"Then I'll help you," I answered.

He blanched at the thought. "Excuse me?"

"I'll carry you," I clarified. "If you really can't walk."

His face turned red, and somehow, I got the feeling he found that suggestion even more humiliating than anything that had happened the night before. "You're not going to carry me," he snapped. "That's ridiculous."

"Then don't linger," I countered.

He scowled at me again, but he didn't protest any further. When he started to get up, I put a hand on his arm to steady him. As soon as he put one foot on the floor, his knees buckled beneath him. I realized he wasn't just being precious after all.

I couldn't help but feel a surge of arousal, and something else far more perplexing at the thought. He really was delicate.

I got out of bed and draped his arm over my shoulders, deciding not to completely humiliate him by picking him up even though that would've been easier. I wasn't even sure why I cared. Humiliating him was something of a pastime for me, but while I wouldn't call it mercy, I was in a strangely lenient mood this morning.

He looked away, sulking, but he didn't argue as he let me help him into the bathroom suite attached to the room. I set him against the wall and went over to turn the shower on, giving the water a moment to warm up. As nice as the cabin was, it was far from new, and the amenities were somewhat lacking. The joys of rural living.

Not that I could really complain too much. The charms certainly outweighed the drawbacks. At least for my current purposes.

I watched as Valentine stepped out of his boxers, unabashedly enjoying the view. He stopped to look over his shoulder, his eyes narrowing in offense. "Could you not gawk?"

"I could," I replied, continuing to stare, just for the hell of it now.

He sighed in exasperation and grabbed the rail on the side of the shower before stepping in. I watched as the water cascaded over his skin, and savored the look of bliss that softened his features as he leaned back, letting the water dampen his hair. It turned dark and bone straight, caressing his shoulder blades with a tenderness I found myself envious of.

Railing him into submission was one thing, but gentleness felt dangerously intimate, if only because it was a completely foreign impulse to me.

When he finally seemed to realize I wasn't going to give him any privacy, he reluctantly began to wash himself, starting with his hair. I watched as he worked the lather into his long strands, combing his fingers through the way I'd done the night before. Grabbing a fistful of his soft tresses to yank his head back was still fresh in my mind and my cock was already hard just from watching him. Thinking about the way he'd whimpered in pain. The way he smelled as I buried my face in the back of his neck and fucked him harder.

He soaped up his body next, and I found myself watching intently as he worked his way down the muscular planes of his shoulders and chest. The water glistened on his skin so enticingly. My own private strip show. Every now and then, he'd cast a furtive glance as if to see if I was still watching, and when he realized the answer was yes, he'd quickly look away again. His skin was flushed all over from the hot water, but I was pretty sure he was blushing, too.

He finally finished and turned the water off, but I easily could've gone on watching him another hour. Theoretically. Assuming I had the willpower not to just get in there and fuck him again, and I was already thinking about it when he got out.

Good timing, Kitten.

I got a towel and a bathrobe that were hanging by the door and brought them over. Valentine looked surprised when I draped the plush white robe around his shoulders and started toweling off his hair. "What are you doing?"

"Grooming my pet," I answered.

That answer turned his face bright red. I expected him to argue, but he didn't. Either he was learning and coming to accept his place, or he knew it was futile.

"Come on," I said. "Go sit on the couch, and I'll make you something to eat."

He did as I said, even though he seemed reluctant, and I stayed close to him on the stairwell just in case he tripped. Once he was settled, I walked into the kitchen to rummage through the refrigerator. I got out a carton of eggs and checked the expiration date on the milk before getting out the rest of the ingredients for omelets.

"I'm surprised you cook," he remarked from the living room.

"I don't," I admitted. "So the results are going to be hit or miss."

He snorted. "Can't be any worse than Silas's last attempt."

"I'm surprised he made one at all," I admitted. "He's not really the type to do any kind of manual labor."

"So I've noticed," he said. "Guess he just likes taking care of my brother."

"He seems to," I agreed.

He was silent for a suspicious amount of time, but when I looked up, he was just watching me curiously. "What do you think about it, anyway?"

"What, Silas making breakfast?"

He gave me a look. "Him marrying Enzo."

I shrugged, stirring the egg and pepper mixture around in the frying pan. "I don't know. It doesn't really matter what I think, does it?"

"No, but everyone has an opinion," he remarked.

I sighed. "I don't really waste time having opinions on things that don't concern me."

"Okay, but if it did concern you?" he pressed. "What would your opinion be, then?"

The boy was relentless. "I think he's happy. And for once, it's not something that's completely self-destructive that's bringing him happiness, so I'm happy for him. Satisfied?"

I could tell he wasn't, but he didn't push any further. "What was he like when you guys were younger?"

I scoffed. "Pretty much the same as he is now. Sarcastic. Callous. Brilliant."

"So he was always a dick," said Valentine.

"Not always," I admitted. "He changed over the years. Hardened."

"It's hard to imagine he was ever anything but."

"Most monsters aren't born, Valentine. They're made."

"What made him one?"

I paused to consider it. And to consider whether I was going to answer him. "How much do you know about our past?"

"Not much," he admitted. "I don't really know how much he's told Enzo, either."

"Probably not a lot," I said. "There's not a whole lot to tell, and what there is isn't the kind of thing anyone likes to talk about. Even him."

"That bad?" he asked.

"Yeah," I said, turning off the burner. "That bad. I'll give you the abridged version. Our mother was an addict who neglected her children and never encountered a substance she didn't want to snort or shoot into her veins, or both. And she was willing to do anything—I mean anything—to get her hands on shit. Lying, stealing, selling herself. Selling her own children."

"Literally?" he asked, his voice cracking slightly.

"Yeah," I said, setting a plate in front of him before I leaned against the counter. "I don't remember all that much before age six or seven, but I remember the first time I stabbed a guy. One of her 'boyfriends' she'd leave me with while she was out stone cold. After that, she didn't bring them around as often. Things got a little better, until one day when Silas was three, I came home from school and found him gone. She wouldn't talk to me, so I took her gun and I put it to her forehead and told her I'd fucking kill her if she didn't tell me where he was. Turned out, she'd sold him to some shitbag dealer for a fucking week's worth of smack."

"I swear to God, sometimes I still wish I'd pulled that trigger, but I didn't," I continued with a bitter laugh. "I left, and I found him. I don't know what fucked-up shit went down in those six or seven hours he was gone, but when I found him, he was hiding in a closet while the creep our mother sold him to was blacked out on the couch. I shot him in his sleep, took everything he had on him, got Silas, and we spent the next few weeks on our own before some cop picked us up. No one ever knew it was me, and I doubt anyone gave a shit what happened to a guy like that, so the rest is one long string of foster homes and bullshit."

I realized he was staring at me, his jaw slightly slack, like... well, pretty much like I'd just told him exactly what I had. And that was the sanitized version.

"Holy fucking shit," he breathed.

"That's one way to put it."

"I don't know what to say."

"Then don't say anything," I told him. "You asked a question, there's your answer. Nothing more to it than that."

"Yeah, but..." He trailed off for a moment. "I'm sorry. I guess it kinda makes sense now."

"What does?"

"Why you and Silas are the way you are."

I snorted. "Silas, maybe. I'm the way I am because that's how I came out of the womb. Wouldn't have mattered if we had grown up in a nice little slice of suburbia with a white picket fence and a dog."

"Maybe," he said doubtfully. "Maybe not."

I rolled my eyes. "There it is."

"There's what?" he asked, frowning.

"The naïveté that's going to get you killed one of these days, if someone doesn't save you from yourself," I said. "Because you believe in fairy tales. Like thinking people are innocent by default."

"They are," he said without a hint of irony. "Children are innocent. And no matter what you became, you were a child once. You said it yourself—monsters are made, not born."

"Most of them," I corrected him. "Not me."

He frowned and seemed like he was about to argue again, so I preempted him. "What about you? Who was it?"

He blinked at me in confusion. "Who?"

"The guy who fucked you up so bad that you get off on being abused," I answered. "Camp counselor, priest, maybe dear old Dad?"

Anger flashed in his eyes, making it clear I had struck a nerve. Which was what I had intended. "You're an ass."

"Sure," I said. "Doesn't answer my question, though."

His lips twitched in agitation and he looked like he was trying to glare a hole in the center of my forehead.

"Teacher," he finally muttered.

"Ah," I said in a knowing tone. "Well, I told you my sob story. Now it's your turn."

"There's not much to tell. I was thirteen," he said with a shrug. "I felt like I was invisible in my own family, like no one ever listened. He did."

"And you never told anyone."

He looked surprised. "How did you—"

"Body language," I said. "You kind of hunker in on yourself when you're embarrassed. When you touch your upper lip, it's like you're subconsciously trying to keep yourself from saying whatever it is you're about to say."

"Just when I start to forget you're a cop," he muttered.

I chuckled. "If it makes you feel any better, I'm not a very good one."

"It doesn't, thanks," he quipped.

"Must not be a very good cook, either. You haven't touched your eggs."

He looked down at his full plate, then back up at me, blinking. "How the hell was I supposed to eat while we were talking about that shit?"

I shrugged. "Never bothered me."

"Of course it doesn't," he said in a flat tone. "Anyway... you're wrong, for the record. I did say something."

"Oh?" I asked. "I take it the freak is dead, then?"

If he wasn't, he was going to be.

"He got in a car accident a few years later," Valentine answered with a shrug, picking at the omelet with his fork. "Karma, I guess."

"Then I guess your old man was even more useless than I thought."

"Oh, he did something about it," Valentine murmured, running a finger down the slight bump on the bridge of his nose. "First time he ever hit me like that. And the last, but it left an impression."

"I'm sure it did," I said, taking a moment to compartmentalize my anger, which had become a very selective problem over the last couple of minutes. "I could fill in, you know."

Valentine hesitated. "What? Fill in for who?"

"Your Daddy," I answered. "Because I think he fucked you up even more than that pervert teacher did."

"Th-that's not... what the fuck, Mal? That's fucked up."

"We're all fucked up one way or another," I said with a shrug. "I get off on causing pain. You get off on feeling it. Seems like a pretty good match to me."

He continued to stare, even redder than before, and I was starting to think that for all my attempts last night, this was the way I'd finally broken him.

"You're serious," he mumbled.

"I'm rarely anything else." I had to admit, the idea of having a little more leeway to explore the more tender urges he inspired in me while still having an excuse was appealing.

He didn't have an answer for that, either, and he'd lost the ability to meet my eyes. "What would that change about our arrangement, exactly?"

I thought about it. Then I realized what the actual cause of his trepidation was and a smile tugged at the corners of my lips. "Don't worry. I'll still be plenty rough. But judging from how hard you got when I had you over my knee, I think you'd enjoy it more if it came in the form of discipline."

So would I, if I was being honest with myself. He looked mortified, but he wasn't saying no. "I... guess. As long as it doesn't make shit weird."

"Oh, it'll be weird," I assured him. "But that's part of the fun."

VALENTINE

It had only been a few days since Malcolm had brought up our altered arrangement, and while I still wasn't walking right, I wasn't in quite as much agony as before. I was in the bath, soaking in epsom salts in the hopes that my ass would be a little less sore by the time he next took me.

And to my complete and utter shame, I was looking forward to it. Even the pain.

No... especially the pain. Malcolm was right about that.

He was gone for the afternoon, as usual. I didn't know what he did in town, only that he expected me to stay put. He had taken additional security measures after repairing the window, and I had been staying in his room ever since, so that had included locking all the other doors I didn't require immediate access to.

It wasn't like I had to worry about boredom anymore, at least. Not when he was home. There was still the matter of finding something to do with myself when he wasn't, and despite the fact that he'd told me I was to stay in bed and rest—making no secret of the fact that it was for the sake of being able to use me again soon rather than actual concern—I ventured downstairs.

It wasn't like he'd know. He didn't have cameras everywhere, just in the places that led outside, like the front door, the backdoor, and in his bedroom, pointed at the windows. And I had checked thoroughly. I'd gleaned at least that much from my brothers and father.

I rummaged through the kitchen and rolled my eyes at the bars on the window that hadn't been there when we arrived. At least Malcolm kept the fridge stocked and the whole pet play thing hadn't extended as far as making me eat kibble out of a bowl, but I knew if I pissed him off enough, that could probably change.

The thing was, it was easy to do. And tempting.

I reminded myself of Johnny's childhood dog. He'd always been one crayon short of a full box, and he liked to chew on wires because the poor idiot liked the buzz. And I liked the inevitable pain and punishment that came with pissing off a madman, so really, who was the bigger idiot?

I'd watched TV for the last few hours when I heard the rumble of Malcolm's motorcycle in the distance and hastily switched it back to the channel it had been on before. After tidying up any evidence of my disobedience, I ran upstairs even though my body paid the price for rushing, and settled on the edge of the bed in a kneeling position, since he seemed to like that.

A few minutes later, after I heard him rummaging around and putting away whatever he'd brought home in the kitchen, I heard his footsteps on the stairs.

My heart skipped with each one.

Calm down, there's no way he'd know.

Malcolm arrived in the doorway, pushing it open slightly and looking around like he suspected something. To be fair, that was always how he acted when he'd been gone for a while. Like he assumed–and hoped–I'd done something he could punish me for.

"You're home... Daddy," I added, even though that word still stuck in my throat a little. That was by far the least concerning physical response it elicited from me, though.

Malcolm raised an eyebrow. Maybe I was laying it on too thick. "Did you behave yourself while I was gone, Kitten?" he asked, the floorboards creaking under his weight as he stepped into the room. He was a solid wall of muscle and just one look at him was enough to make me feel like I was going to snap in half.

When his dick had been rammed inside me, it felt like that might be more literal than figurative.

"Yes, Daddy," I said, doing my best to appear innocent even though I felt like he might somehow hear my heart hammering away in my ears.

He walked closer and when he reached into his interior jacket pocket, I tensed up in nervous anticipation. "I brought you something," he said, pulling out a long black box.

My eyes widened as he drew even closer, coming to a stop at the edge of the bed. I waited for him to give me the box, and listened closely for the sound of ticking, but instead, he took the lid off to reveal the thick leather collar within. There was a silver tag hanging down off it that read KITTEN in bold engraved script.

"A collar?" I asked warily.

"You are my pet," he said, as if it should be obvious. He took the collar out of the box and ordered, "Pull your hair back."

I knew better than to hesitate even a fraction of a second when he gave a direct order, so I did as he said and gathered my hair up and off my neck. My throat tightened as his fingers brushed against it while he fastened the collar around my neck. It was a bit tight, especially when I swallowed, but I also knew to pick my battles.

"There," he said, stepping back to survey his work and taking the tag between his fingers. The light of satisfaction in his eyes made my stomach twist into knots and I had to bite down on my bottom lip to keep from smiling like an idiot.

God, I was so pathetic.

"How's your ass feeling?" he asked, shattering the delicacy of the moment with a sledgehammer.

"It's fine," I mumbled.

"Oh?" he challenged, like he knew it was a lie. "Then this won't be that bad."

"What won't be that bad?" I asked warily, moving over as he sat next to me on the bed and it depressed heavily from his sturdy frame.

"Take your clothes off," he ordered, ignoring my question. That, I had grown used to, but it didn't make it any less annoying.

I clenched my jaw and bit my tongue, getting up off the bed. Was he going to fuck me this soon?

It wasn't like he'd limited himself to one time the first night, though... guess I should have expected that. And now I was regretting my decision to lie about taking it easy.

I pulled my shirt over my head and when I started unbuttoning my jeans, I could feel his gaze traveling over my bare flesh, hungry and appraising. Being observed like this stirred conflicting feelings of giddy pride and apprehension.

It was far from a strip tease. I was way too awkward and unsure of myself to even try seducing him like that, but he seemed like the kind of man who wouldn't find that appealing, anyway. Maybe from a lover, but not from his pet.

Once my jeans hit the floor, along with my boxers, and I was left completely exposed before him, he gave no further orders. He just let me stand there, squirming in discomfort as he looked his fill. He finally took me by the wrist and yanked hard, drawing me over his knee.

My head spun from the sudden shift and I tried to look over my shoulder, but his hand was already on the small of my back, keeping me there. "What? What are you doing?"

"Your punishment," he answered.

"Punishment?" I cried. "But I didn't do anything!"

"No? You didn't go downstairs after I told you to stay in bed?"

I gritted my teeth, scrambling for a suitable excuse. How the hell did he know? I'd been careful. "I—"

"Lie to me and it'll be three times as bad," he warned.

All I could do was stare at him, jaw slightly slack, as I weighed my options. No matter what he said, denying it still felt like my best option. "I didn't."

Malcolm's lips turned downward, but the frown didn't match the glee in his eyes. "No?" he challenged, his hand traveling down. My cheeks clenched in anticipation of the stinging blow, and I was already hard from thinking about it, but instead, he slipped his finger into my cleft and pressed it against my aching hole. "Then this shouldn't hurt that bad."

I turned my head toward the floor and pressed my lips together to hold back the strangled sound welling in the back of my throat. All the blood rushed to my head. At least, most of it. I didn't dare respond because I knew anything I said could and would be used against me in the Devil's court, where Malcolm was judge, jury, and executioner.

He pushed his finger deeper in and wiggled the tip around inside me. When he pressed against a tear inside, I couldn't hold back the cry any longer.

He froze and pulled out the tip of his finger, resting his hand on my bottom. "That's what I thought."

Bastard.

"How did you know?" I gritted out.

"I didn't," he answered, and my heart dropped right into the pit of my stomach. "Not until just now."

Son of a—

Thwack!

A cry of alarm escaped me as his hand connected with my outer thigh, even though the strike wasn't nearly as hard as the first time he'd spanked me. It certainly paled in comparison to anything he'd done to me the other night, and that hadn't even been a punishment. More shocking than anything.

"I told you it would be worse if you lied," he said in a calm, matter-of-fact manner I had come to realize preceded things so much worse than his anger did. "But you can't help it, can you, Kitten? Or maybe..." He leaned down, his breath disturbing the hairs at the nape of my neck since the rest of it had fallen over my shoulder. "You just crave the discipline you so badly lack."

His words sent a shiver down my spine, but before I could even prepare myself, his hand connected with my ass again. This time, I managed to grit my teeth and hold my cries back, at least for now. My response to clench down after each successive blow meant my ass hurt inside even more than the stinging pain of his palm meeting my flesh. The first time, he'd at least warned me of how many blows were coming, but not this time. One strike followed the other and each seemed harder than the last, even though I knew for a fact he was holding back. Using only a fraction of his strength.

If he wanted to, he could snap my neck like a fucking twig, and there had been plenty of times the look in his eyes told me he wanted to. Very much so.

That knowledge somehow made the traitorous lust within me flare up even more in response to his brutality. I gave up counting how many times he'd struck me when he suddenly stopped and asked, "Had enough, Kitten?"

My head was still spinning and the pain had eaten up the majority of my mental bandwidth, so it took me a second to process what he was asking.

"Are you ready to use your safe word?" he clarified.

It hadn't been long at all since we'd come to that arrangement, but I had forgotten it all the same, as if a year had passed. It was a life preserver tossed in a choppy, stormy ocean, a promise of relief, even if I was surprised it was one he was still willing to keep.

Part of me resented him for reminding me of it, but the sensible thing would have been to take him up on it. To recognize how far out of my depth I was and call it a day.

Instead, I shook my head like a stubborn child.

Malcolm gave a knowing chuckle. Like he knew that would be my answer. "Well, then," he said, smoothing his hand over my ass. The tenderness was pure torture brushing against my stinging flesh. "I think that's enough for the night."

He lifted me off his lap and set me back on my feet, even though my knees felt wobbly beneath me. Before I had the courage to test my footing, he stood and scooped me into his arms. He somehow managed to yank back the covers before placing me down, absurdly gentle after everything he'd just done.

"Th-that's all?" I asked, still trembling and breathless. I only realized then that tears were stinging my eyes and I could feel the tightness of a few streaks of them drying on my cheeks.

"You want more?" he asked, raising an eyebrow.

"No!" I cried.

Maybe.

His lips twitched, betraying the amusement his dead eyes gave up so seldom. "I have work to do downstairs," he informed me. "Get some rest or don't, but either way, I'm taking your sweet little ass tomorrow. I suggest you take me up on my generosity."

With that, he left the room and I waited until I heard his footsteps travel all the way downstairs before burying my face in the pillow, trying not to be as turned on as I was by his scent on the linens and the aftermath of...

Whatever the hell that was.

It occurred to me that this was my real punishment. Doing *that* and then leaving me like this, desperate and just too proud to beg. Barely. Instead, I wrapped my hand around my own cock and started stroking, only fueled by the lingering pain.

It didn't take long. I cursed the son of a bitch's name under my breath even as I came, and collapsed, deciding to give myself a moment before I cleaned up the evidence. He wasn't coming back for a while, anyway.

He knew exactly how to torture me, and this was by far one of his cruelest methods yet.

VALENTINE

We had been at the villa for a couple of weeks, give or take. My perception of time was skewed from having no discernible routine to adhere to, save for whatever Malcolm felt like handing down for the day. While my initial trepidations had mostly revolved around what Malcolm was going to do to me, after that first brutal night, I had been more concerned with what he hadn't done.

It wasn't that we hadn't been fucking like rabbits or anything. And while I didn't exactly have experience with sleeping with men outside of him, I was pretty sure he was still rough compared to most people, but compared to that first night, things had been almost tame. Gentle, even.

The fact that this was Malcolm when he was trying to be gentle should have been unnerving in its own right, but not for the reasons it was. Of course, I had to go and feel insecure because he wasn't pinning me against the wall and fucking my brains out like he was a jackhammer and I was the pavement.

Every day, I found new depths to sink to, but fuck it, I had already made a deal with the devil, and the least he could do was deliver on his part of the bargain.

That afternoon, I'd been warring with myself all day while he was downstairs at the kitchen table working on a laptop he'd bought in the nearby town at some point. Because he was allowed to have technology while I had to live like a fifteenth-century peasant.

"You can't be trusted, Valentine."

"You don't even know what a VPN is, Valentine."

"All you're going to do is look at furry porn all day, Valentine."

And yeah, okay, that was all true, but it was still hypocrisy and he wasn't exactly keeping me entertained.

When I finally mustered the courage to venture downstairs and saw him sipping a glass of whiskey while doing whatever the hell it was the chief of police even did when he was supposed to be on leave, I hesitated. All of a sudden, my courage faded, and I was left unsure of myself, which was my default state in his presence.

Most people probably would've felt more comfortable around someone after they'd bared their soul, or at least, whatever passed for his. But our conversation had had the opposite effect. Now he knew all my dark and dirty little secrets, and I knew he'd killed a man while he was still in elementary school. I wasn't sure that exactly qualified as vulnerability if it made him even more terrifying.

And like a complete fucking headcase, I wanted more. More of him, more of his touch, more of his brutality. I wanted as much as I could get for as long as I could get it, because if I didn't figure out a way to purge this sickness he'd been the vector of before we left Romania, I was going to be in a world of trouble back home.

I found myself worrying at the tag hanging from my collar, rubbing it between my thumb and forefinger. He hadn't noticed me yet, or he was pretending he hadn't, which gave me plenty of time to abort mission and head back upstairs before I outed myself as the complete attention whore I was.

Instead, I sank down onto my hands and knees and crawled toward him into the kitchen, trying to look sultry even though I felt completely and utterly ridiculous.

"Meow?"

Malcolm looked up in confusion before his gunmetal eyes traveled down to me as I approached his chair and pawed at his leg. For the longest few seconds of my life, he just sat there staring at me, as I blinked at him slowly and rubbed my cheek against his leg.

I'd worked on purring earlier, but it just came out sounding like I was trying to start an energy-efficient lawnmower, and this felt ridiculous enough. Just when I thought he was going to scold me for bothering him while he was working again and crush what was left of my already miniscule self-esteem, his eyes darkened in that familiar way that made my heart flutter and sink like a rock at the same time.

He reached out, cupping my chin in his palm and tilting my head up to force me to look at him. "What's this?" he asked, his voice rough with something I was too hesitant to read as desire. "I take it my Kitten wants attention?"

Encouraged, I pushed my cheek into his palm and sidled up to him, trilling, "Meow?"

His lips curved at one end, a crooked smirk I'd been on the receiving end of a thousand times over, and each time, it struck the same exact chord of lust within me as violently as the first.

"Well, can't have that, can we?" he asked, closing his laptop before he turned to face me, running his fingers through my hair. His nails lightly grazing my scalp sent an instant surge of bliss through me, and all of a sudden, I had no trouble purring at all.

"What a good boy," he said in a gravelly tone I finally allowed myself to accept was desire. He pushed his chair back from the table and started unfastening his belt with his right hand, his left still buried in my hair, stroking affectionately. "You know, if you wanted Daddy's attention, all you had to do was say."

I wasn't about to break character and admit that, believe it or not, this had seemed like the less humiliating option.

As he freed his cock from his jeans, my thoughts were racing, all of them contradictory. I'd never sucked a guy off before, and until him, I hadn't really thought about it. Getting fucked by him should have felt like a bigger deal, but I really hadn't had all that much to do about it, save for just laying there and getting absolutely wrecked. No skill involved in that. At least, not the way he fucked.

This, though...

He must have noticed my hesitation, because he gave a dangerous little smirk and cradled the back of my head. "Be a good boy and lick it for Daddy."

My face turned so hot I felt like I was going to pass out, but I put my hand around the base of his shaft and flicked my tongue tentatively against the head of his cock. When my eyes flicked up to meet his, they were dark with approval, so I ran my tongue up along the underside, and the taste of the precome waiting for me when I made it back to the tip was far more pleasant than I had expected. Strong and kind of salty, just like him. I wrapped my lips around the head and sucked lightly, getting a feel for it. I'd just started to relax when he pushed down on my head, pushing his cock deeper into my mouth and stretching my jaw open.

I gave a muffled cry of alarm, but he just tightened his fingers in my hair and settled back in his seat. "You can take it," he said, his voice rough with arousal that sent a surge of heat down my own cock like a lightning rod.

Could, maybe. But I wasn't sure I was going to be able to shut my jaw again if I kept it up for long, and I already knew his endurance was impressive, to say the least. I tried to adjust, sitting up a bit further on my knees with both hands wrapped around his shaft, and before the crown could pass my lips again on the way out, he pushed my head back down until it hit the back of my throat and made me gag.

I pulled back and fell flat on my ass, bumping my head on the side of the table as I coughed.

Malcolm stared down at me, one eyebrow lifted in a slightly bemused expression. "We're going to have to work on that gag reflex."

"You can't just deepthroat someone without warning," I protested. "Or... reverse deepthroat. Whatever."

"Did you bring lube?" he asked, ignoring my comment.

I nodded, still flustered as I reached into my pocket and pulled out the small bottle. I also knew better than to risk an encounter with him without being fully prepared, because I was pretty sure he'd jump at the first opportunity to take me raw.

"Good boy," he said, taking the bottle from me. He grabbed my hips and turned me toward the table, bending me over it so swiftly I barely had time to process what he was doing before he yanked my pants down, and I heard him squirt out some clear jelly before I felt his fingers push against my hole. I clenched down in response, but he was gentler than before, easing them in past the first knuckle. I felt him standing behind me, kicking back the chair as he prepped me.

I should have been grateful. Even though he was going slow, it still hurt bad enough, and I knew just how much worse it was going to be when he put his cock in. My jaw was still sore and I hadn't even taken half of it into my mouth. Even so, my self-destructive impulses were getting the best of me again and I found myself longing for more.

By the time he managed to work a third finger into me, my hips were bucking and my own cock was weeping precome, desperate for release.

"There," he purred, finally pulling his fingers out.

I braced myself for the impending invasion I knew was coming as he poured out some more lube and I felt his newly slick crown slip between my cheeks.

He entered me slowly this time, but I still gave a strangled cry and gripped the other edge of the table as he stretched me open. His hands settled on my hips, the right one still slick with lubricant as he started guiding his cock deeper into me, and as much as I wanted it, my body naturally resisted.

"So fucking tight," he gritted out, his voice strained like he was the one getting the rough end of the stick.

More like a fucking tree trunk.

And here I was, bitter that he was being "gentle." I didn't dare say a word, and when he combed his fingers through my hair and bent his body over mine, kissing the side of my neck, I melted.

"How's that feel, Kitten?"

My breath faltered on my lips. "I... good?"

My words came out kind of squeaky, but I didn't think he'd think anything of it, considering what we were doing. When he froze altogether, I wasn't sure.

"Something's wrong."

I swallowed. "N-no. Nothing."

I never thought it was possible to hear a glare, but everything Mal did was a multisensory experience, from his burning stares to the bittersweet taste of the pain he inflicted.

He gripped my hair tightly all of a sudden and yanked my head back, leaning in so I could feel his lips brush against my throat. "What did I tell you about lying to me?"

I gasped in alarm as the abrupt change in angle drove his cock into my prostate. "I'm sorry, Daddy."

"You're damn right," he muttered. "Now tell me what's wrong."

I pursed my lips, my pulse hammering in my chest and his equally deep inside me. "It's just... it's different. That's all."

Malcolm paused for a few torturous seconds before he pulled out and spun me around to face him, a hard, dangerous look on his face that did even more to my cock than what he had just been doing.

"What's different?" he demanded.

I tried to swallow the knot in my throat, but it wouldn't budge. "The way you fuck me."

My voice sounded small and timid, which was accurate enough.

He raised an eyebrow. "And how is that?"

Well, he was already pissed and I was already mortified. Lying could only make it worse. "You're gentle," I finally answered.

His expression didn't shift, and he said nothing. Not a damn thing, and he was silent for long enough that I felt like I might spontaneously combust from the tension in the room. I didn't even care what he did or said, as long as he did something, and when he finally spoke, his voice was less biting than I had anticipated.

"And that's a problem."

I swallowed again, but my mouth had forgotten how to produce saliva, apparently. "I mean, I guess I just figured you were... I don't know, bored or something."

"Bored?" he echoed.

Fuck, I really wished he was easier to read. My Latin textbooks had nothing on his poker face.

"Yeah," I said with a shrug, my arms folded over myself, like that was somehow going to put any sufficient kind of barrier between us.

His eyes darkened with something like understanding and he reached out, tilting my chin up so I had to meet his eyes. "Let me make one thing clear. I do what and who I want, when I want to. No exceptions. And I don't play games. If I were bored, you'd know. As for me being 'gentle,' after the conversation we had the other day, I figured that was what you'd want."

It took me a second to realize what he was talking about, and when it hit me, I felt like an idiot. "My teacher?"

"What else?" he asked gruffly. "You're already a mess, I didn't want to re-traumatize you even further."

It took another few seconds for me to process that revelation, at once insulting and touching, and all the implications that flowed from it. Namely the fact that he was being careful to avoid re-traumatizing me or whatever. "That's kind of sweet. But I think I kind of like being traumatized. When it's you."

He rolled his eyes. "Clearly, it was misguided. And if I've been holding back all this time for no reason, then I'm going to make up for lost time."

I felt my eyes grow wide as I stared at him, and when that familiar sinister look came over his face, I wondered what the hell I'd just gotten myself into. "Oh."

I'd barely gotten that one little word out of my mouth before he grabbed me by the throat and had me pinned against the table so swiftly I couldn't even register that I'd smacked my head on it until he was on top of me, looming.

"That turned you on before, didn't it?" he asked, his voice a malevolent rumble. "Me choking you. You certainly got hard enough."

"Pretty sure that's a natural physical response to being strangled," I muttered, instinctively grabbing his wrists even though I knew trying to pry them off was a lost cause. And a pointless one, considering he was right, incidentally. It did turn me on. And I was already rock fucking hard again, which he knew perfectly well, considering the fact that he was already between my legs, pushing them open.

His hand tightened around my throat, and I gasped voluntarily, trying to force air into my lungs while I still had the chance. I squirmed, but he was leaning in enough to pin my lower body, too, and somehow, I'd ended up with my left foot up on the edge of the table, making it even easier for him to position his cock at my entrance. Just the right angle, just the right configuration, but when it was him, I knew better than to think anything happened by accident.

"You're cute when you struggle, Kitten," he remarked, his eyes darkening with the approval that had become my drug. My fucking catnip, to put it in terms appropriate for this utterly fucked-up little roleplay of ours. And me walking around on all fours meowing like a damn cat wasn't even anywhere near the most fucked part. "When you're gasping for breath."

Instinctively, I gasped in response and found it more difficult this time to take even the slightest breath. Just enough to give my brain the minimum amount of oxygen I needed to call for a surge of adrenaline as I realized just how precarious this situation was. Not that a whole lot of blood was making it to my brain anyway when it all seemed to have rushed to my cock.

I whimpered as the buckle of my collar dug into my Adam's apple from the force of his tightening grip, but it became a strangled cry of pain as he pushed his cock into me. Unlike before, he did it all in one swift motion, and he hadn't bothered to re-apply the lube after he pulled out, so I was left to make do with the remnants.

I felt the telltale sharpness where there was supposed to be only a dull ache and knew he'd torn me. He hadn't even started thrusting yet, but when he did, I felt something warm and sticky trickle down my thigh, and there was too much of it to just be lubricant. Blood was clearly an aphrodisiac to him on par with pain and choking, and the fact that all three were in the mix seemed to send him over the edge. I couldn't even scream properly, and just when I felt sure I was going to black out, he loosened his grip just enough that the black beginning to form around the corners of my vision ebbed away.

With the near blackout came a kind of euphoria like I'd never known before. Judging from the look on Malcolm's face as he stared down at me like an angry god claiming his human sacrifice, he was feeling his own version.

"I love the way you bleed for me," he purred.

I'll take things serial killers say for a hundred.

And the fact that those words stroked my cock like a lover's caress was just proof I was as twisted as he was. Everything I'd ever thought I knew about myself had been left a mangled, misshapen wreckage the moment the head-on collision that was our relationship had happened.

Hell, I wasn't even sure what it was. We certainly weren't boyfriends—or friends, even. But at some point, he'd ceased to be just my dick of a brother-in-law I saw only at the odd family gathering, usually where he was judging the shit out of me for piling five dinner rolls on my plate, or I was snort-laughing at whatever tasteless joke Chuck or Johnny had just told.

I was pretty sure there wasn't even a word for where we'd ended up. Somewhere between Stockholm syndrome and enemies with benefits for sure.

It didn't matter what the official definition was, though. All that mattered was the fact that at this very moment, choking me breathless and fucking me senseless, he was mine.

My Master.

My Daddy.

My worst nightmare and my filthiest dream all wrapped up in one person.

I didn't know what I was to him, but I'd be it. His boy, his kitten, his fucktoy. I'd be whatever he asked me for as long as he wanted me, because more than anything, I was crazy. Crazy enough to want him. Crazy enough to need him. Crazy enough to let him own me, wreck me, break me, because when I was his, it was the closest my world had ever been to sane.

And that was the most fucked-up part of all.

At some point, he released his grip on my throat, and I only realized it because he bent down to kiss me and what little was left of my composure shattered into a thousand pieces. Despite everything we'd done, it occurred to me that I didn't think he'd ever actually kissed me before. Not like this. He'd licked and sucked and nipped and bitten and ravaged every part of me with nearly every part of him, but had his lips ever crushed mine like this, hard enough to bruise? He'd fucked my ass with his tongue, but somehow, that tongue flicking against my bottom lip for entrance felt even more intimate. And the juxtaposition of that tender thing on the relentless rhythm of his thrusting unwound something in me like a damn spring and I just...

Broke.

I kissed him back, and now that I wasn't instinctively trying to pry his hands off my throat, my hands found his hair and my fingers rifled through it greedily, but my body was acting on its own. I couldn't formulate a single rational thought, let alone a command, but I decided it didn't matter. When you were in the path of a hurricane, you didn't fight it, you ducked for cover wherever you could find it, but I couldn't even do that. No, I just surrendered myself to the storm entirely, and let him crash over me again and again until I lost track of where my body ended and his began.

When he finally broke the kiss, I was left gasping again, but this time, not for air. For him. For that strange, aching, tender thing I'd held such a tentative grasp on for such a short time, but it was long enough. Long enough for an addiction to form. Long enough to spark an obsession.

He gave me a knowing look as he dug one hand into my hair and wrapped his other hand around my throat once more. "Touch yourself," he ordered, leaving just enough space between our bodies for me to execute his command, and I did without thinking, because he was perfectly capable of bypassing my brain and controlling my body through some form of twisted sex telepathy. "I want you to touch yourself while I choke you, and in the morning, I want my hands to leave a bruise that wraps around your throat so even if you take off that collar, everyone will know you're mine."

Every now and then, as deep in this thing as I was, he'd say something that made me stop and wonder, "What the hell would a normal, rational, not completely fucked in the head person's reaction be to that?" And for the life of me, I couldn't say. But it sure as hell wasn't my reaction, which was to stroke myself faster even as his grip tightened and my head started swimming again, because I had never been more turned on in my fucking life.

Malcolm's breathing grew as heavy as his thrusts, and as I stared up at him, the kitchen lights stretched and blurry behind him like some kind of ironic halo, I found myself thinking it'd be okay if this was how it ended. I didn't want to die anymore, and I really wasn't sure when that had happened, but the thought of it ending like this was still far more palatable than the thought of this ending at all. And through the haze of sex and lust, I knew it would eventually. It had to. Nothing good could ever last. Even if it was the most decadent, delicious sin I'd ever tasted on my tongue.

At that moment, furiously stroking myself to race my dwindling consciousness and his quickening thrusts, I had a kind of epiphany. I'd heard somewhere the French euphemism for orgasm was *la petite mort*—the little death. And at the time, I'd kind of just shrugged it off and figured it was one of those French things I would never understand, like escargot, but now, I got it.

As I came harder than I ever had, and the pleasure and pain both merged into a kind of euphoria so intense it didn't seem like anything else could possibly be left in its wake, I was sure I died. I just ceased to be whatever I had been before, and at some point, I must have actually blacked out, even if it was only for a fraction of a second. Mal was kissing me again, his tongue buried in my mouth, and I was kissing him back, like someone else had been piloting my body while I floated somewhere just beyond it.

He growled against my lips as his come filled me, and I gave a pained cry because it fucking burned, but he swallowed the sound down as hungrily as his tongue was exploring mine. Even as his thrusts slowed and my whimpers became plaintive purrs, the ecstasy hummed within me like a siren's song. The euphoria lingered, and I found in it the kind of escape no drug or drunken binge had ever come close to providing. I died in his arms, and I was reborn in them, too. As he held me, stroking my hair down to the marks that had to be forming on my throat, the perfect blend of tenderness and pain seemed to draw it all out indefinitely. I found myself thinking if I could just stay like this forever, held by him, maybe it never had to end after all.

But that was a fantasy. And no matter how grim and twisted the fairy tale, all fantasies have to come to an end eventually.

He pulled out, and I felt a fresh trickle of blood and come run down my thigh as I rolled onto my side, realizing at some point, we'd knocked all his shit off the table, his laptop included.

"Hope you got a warranty on that," I mumbled.

Malcolm gave a coarse laugh, raking a hand through his sweat-drenched hair. "Probably in better condition than you right now."

I could only offer a moan of apathetic agreement, my eyes fluttering shut since the lights above were dancing too brightly to be tolerable without him blocking them at least partially. As the orgasm faded, the analgesic effects along with it, the pain remained and I ached and throbbed in places I didn't even know existed.

"Come on," Mal said, gathering me into his arms before I had the chance to even think of resisting. He lifted me as easily as if I was a child, cradling me against his strong chest as he carried me toward the downstairs bathroom. "Let's get you cleaned up."

"Nooo," I groaned in half-hearted protest, because I couldn't even muster the proper embarrassment that should have been kicking in right now.

He ignored me, of course, and placed me down in the clawfoot bathtub. I winced even though he'd placed me on my side, and realized there was no way I'd actually have been able to walk on my own. He turned on the water and adjusted the detachable showerhead on the wall so the stream was gentle. I hissed as even the cold droplets cascading over my skin were painful, but the heat was soon too soothing to care.

Malcolm actually climbed into the tub with me this time and sank back against the back of the tub, adjusting me so I was still curled up on my side against his chest. I breathed a deep sigh of relief as the water washed the blood and come and insufficient traces of lubricant down the drain, and I let my head fall against his chest, lulled into a quiet trance by the steady sound of his heartbeat and the rush of the water.

"You regret asking me not to be gentle?" Malcolm finally asked in a knowing tone.

I considered it for a moment, snuggling into him even though that was probably the gayest thing I'd done so far. "No," I admitted, sighing deeply. "But this is nice."

I could get used to both sides of him. If I was being honest with myself, I already had.

20

MALCOLM

It had been over a month since I'd taken Valentine in the kitchen that first time, and there had been plenty of times since. In the kitchen. The living room. The shower. The bath. The stairs once, which had been an interesting challenge of dexterity. Even the bedroom occasionally, when I could summon the patience to get that far without ravaging him.

In the beginning, I'd been sure that a little force was all it would take to break him. I had wanted to, but at some point, I'd become afraid of it. I had been pleasantly surprised by just how much he could take. He was so fragile and unstable in so many ways, and yet, in others, he was a hell of a lot stronger than I'd ever imagined.

Most concerning of all, he actually seemed to crave the brutality that came so easily to me, but never more so than when I had him in my grasp. He'd called me by so many names, both cried out in ecstasy and cursed under his breath, but he'd yet to call me by the one name that would end it all. I found myself hoping he never would, pushing it a little further each time.

The problem was, everyone had a limit eventually. And I hadn't yet decided what I would do when I finally found his.

I wouldn't take him by force, but shy of that, anything was fair game.

Even if he didn't tap out during our time here, after I'd subjected him to the myriad of depravities I still had plans to exorcize from my fantasies, we couldn't stay here forever.

I wasn't sure what to make of the fact that part of me wanted to.

That morning, while Valentine was still asleep and I knew he would be for another couple of hours at least, I decided to call and check in with Elijah. It had been a few days since he had given any updates, and like any other asset, he had to be handheld and babysat through the whole thing.

He was bold to let the phone ring a few times before he picked up, but at least he had the sense to not let it go to voicemail. I didn't take kindly to being ignored.

"Malcolm," he said, sounding breathless, although considering he was a doughy professor, that might easily have been the result of him walking up a flight of stairs rather than anything eventful. It was hard to be appropriately irritated with a guy who looked like a living teddy bear, but if he kept fucking around, I would manage. "How can I help you?"

"I think you already know the answer to that, Professor," I said, keeping my voice down just in case Valentine was a lighter sleeper than he let on.

He swallowed audibly. "Yes, I... Well, there is something. I was going to call you shortly, actually. I just wasn't sure it was a good time."

"I think I made it pretty clear there's never a bad time for this kind of thing," I said, struggling to keep my tone level. There was only so far he could be threatened without becoming useless.

"Of course," he said, sounding very much on the verge of passing out. "Well, here goes. I succeeded at decrypting the chip."

I frowned. "Then why the hell did you wait until now to tell me that?"

The silence on the other end told me I wasn't going to like the answer. "Elijah—"

"It's nothing," he blurted out. "I decrypted it, but there's nothing."

"What do you mean, there's nothing?" I hissed. "That's not possible."

"Trust me, I've been working the last two days nonstop, trying to find any hidden firewalls, any sign of a tripwire I might've activated that would wipe the chip as a failsafe, but there's nothing. Nothing but..."

"Nothing but what?" I demanded.

He paused again for long enough that I was about to ream him out before he added, "There was a message. Just a single line of text. It was in code, but it was easy enough to crack. He clearly wanted you to see it."

"And what is the message?" I asked coldly.

"'Did you really think it would be that easy? Don't worry, we'll be seeing each other again soon enough.'"

I fell silent, considering the message and measuring my own response.

"Malcolm?" he asked after a moment.

"I'm here," I said gruffly.

"What should I do?" he asked. "Do you want me to try—"

"No," I answered. "Destroy it. You know how, I assume."

"Of course, but–"

I hung up before he could say anything else because I could already feel the anger boiling over. I flipped the table, letting out a snarl more fit for an animal than a man. It was rare that I let myself get out of control—though less so lately—but if anyone was capable of pushing me to that, it was Demon.

I looked up from my rampage to find the only other person who possessed that rare and unique skill set standing in the doorway to the kitchen, staring at me with the first appropriate tinge of fear that had been in his eyes for weeks.

"Malcolm?" Valentine asked warily.

"What did you call me?" I asked. I needed an outlet for my anger, and that was a sufficient excuse to make it him. Before he could answer, I closed the distance between us in a few long strides and had him pinned against the wall by the throat.

Valentine's eyes widened in genuine fear, and I'd missed the tang of it on the tip of my tongue, but my body was pressed close enough to his that I could feel his hard-on. Right where I liked to keep him, somewhere between arousal and terror.

"D-Daddy," he choked out even though I wasn't applying nearly enough pressure to affect his breathing.

Yet.

"Damn right," I said through my teeth, before capturing his lips in a violent kiss and pinning his wrists to the walls.

He gasped as I turned my attention to his neck just above his collar, nipping and sucking hard in alternation with the goal of leaving my mark on him as clearly as possible.

"What happened?" he asked, already breathless as I tore his shirt open, groping every inch of him I could get my hands on.

I ignored his question and muttered, "Stay," against his throat before I disappeared just long enough to grab the lube sitting in the drawer of the side table in the living room. When I returned, he was right where I'd left him, his back pressed against the wall as he stared at me in wide-eyed curiosity.

He took one look at the bottle in my hand and gulped. I smirked, setting it aside to yank down his pajama pants and force him to step out of them. I applied a bit of lube to my fingers and pushed two of them into him without warning, grabbing his hair with my other hand and swallowing down his startled cry with another kiss.

He tasted like fear and desire, and I couldn't get enough of it. I pushed my fingers in deeper, scissoring them inside him to loosen him enough that I would be able to go in without tearing him. That was the idea, at any rate. Given how worked up I was, I wasn't sure that was a plan I'd be able to follow through on, but he didn't complain as I pulled my fingers out suddenly, even though I'd usually give him a bit more prep.

Valentine's hands settled on my shoulders, his eyes heavy and his lips parted with his already shallow breath. I hitched his thigh up over my hip, and he whimpered a little in anticipation, which had the exact opposite effect of whatever misguided prey response that was. When I pushed into him halfway, his tight ass clenched down on my cock, and I drove into him harder until I was balls deep, pinning him to the wall like a fucking butterfly on a corkboard, delicate and ruined.

Another strangled cry tore from his beautiful mouth and his head fell back, baring his throat. It was just begging to be claimed with my teeth, and I wasn't in the mood to deny myself any of the carnal impulses this boy stirred within me so easily.

"Fuck," he gritted out as a metallic taste hit my tongue and I realized I'd bitten him a little harder than I'd intended. I couldn't bring myself to apologize, other than running my tongue up the small puncture to collect the droplet of blood that was already trickling down toward his collar. Couldn't have it go to waste.

"Still so tight for Daddy," I growled next to his ear before taking his earlobe between my teeth. I let it go before I started thrusting into him since I didn't trust myself not to bite clean through.

Valentine wrapped his arms around my neck, burying his face in my shoulder, but not before I caught a glimpse of his pained grimace. I was being rougher than usual, and we both knew it, but he hadn't used his safe word. Part of me wondered if he'd forgotten that part of our little arrangement, and I wasn't good enough to risk reminding him. He hadn't said no, either, or asked me to stop, and I figured he would have at least done that if it was too much.

His cock was hard against my stomach as I thrust into him, though, our bodies pressed so close he was leaking precome from the friction of each movement. His fingers clutched and released my hair to the same rhythmic grinding of his hips, even though he was only making it worse for himself. It seemed to be instinct more than anything. Then again, I'd been pleasantly surprised by just how much he could take. How much pain he craved.

I knew the depths of my sadistic tendencies surely ran deeper than his masochistic ones, but he was the closest I had ever come to finding an equal. The closest I ever would. I knew that, even now as I lost myself in his body, in the bittersweet nectar of his blood on my tongue.

The truth was, if there was a better match out there somewhere in the seven billion or so motherfuckers wasting air on this earth, I wasn't interested in finding him. I wanted *him*. Now. Tomorrow. Forever. I wanted him with such intensity that it drowned out the rage from earlier. It felt like five minutes ago and five years ago all at once. Time was a concept that lost all meaning when I had him in my arms, but that didn't stop the clock from ticking. Counting down the timer that had been on this thing from the beginning.

Tick.

Tock.

He gasped as I drove him into the wall harder than before, like I wasn't already buried balls-deep in his perfect ass. Just to hear him scream. I wasn't sure which name he'd even called out when I heard the sound of the front door falling shut, but when I looked up, I realized we were very much not alone.

Before I could even reach for my gun, I processed the fact that it was Silas, but that was far from a relief in a thousand other ways.

"What the fuck?" I seethed.

"Silas?" Valentine croaked out at the same time, his voice still strangled and breathless. Considering the way he looked, and the fact that I probably looked like I was halfway through transforming into some kind of demon, I wouldn't have been surprised if he'd gotten the wrong idea.

Or the right one.

For his part, Silas was just standing there, looking like someone had just wiped his mind blank. Or wishing they would. I could count on one hand the number of times I had ever seen my brother frozen in shock, and this was one of them.

I pulled out and Valentine gave a pained yelp, but I kept my hands on his arms to keep him steady since he didn't look quite capable of standing yet. "You okay?" I asked, my voice gruffer than I wanted it to be.

He just nodded shakily, so I zipped up before grabbing his clothes and handing them to him. "Go upstairs and get cleaned up," I muttered.

Valentine clutched his clothes to his front and seemed like he was trying to figure out a way to get to the stairs without baring his ass, but he quickly gave up and just scampered up them with a limp obvious enough Silas was sure to pick up on it.

Great.

"You ever heard of fucking knocking?" I snarled, turning to face him once we were alone.

"You weren't answering your phone," Silas said, holding his up pointedly. "Although now I certainly understand why you didn't hear the door. And I thought the boy was loud under normal circumstances."

I scoffed a laugh, walking over to lean against the wall, my adrenaline still racing from the interrupted orgasm. "You could've called before you got on the fucking plane."

"What would be the point of checking in on you, then?"

I felt a surge of rage that he was just coming out and admitting it. Not that I could really say I blamed him, considering what he'd walked in on.

"What was that, Malcolm?" he pressed.

"Before you showed up, it was a good fucking morning."

"Oh, you've got jokes," he said with a bitter sneer. "That's good. I'm glad one of us finds this funny. Enzo's brother? Really? Are you out of your fucking mind?"

"What did you think was going to happen when you left the lion in charge of the lamb?" I challenged.

Anger I hadn't seen in years flashed in Silas's eyes, and for a moment, I found myself wondering if he was going to attack me. It had been a long time since we'd actually fought, but I had a sudden excess of adrenaline to burn off, so if he wanted to throw the first punch, so be it.

Instead, the flame in his silver eyes went cold and hard. That look, I knew well. "Please tell me this was a one-time lapse in judgment, and I just happen to have the world's worst timing."

"Sure," I said with a shrug. "If that makes you feel better."

His eyes narrowed. "Well, it ends tonight."

"You don't get to make that call," I said with a dry laugh. "He's an adult."

"He's a child all the same," he snapped. "The fact that he doesn't have the sense to stay away from you is proof enough of that."

I took a step forward. "Tell me, Silas, are you pissed on Enzo's behalf or yours? Because this sure seems personal."

"Both," he answered, not taking the bait. "He's Enzo's responsibility, which makes him mine by proxy, and if there's one thing you and I have in common, it's how we feel about other people touching our things. Which is all the more reason you should fucking know better."

Now I was the one on the verge of throwing that first punch. It seemed like Valentine was capable of igniting that side of me even when he wasn't directly involved. "You act like I'm a bigger threat to him than Demon."

"You are," he said without hesitation. "Demon is a physical threat, not an existential one. You're both."

I rolled my eyes. "You're being dramatic."

"Am I?"

"Why don't you let him be the one to decide that?" I asked, even though there was part of me that wasn't sure what his answer would be.

Silas said nothing for a long while, just standing there watching me with that look even I couldn't read. "Oh, God," he murmured. "It's not just about sex, is it?"

"What?" I demanded, already on edge.

"It was bad enough when I thought you were just fucking around for the hell of it," he answered. "Because he's the one thing you can't have. But that's not it, is it? You actually think you care about him."

For some reason, that of all things was what I took offense to. "And what if I do?" I asked with a shrug, refusing to let him know he'd gotten to me. "You're allowed to have a pet, but I'm not?"

"No," he answered immediately. "Not him. Sex is one thing, but you can't have him. You know that."

I clenched my jaw, furious even though he wasn't doing anything more than voicing the same arguments I'd been having with myself all along. "And why the hell not? I can't be any worse for him than you are for Enzo."

Another laugh escaped him, this one sharp as he raked a hand through his hair in disbelief. "God, I think the altitude is fucking with your head. Of course you are! I live my life in the shadows and I always have. I keep the people I love as far from my work as possible. I compartmentalize, but you... you *are* your work. You live for the prestige and the infamy and all that comes with it."

"You don't know shit," I muttered.

"No?" he asked. "You've made enough money that you could have retired a decade ago if you wanted to, and I know it isn't because you care about 'justice.'"

"You're walking a fine line, Silas," I warned him.

"And you've crossed it," he shot back. "I've never cared about your little power games and I'm not going to start now, but this isn't one of them. Not him."

"I know that," I snapped. "You don't think I fucking know that? We didn't talk for five years. You think I'd risk losing you again for a game?"

Silas didn't seem to know what to make of that. "No," he finally said, his voice quieter. "I don't. And that's what scares me."

"You're the one who asked me to watch him," I reminded him. "You trusted me with his life, but caring about him —wanting him—*that's* too far?"

"Wanting him as what, Malcolm?" he asked. "A toy? A boyfriend? A dirty little secret?"

"No," I said through my teeth. It was only hearing each of those labels out loud that I realized just how inadequate they all were. How they failed to describe what I felt for Valentine. "He's more than that. He's... he means more than that, okay?"

Silas frowned, something like pity coming into his gaze, which pissed me off more than anything. "Then that's all the more reason you have to let him go," he said firmly. "Unless you want him to end up like Owen."

His words were a slap in the face, and it took all my willpower not to lunge at him right then. "Fuck you," I spat, shoving him back. He staggered, but righted himself quickly enough, infuriatingly calm. "You of all people have no fucking right to even say his name. Not when you're the reason he's dead."

"You think I don't know that?" Silas asked, his tone softening. "That's my entire point. Demon used you to get to me, and he knew the best way to do that was through Owen. And you made it easy enough, didn't you? Parading him around at parties. That flashy sports car you bought him. That's what you do when you love something—you put it on a pedestal. You lock it in a display case so the whole world can see it, and eventually, the wrong person will. If it isn't Demon, it'll be someone else. One of the countless enemies you've made, all of whom know exactly where you live. Maybe you can keep him from them, but even if you succeed, what kind of life is he going to have living on a shelf, Malcolm? He's not another award to hang up in your office."

His words were a constant barrage of everything I already knew. Every voice of reason whispering venomously in the back of my mind, drowned out by the noise of passion and selfish ambition that was always so much louder.

"Demon is a ghost that haunts us both," he continued, because he knew he'd hit his mark the moment he brought up Owen. "I take full responsibility for bringing him into your world, and I swear to you, I will do whatever it takes to take him out of it. For Enzo, for you, for

Valentine. But when that ghost is laid to rest, the people *I* love will be safe. Everyone but you. Everyone but Valentine, if you go through with this. If you make him yours. Demon will be gone, but all the other ghosts that haunt you will still be there, and I know you can handle them, but can he? Should he have to?"

All I could really do was stare at him, because for every argument on the tip of my tongue, he'd already made a better one in the back of my mind. And when a bona fide sociopath was your stand-in for a conscience, you were already fighting a losing battle.

"I'm taking him back," Silas said softly. It wasn't a challenge this time. It was a plea.

I stood there frozen for a long while, coming to terms with the decision I'd already made, knowing it would be the only good, decent thing I'd ever done. And I fucking hated it. I finally nodded, because I didn't have the breath to speak. Even though he'd never thrown that punch, he'd knocked the wind out of me all the same.

But he hadn't told me anything I didn't already know. Nothing I hadn't known from the very beginning.

VALENTINE

I showered as quickly as I could, washing as much of my shame down the drain as possible, before I got dressed and went back downstairs just to make sure Silas and Malcolm hadn't killed each other. That seemed like a possibility whenever something involved two men with antisocial personality disorder and histories of violent crimes that rolled like movie credits.

When I found them both standing around in the living room, dead silent, I wasn't sure that was much better than actual physical violence.

"Okay, who died?" I asked warily. There was always a good chance that wasn't a hyperbolic question, either.

Neither of them answered for a moment, and I was beginning to think I had hit the nail on the head. I was starting to freak out a little bit when Silas spoke up.

"You're coming back with me."

"What?" I asked, looking between them. "We're going back?"

"Just you," said Malcolm.

It took me a second to process what he was saying because it had completely come out of left field. "What? What do you mean, just me?" I demanded. "Did you find Demon?"

"No," Silas said carefully. "Not yet."

"Then what?" I pressed. I was sick of everyone always having conversations behind my back, especially when those conversations directly affected the course of my life. I thought we were past that, but one look at Malcolm's solemn expression and I knew better. I couldn't help but feel the sting of betrayal, but I told myself he had a reason.

Right?

"Mal?" I asked hopefully.

I knew it was a risk not to call him Daddy, even in front of Silas, but part of me was hoping he would scold me on it. That he would be eager to claim me as his, because right now, I didn't feel sure of much of anything.

He just shook his head.

"I don't understand," I said. "If nothing has changed, why? Why now?"

"Because there's no point," said Silas. "For one thing, Demon hasn't made any moves recently, and for another, I've made arrangements to ensure you can be kept safely at home."

"But I don't want to go back. Not without you," I said to Malcolm, knowing I probably sounded like a spoiled child throwing a tantrum. But that was kind of how I felt right now, and I didn't care. Not if it meant I didn't have to leave the hell that had turned into an unexpected heaven, because apparently, the devil was the only one capable of saving me.

And yeah, it was fucked up, but I didn't care. It was also the safest and most at home I had ever felt, and I didn't want to give that up. Not without a fight.

The problem was, I was pretty sure I was the only one fighting.

Malcolm just stared at me in silence for a few moments, and I was back to not being able to tell what the fuck he was thinking. When he finally spoke, his voice was measured and devoid of emotion, just like it had been the day we met. Even before he gave his answer, though, I knew something had shifted. I had felt it from the moment I walked into the room.

"I know," he finally said. "But this was always temporary."

"Yeah, but..."

I trailed off because I realized I couldn't finish that thought without betraying how completely and utterly pathetic I was.

Fuck that, though. I had been far more vulnerable with far less provocation around him—and if that was what it took to make sure this thing, whatever it even was, didn't come to an end, so be it. It wasn't like it would be the first time I'd made a fool of myself in front of him—or Silas, for that matter.

"I thought things had changed," I admitted, my voice sounding hoarse and cracking, like a nervous teenager and not a grown man with a fucking medical degree, but that was just what Malcolm turned me into.

"You thought wrong, then," Malcolm said in an apathetic tone I knew well. It stung more than his belt ever had. "Look, we've both had our fun, but I'm getting bored and I'm not cut out for full-time babysitting. It's better to end this thing while it's still a pleasant memory. You'll be better off back with your brothers."

If I were bored, you'd know.

His words didn't just hit me like a punch in the gut, they hit me like a fucking freight train. They physically hurt, but even now, even though he had just spelled it out in terms so crystal clear even I couldn't deny them, I didn't want to believe him. My mind understood his words perfectly, but my heart wouldn't latch on to them.

"What?" I choked.

He rolled his eyes. "Come on, Valentine, what did you think this was? A relationship?" There was such a dismissive tone in his voice that it, too, felt like a blow I would never recover from. "You have your pretentious doctor waiting for you back home, anyway. He clearly has a higher tolerance for caretaking than I do. He made a profession out of it."

That was it. That was the last I could take. I felt like a vice was tightening around my chest, and I could hardly breathe. Like the room was closing in, and if I didn't get some fresh air immediately, I was going to suffocate.

That actually seemed entirely possible as I stalked out of the cabin without another word. Before he could land a devastating blow I knew would break me forever, assuming there was anything left to shatter.

I was vaguely aware of someone following me outside, at once relieved and heartbroken to realize it was Silas.

"Come on," he said in an uncharacteristically gentle tone. At least, he'd never used it on me before, so I knew I probably looked even more pathetic than I felt. He put a hand on my shoulder and nodded up ahead to the black SUV waiting for us. "Let's get you home."

As innocuous as those words were probably meant to be, they were the last straw. The knife in my gut twisted sharply, and it felt like someone had knocked the breath from my lungs.

Home.

I realized only then that was exactly what the cabin in the mountains, the cabin I hadn't even wanted to be at, had become.

No, that wasn't true. It wasn't the cabin. It was him. Malcolm. Somehow, without even realizing it, I had given him more than just my body and absolute control, which was a mindnumbingly stupid decision in and of itself. I had gone and done something even more foolish. I had given him my heart.

And he was bored. That was what I was to him now. A toy—not even a pet—that had already begun to lose its novelty. One he couldn't wait to toss out the first chance he got.

I got into the car with Silas, and it started up immediately. I couldn't see the driver through the dark partition, which made this whole thing seem even more like a fever dream. None of it felt real. Part of me still felt convinced that I was back in the cabin, and any minute, I was going to wake up and find it was just a bad dream born of insecurity and neurosis. God knew I had plenty of those.

"I'm sorry," Silas said once we had been on the winding mountain path for a while. The landscape was just a vague outline of mountains obscured almost entirely by the snow, like some great, spiny dragon about to rise up from its frosty ashes at any moment.

"For what?" I asked. My voice sounded blank. Detached. Guess that was what I was now. What I needed to be.

"For leaving you with him," he answered. "It's clear that was a mistake."

Well, that made sense. He was right. It was a mistake. Just not for the reasons he could possibly fathom. Not for reasons I could fathom in the beginning, either.

"If it's any consolation, it's for the best," he continued. "That thing you're feeling now, that dull, empty pit in the center of your stomach... it would be the same, whether it happened now or in a year. You feel empty because that's what people like Malcolm do. They use you until they get bored, or until there is nothing left to consume. Be grateful that in your case, it was the former."

I stared at him for a moment. "You know, you're not very good at pep talks."

He breathed a laugh. "I'll concede, my empathy is limited to your brother, but I'm sorry all the same."

I turned to look out the window, trying not to think about how it still felt like a part of me was left behind. And it wasn't just because we had left too quickly for me to even pack my things, few and far between as they were. My whole life was back in Boston, and yet, I hadn't felt like I was missing anything here. Not until now.

"There's something I've been meaning to ask you," I said, because I desperately needed to change the subject to anything else. And I was pretty sure this was the best chance I would ever stand at getting an honest answer out of him. It figured even a sociopath would find a way to pity me. Because I was just that pathetic.

"Yes?" he asked.

I forced myself to look back at him, but it wasn't hard for the usual reasons. It wasn't hard because of that coldness in his gaze that was always there, always lurking beneath the surface, with the notable exception of when his eyes were fixed on my brother. It was because of how closely they resembled the ones I'd grown used to waking up to.

"Did you really kill him?" I asked. "Demon?"

Silas looked surprised, even though that only lasted for as long as any other emotion did where he was concerned.

He didn't respond for long enough that I thought he wasn't going to at all.

When he finally opened his mouth as if he was going to answer, something else happened. I felt a sudden lurch as if the car had hit the brakes suddenly, and then, the next thing I knew, we were hurtling through the air. Silas reached out as if to grab me, but my head struck the window, and the next thing I knew, I was on my back.

Or maybe I was upside down. That would explain why it felt like all the blood was rushing to my head.

There was glass everywhere. The windows were shattered. I tried to raise my head, even though I wasn't quite sure I remembered which way was up, but it felt like it was made of solid stone. Out of the corner of my eye, I could see Silas hanging from his seat, too, but before I could work out whether he was still breathing, I heard footsteps crunching through glass and snow.

My vision was blurred, and I could see two pairs of black boots trudging through the snow toward me. But when they finally came to a stop right in front of the SUV, I realized I was just seeing double.

I tried to open my mouth to call to whoever it was for help, even though somewhere in the back of my mind, past the head trauma and the confusion, I knew it was just a little too convenient. When the man knelt down to look into the shattered window, I was convinced he was nothing more than a hallucination.

"Chris?" I managed to croak out before it all went black.

22

MALCOLM

The moment they left, my fists found the wall and hit it hard enough that the entire cabin shook. The next few minutes were a blackout blur, or maybe it was hours. By the end of the night, the entire place was trashed, and I had downed enough whiskey to put down a horse. But I was still no closer to hating myself any less.

I told myself I was doing the right thing, and for once in my fucking life, I actually cared. I actually cared about the right thing for him, what was best for him, even if it meant my world was falling apart.

It wasn't hyperbole. I didn't know exactly when Valentine had managed to carve up such a significant space in my life, but he had. The little weasel had to work his way in past every ten-foot wall, and I hated it.

I hated *him*. I hated him, because I had realized only when he was walking out the door that I loved him. And that was, by far, the cruelest thing anyone had ever done to me.

The worst part was, I thought I had loved Owen. I really fucking did. And I cared for him, at least, as much as I was capable of back then. The problem was, I was capable of more now. I was capable of it because of Valentine. He had given himself to me, fully and without reservation, and yet, at some point without me even realizing it, he was the one who had taken control. I possessed him, body and mind, but he had taken something even more intimate. Something I only realized I had lost when I saw him walking out the door.

At some point, I blacked myself out if only because I didn't want to have the option of going after him. I didn't trust that my selflessness would last once he was far enough out of reach, and whatever forcefield of decency and goodness he'd projected onto me was gone.

When I finally opened my eyes, it was morning, so I hadn't done quite enough damage to my liver to slip into an alcohol-induced coma. I looked around at the wreckage surrounding me and decided I wasn't even going to bother with the cleanup. I was the one who was usually cleaning up Silas's messes, so he could deal with mine for once.

Technically, I knew I should have been grateful to him for keeping me from making the one mistake that could never be undone. The one thing I would never forgive myself for.

Because he was right. If that boy stayed in my care any longer, I was going to taint him. Corrupt him. Break him. At first, it had been a challenge, but now, I realized it was just second nature. I was a predator, and no matter how much I had grown fond of my little lamb, a wolf could never be trusted as a shepherd. Sure, I could protect him from the other wolves, but did that matter if the one who was the greatest threat to him was the one whose bed he went to every night?

Sooner or later, I would destroy him. Because that was what I did when I cared about something. Something fragile and human and capable of being wounded. The only reason I hadn't ruined Silas was simply because there was nothing left to break in him. And hell, maybe that wasn't true anymore, either. Maybe I was the one who should stay away from him, and his family. As far away from them as possible, one in particular, because if there was one thing Owen should've taught me, it was that being loved by a monster was a curse—and if I wanted to protect Valentine, I had to make him hate me.

Fortunately for me, that was easy enough to accomplish.

I ran a hand down my face and tried to compose myself enough to call Silas, since he hadn't bothered to text me to let me know that they had gotten there safely. A needling voice told me something was wrong, but I pushed it aside for my own sanity's sake.

There was no answer, and by the third time his phone went straight to voicemail, I cursed him out until the machine beeped and cut me off.

I warred with myself for a second over calling Valentine, but if Silas wanted to bitch about that, he should've sent me a damn text message. Because apparently, now I was the worried, overprotective boyfriend, except I wasn't. I wasn't anything to Valentine, and I had just made sure of that. His continued survival—or at least, the continuation of any life that was worth living—depended on it.

When he didn't answer, either, I started to feel another emotion that was entirely novel.

Panic.

I reminded myself that it really wasn't all that strange that he would be ignoring my phone calls, but rationality was not something that seemed to have any significant role in my life anymore.

Desperate and out of options, I called Enzo, all the while telling myself I was just being paranoid. He answered immediately, and said, "Malcolm? Thank God, I was just about to call you."

I frowned. That definitely was not a response I had elicited in anyone before, certainly not a DiFiore. "Why?" I asked warily. "Actually, scratch that. Is Valentine with you?"

He paused for a suspicious amount of time before he said, his voice slow and deliberate, "You're joking, right?"

"Comedy really isn't my thing," I informed him. Certainly not where this was concerned. "He and Silas should've been back this morning at the latest. You're telling me they're not there?"

"No," Enzo said, his voice growing tight with the same fear I now knew in abundance.

Holy shit, this fucking sucked. How did people deal with this? I had never had a particularly strong survival instinct, it was just something that I happened to be good at. But it felt like the most vulnerable part of me was walking around outside my body, and there was nothing I could do about it.

And I actually cared.

"When was the last time you heard from them?"

"Last night," Enzo answered. "Silas called me right when he got to the cabin."

"Son of a bitch," I seethed.

"When did they leave?" Enzo demanded as I was already on my way to the car.

"Last night," I said. "Between eight and nine here."

Enzo's silence spoke volumes. "He wouldn't do that," he finally said, his voice hoarse. "Silas wouldn't do that to either of us, he'd call."

"I'm inclined to agree with you," I muttered. Or at least, I knew he wouldn't do that to Enzo. I could probably go either way, depending on how pissed off he was.

"I'm coming to Romania," Enzo said suddenly. I knew Silas would want me to tell him no, but at the moment, I didn't care.

"I'd better go," I said.

I hung up before he could answer, feeling like I was going to be sick.

As soon as I got on the road, I realized it had been snowing too hard for there to be any hope of tracking the car beyond the most logical route I knew it had to have taken. The mountain slopes were rough, even with a car meant to weather the snow, so as I drove through the drift, my mind treated me to all kinds of scenarios about what could've happened.

What if they had gone off the mountain?

What if they had gotten into a head-on collision?

What if it was Demon?

The questions were literally going to drive me insane, so I forced myself to stop and try to remember what it was like to be my usual rational self. If only for the sake of the person who had taken those faculties from me.

I had been driving for a good twenty or thirty minutes when I was considering more efficient means of transportation. Something caught my attention out of the corner of my eye, but it was so hard to see through the snow that I almost dismissed it as a trick of the light. As I drove closer, though, and saw the telltale signs of a wreckage—a strip of metal, and a chunk of a tire just big enough to stick out of the snow, a mere hour or two away from being covered completely—I froze.

I barely even managed to put the car in park before I got out, leaving the engine running as I dove into the drift, searching frantically. It didn't take long to trace the debris to the wreckage itself.

A black SUV, flipped over onto its side and barely visible, completely obscured from the road.

Even as I ran, I could hear something through the howling of the wind, and at first, I was convinced it was my imagination, or maybe some kind of panic-induced hallucination. I assumed that could happen, even if I didn't have any firsthand experience with it.

As I drew closer, the sound grew clearer, and I realized it was coming from the car radio. The sound of a man's screams, familiar in their tenor, sickeningly so. Even though I had never heard the recording itself, I knew who the voice belonged to.

A ghost.

I threw the door open, not even trying to make sense of the phenomenon at the moment. When I found the driver of the car dead, I felt relief that probably would've shamed most people, because I didn't recognize him. At least, I felt relief until I realized it wasn't the accident that had killed him. It was the bullethole right in the center of his forehead, execution-style.

Dread washed over me anew as I opened the back door, at once relieved and bewildered to find that it was empty. No sign of Silas, or Valentine, except...

I reached for the bloodied roof of the SUV and picked up a familiar strip of leather, feeling my heart bottom out into my chest. I touched the droplet of crimson staining the silver tag, still tacky, and realized my hands were shaking. With fear, with rage. God only knew there were plenty of both coursing through my veins.

My Kitten. My brother. They were gone. Both of them. They must have been injured rather than killed, because why would he have taken their bodies? And there was no doubt in my mind who had done it, of course. Demon, if not a proxy.

The ringing in my ears had mostly drowned out the sound of the familiar screams, which I had barely even registered before because I was fixated on Valentine, but now, I realized the connection between them. Between the gruesome recording playing through the car stereo and what was happening right now. Maybe at this very moment.

No... no, if he had gone to all this trouble to find me and take Valentine and Silas, there was a reason. He wanted to use them against me. That meant he would keep them alive, at least for as long as he had to.

I listened to the recording and realized it was playing on a loop. A solid five minutes of Owen's agonized screams, undoubtedly recorded moments before his actual death at the hands of the monster who now had the other two men I had failed, if only by daring to love them.

I was still trying to figure out what to do when static interrupted the repeating broadcast. I froze as a strangely familiar voice greeted me. At first, I thought maybe it was just an interruption of whatever pirated frequency Demon had hijacked, but it soon became clear that it wasn't.

"Well, it took you long enough, didn't it?" the voice taunted. "Let me guess, you were busy drinking yourself into a drunken stupor. I hear that's how you passed the first few months after Owen's death. And look how you've come full circle. I've got my hands on your brother—and your new pet. Imagine that. You really need to learn to take better care of your things."

I looked around for any sign of a tower in the distance he might have been using to broadcast from, but a second later, I got a direct answer. "Oh, don't bother with that, Malcolm," he said boredly. "Do you really think I'd be in the area? Yes, right now, I have my sights on you from a distance. But let's focus on what's important, shall we? If you want to see either of them again, we're going to play a little game. And if you refuse to play along, I'll just have to play with them. The same game I played with Owen."

I clench my jaw, struggling to see through my rage. Doing nothing wasn't something I could handle, but he was right. He was in control, and we were playing his game.

"That's good," he taunted. "I see I've gotten your attention. I had hoped it would be easy enough, considering your obsession. And really, how pitiful is it when a monster falls in love? It can only ever end in tragedy. I wonder, does he know that, Malcolm? Does he know you love him, or is that why you let him go? Did you think you were protecting him? That you could keep him from me?"

He paused, chuckling. "Don't worry, I'll cut to the chase. Our game. Every game worth playing has its stakes, so to make it interesting, I'll make you a particularly generous wager. I'll let you have one of them. But you have to come and get him. And you have to choose—your brother or your lover. Now, I know what you're thinking. How do you even know I haven't killed them? Well, I'm a reasonable man, and I'm happy to provide the proof your analytical mind requires. Allow me a moment."

I heard familiar, muffled screams. Valentine. All of a sudden, they became clear words, but his voice was hoarse, like he had been screaming for hours. "Malcolm, don't—" His voice broke off into a blood-curdling cry that had an exponentially greater effect on me than the ones that had been playing on a loop. Because I couldn't even love one man without betraying another.

"Valentine!" I seethed, gripping the dashboard, his collar still dangling from my hand. I could barely see through my rage.

Being shot was nothing compared to this. That pain had registered as belonging to my body less than his sound of agony, and when I heard his voice muffled again, I felt like I was going to lose my fucking mind. The only thing keeping it together was the knowledge that I had to find him. It wasn't too late. He was still alive. He was still alive, and that meant there was time to play Demon's fucking game.

"And now, your brother," Demon continued.

All I heard after was the sound of something sharp—maybe a knife—piercing flesh, and a strangled groan, followed by Silas's voice. "You have to get Valentine, Malcolm," he said, his voice strained. "It's our old house."

"Chatty tonight," Demon said bitterly. "No matter. Nothing more than I was going to tell you, anyway. He's right, of course. I assume you still remember the address?" he asked in a mocking tone, pausing as if waiting for me to answer. "That's wonderful, because the clock is ticking, and as you all know, I don't like to be kept waiting. Remember, I am a man of my word. The choice is yours."

The radio cut out and resumed playing that noxious melody of torment, but it was almost a relief. Valentine's screams echoed in my ears, so much louder.

I walked away from the wreckage and picked up my phone with my other hand, because I couldn't bring myself to let go of Valentine's collar. I dialed Enzo's number, and he answered on the first ring again.

"Malcolm? What's going on? Did you—"

"Cancel your flight," I said hoarsely. "I know where they are."

23

VALENTINE

At some point after Chris's—or rather, Demon's—little performance for Malcolm, I must have passed out. The next thing I remembered, I woke up to find that my leg was bandaged, and I hadn't died from blood loss, which meant Chris wasn't finished using me yet.

I could barely lift my head, and my thoughts were so disjointed and strange that I realized he must've drugged me. I had no idea how much time had passed, but it felt like a long damn time. When I looked over, I was relieved to see that Silas was still breathing and awake.

I never could have imagined that was something I would feel toward him, but there was a first time for everything.

Everything that had happened still felt surreal. It had to be a dream, or rather, a nightmare. I couldn't bring myself to believe this was actually happening.

"Where is he?" I asked.

Silas looked like he was about to answer, but when I saw the shift in his expression to one of pure hatred, I realized that, despite what I used to think, he didn't really hate me at all. Not even close.

"You're awake," Chris said in a familiar, eerily pleasant tone. I looked up at him, still struggling to come to terms with the fact that it was the same man I had worked alongside for the last few years. My boss. A fucking doctor. He and the infamous, twisted Demon were one and the same. "That's good. I imagine Malcolm will be here any moment, and then the fun can really get started."

"Why?" I asked, because that was the foremost question on my mind. There were so many others, but that was what they all boiled down to.

"Why?" he echoed. "I'm afraid you'll have to be a little more specific than that."

I paused to think about it. I wasn't really in the frame of mind to put my question into more specific terms. It encapsulated the complete, utter confusion I felt, now more than ever after his speech.

"Why did you do all this?" I asked. "Having me work for you... earning my trust... what the hell was the point of any of it if you're just going to kill me? You could've done that any time, as yourself. Why pretend to be someone else?"

To be fair, he had tried to kill me himself on several occasions, but it seemed a little delayed.

"That is a good question," he remarked, turning to Silas. "Are you going to answer that for your brother-in-law? Or have you not figured it out yet?" When he saw the look of confusion on Silas's face, he shook his head. "You really are losing your edge. How long have you and Enzo been together now, Silas?"

A look of realization dawned on his face, and he murmured, "The same length of time we were together."

"There it is," Chris said, walking over to cup Silas's face in his hand. "Took you a little while, but you always figure it out in the end. Exactly the same amount of time I was with you, as your student. Your protégé. Your lover. Exactly as long as it took you to grow bored and throw me away. Long enough for you to know what it's like to love someone as long as I loved you, so you can fully appreciate it when I take him away from you. Rather poetic, don't you think?"

A look of pure, unadulterated rage I'd never seen before flashed in Silas's gaze. "You won't touch him," he seethed. "I don't know how you're alive, but you're going to wish you had never come back from the dead if you so much as lay a hand on him."

"Touching," Chris taunted, even though the bitterness in his tone belied his sarcasm. "But I don't think you're in any position to be making threats right now. Any moment now, I'll be in possession of every weakness you've ever had. Your husband. Your brother. I don't think I'll stop there–not until you've watched every last one of them die. Enzo, Valentine, Luca... the entire precious family. Everyone you have so much as interacted with. Everyone your beloved cares about, and you by extension, because that's what you taught me to do before you decided to punish me for being the monster *you* made me into."

"You were out of control," Silas said bitterly. "You were losing your mind. I had you put down before you destroyed everything."

I grimaced. He was really not good at placating psychopaths, considering his line of work.

I was sure Chris was going to strike Silas when he raised his hand, but instead, he fisted a handful of the man's bone-white hair and climbed onto his lap, yanking his head back.

"You used me," he spat. "I would've done anything for you. I would've died for you. I would've put the bullet in my own skull if you'd asked me, but you didn't, did you? I ceased to be of use to you, and you threw me away. Like trash."

Silas glared at him in silence for a long time, like his life wasn't literally in this man's hands. Guess he was still crazy, after all. He just hid it better than before. "You're right," he said at length, his voice quiet. "I did. Is that what you want to hear? That I'm sorry?"

"I don't want your fucking apologies," Chris seethed. "I want to know why. I want to know why you couldn't even do it yourself. You rigged my car with explosives like a fucking coward. You couldn't even pull the trigger."

My heart raced. Silas had gone through with it. He *had* killed him, or at least he'd tried. Clearly, he had failed, but he hadn't betrayed Malcolm, and he hadn't lied to Enzo. Guess that counted for something.

Silas paused as if he was considering it. "Because I was weak," he answered in a matter-of-fact tone. "You were a monster, but you were mine. I made you, and it was my responsibility to deal with you. To give you a decent death, if nothing else—and I didn't because I didn't have the stomach for it. You're right. I was too much of a coward. And I've regretted it every day since."

Chris had been listening up until that point, but I wasn't really all that surprised when he pulled his gun and struck Silas across the face with it. He wasn't exactly helping his cause.

Silas swooned for a second before he came to, his eyebrow split open. He gave a dry laugh. "Don't ask questions you don't want the answers to. It's not a game you'll ever win."

Chris's eyes darkened with disgust, but his snarl became a sneer. "It doesn't matter if you love him more than you ever loved me, or if you loved me at all, because soon enough, it'll just be the two of us. Forever, like you promised. If I have to keep you as my prisoner and cut off all your fucking limbs to keep you here, I will."

Silas laughed again. It was the sharpest, most genuine laugh I had ever heard from him. Even Demon seemed caught off guard. "You should just kill me, then," he said. "Because that's not how love works. I pitied you, yes, like a mad scientist pities the abomination he just created, but that's it. I never loved you then, and I never will."

Chris got up, and this time, he struck Silas hard enough across the face to almost knock him over. Chris was on him immediately, bringing his fist down onto the other man's head over and over until I screamed, "Stop! Please, stop!"

Chris froze, slowly looking over his shoulder. His hair was in his eyes, but I could still see enough of them to recognize the madness in them. He stared me down, rising slowly off Silas, who still seemed to be partially conscious, even though his face had been beaten bloody.

As Chris walked over to me, I was relieved that I had managed to distract him from Silas before he could kill him, but I was also petrified. Because how could I not be?

"Oh, Valentine," Chris said, coming to a stop in front of me. His voice was soft and gentle, a side I had only recently seen of him, even though I now knew it to be completely artificial. Just like everything else. "My sweet Valentine. You know, for what it's worth, I really did get attached to you. Honestly, I might even keep you as a pet. To keep him in line. I think you could be molded. Shaped. And you'd be better off for it. Malcolm could only ever break you—he could never help you reach your full potential. But he doesn't know what I do. A healer has more potential to be a killer than anyone. After all, I studied human anatomy in my work more than any med student." He chuckled. "An endless supply of cadavers.

That would toughen you up, wouldn't it? If I could masquerade in your world, I can teach you to thrive in mine. They're not really so different."

The fact that a fucking serial killer had managed to masquerade as a healer for so long was disturbing as hell, but he had a point. Few surgeons had carved up as many people as the infamous Demon must have in order for him to end up on Silas's radar.

"You don't have to do this," I said, even though I knew deep down he was too far gone to reason with. I had to try anyway, and the more time he spent on me, the less he would have to spend on Silas. If we stood a chance at getting out of this place, it was him, and if not, well... there was also a part of me that was hoping Malcolm wouldn't show up at all. "I know you. I don't believe it was an act. All the people you helped... maybe you think it was all fake, all part of a persona, but there's truth in everything. Even a lie."

Chris stared at me for a moment, his expression unreadable. When he finally laughed again, there was something about the sound that made it clear just how sick he was. And I knew at that moment that there was no reasoning with him. There was no better nature to appeal to, and if there was, it was buried so deep below the madness as to be hopeless.

I'd assumed Demon had to be like Silas and Malcolm. That the nature of his monstrosity was like theirs, cold and unfeeling, but I was beginning to think that wasn't the case. He did feel. It was clear from the moment he looked at Silas the way he had. I knew intimately what pent-up anger, longing, hurt, and insecurity looked like, even if I was usually on the other side of the equation. While Silas and Malcolm were the eye of the storm, still and silent, this man was pure, raging chaos in human flesh. I saw myself in him, and somehow, that made him far more terrifying.

"Oh, you're precious," he replied. "Even if you do turn out to be a dud, you'll be endless entertainment. But don't worry, I'm going to do you a favor I wish someone had done for me, and I'm going to show you exactly who your lover is. I'm going to go through with the little charade I promised, and I'm going to let Malcolm think he actually gets to choose, just so you can see. Because in case you haven't figured it out, he's going to choose Silas. He'll always choose Silas, because blood is the closest thing a man like him knows to love and loyalty."

Before I could respond, Chris looked up as if he heard something. And judging from the fact that Silas had just lifted his head off the floor, they were both more perceptive than I was in a myriad of ways.

"Perfect timing. He's here," Chris said, turning away from me. "You don't have to take my word for it. You'll see soon enough."

He seemed to think that was a threat, but it wasn't. Not the way he thought. Because if Malcolm was here, and he could only save one of us, I wanted it to be Silas. Even if I had only recently stopped hating him, my brother loved him, and that was enough. Enough reason for me to want him around, regardless of how I felt about him personally.

I still wanted to believe that Malcolm had actually cared about me. I knew now that his apparent feelings for me had all been bullshit, but that didn't change the way I felt. I knew that would probably make me an even bigger fool in his eyes as well as Chris's, but it didn't matter.

Knowing he didn't really care about me at all changed nothing.

24

MALCOLM

While part of me debated whether I should give Enzo the actual location of the house, if only for the sake of having backup when I walked into Demon's lair, I ultimately decided against it. For one thing, Silas wouldn't want me to put him in harm's way, and for another, he could easily turn into a liability. I didn't really know what Leon DiFiore had been teaching his boys, but it sure as hell wasn't how to function in high-pressure situations.

As I drove into the dilapidated, long abandoned neighborhood where Silas and I had grown up, I found myself wondering how much he even remembered. The house had been center stage to the hell of our shared childhood, and while we hadn't lived here long, this place had somehow managed to accumulate a majority of my worst memories.

It figured Demon would pick this location to serve as the backdrop for what might easily become another. Or the last.

I drew my gun, since there was no way he was going to fantasize that I would walk into this place unarmed. It was anyone's guess whether Demon would have a team waiting.

Then again, this was clearly personal, and he had learned to be paranoid from the best, so maybe not.

I opened the front door, not surprised to find it unlocked even though it was hanging off its hinges. I kicked it open the rest of the way and looked inside the mostly dark hallway, the floorboards creaking beneath my weight as I stepped in further.

The dust in this place was so thick that I could hardly breathe, but something told me they wouldn't be on the first floor. I looked anyway, just so nothing could jump out at me, but just walking in like this was suicide. I didn't care if I got out alive or not as long as I took Demon out with me, and I knew Silas would get my boy home safely.

And I would do the same for him.

"All right, you freak," I snarled. "I did what you asked, and I came alone, so why don't you be a man for once and come out and face me?"

"Always so impatient," Demon taunted. I could hear his voice coming from upstairs, but it was echoing, making it clear the old walls weren't quite as thick as I remembered. I knew I was walking into a trap, but what choice did I really have?

For all I knew, Valentine wasn't even here.

When I climbed the stairs, they groaned so much that I wondered if I was going to fall through them, but I continued on regardless, keeping my gun at the ready.

The attic door at the top of the stairs was propped open slightly. Yeah, definitely a trap.

Oh, well.

I kicked the door open, freezing at the sight awaiting me. I wasn't sure what I was expecting, but I was definitely not expecting the setup Demon had arranged.

There were two clear glass cases sitting on the far end of the room, on floorboards that didn't look anywhere near secure enough to hold their weight. Tied to chairs and gagged, Valentine was in the one on the left, while Silas was bound in the one on the right.

There was little else in the room, but I knew Demon had to be watching from somewhere. The moment I made eye contact with Valentine, my heart lurched in a newly familiar way.

He was alive. There was a cut on his forehead that would definitely need stitches, and there was a bloodied bandage on his leg, but apart from those two wounds, he didn't seem to have been severely harmed. The wounds and injuries I could see might easily have been caused by the accident itself, but I knew that didn't mean Demon had spared him from the torture he had subjected Owen to.

Or maybe he simply wanted to do that in front of me.

I saw the look of panic in Valentine's eyes, so I wasn't surprised when I turned around to find someone standing behind me.

What I was surprised by, however, was *who* was standing behind me.

Chris.

Or rather, James. Of fucking course it was. My surprise lasted all of two seconds before I said, "Well, that makes perfect sense. Let me guess... you killed a guy and stole his identity just to get close to Val? And Silas, by extension."

He sneered. "He was thoughtful enough to die of natural causes, actually, but you're right on the other counts. And it was easy enough. I'd all but finished med school when I started... freelancing, so to speak. I certainly had the intimate knowledge of human anatomy to pull it off, and I've always been fond of hiding in plain sight. Your brother taught me that."

"I'm sure he taught you a lot of things," I muttered, aiming the gun at him. I wasn't sure why he didn't have one himself, but that lent credence to the possibility that he had someone watching me from an unseen vantage point.

"Don't worry," he said as if reading my thoughts. "There's no one else. Just you and me, one on one. What's the point of a game if it isn't fair?"

"You know, Silas might've tolerated the Joker bullshit, but I'm not as patient with theatrics as he is," I said through my teeth. "So why don't you just save us both the trouble and tell me what the catch is?"

"There's no catch," he said with a shrug, his hands tucked into the pockets of his coat as if we were having a casual conversation. "You can shoot me right now if you'd like, but I think you would find that to be a mistake. You see, those chairs are rigged with sensors, and the moment pressure is removed from one, a deadly gas will be released into the other chamber, killing the occupant within seconds. And if neither chamber is deactivated in the next fifteen minutes, they will activate automatically. And of course, I'm the only one who can stop that unfortunate event from happening. But by all means, be my guest."

I narrowed my eyes. "Exactly what is the point of any of this?"

"You should've figured that out by now," he remarked. "None of it is personal." He paused. "Actually, that's not true. Owen wasn't personal, but now that I've gotten to know you a little bit, quite frankly, I don't like you. So making you miserable is one hell of a plus side."

"You flatter me," I said flatly.

He smirked. "Go ahead, Malcolm. I won't belabor the point any longer. Make your choice. Your brother, or your lover. That is, unless you'd like to avail yourself of the opportunity to be rid of the last vestiges of your human weakness and abandon them both. I could certainly respect that."

"Fuck you," I spat.

"The clock is ticking," he said in a singsong, walking the length of the room. "My apologies for not choosing a more theatrical location, as you put it, but who doesn't love a walk down memory lane?"

I turned back to both cases, studying them for any sign of weakness. I fired a bullet into Silas's, but when the glass merely cracked in a spiderweb pattern, it confirmed my suspicion that it was bulletproof. Worth a shot.

"I'm insulted," Demon said in a tone of irritation. "What do you take me for, a fool?"

"No, that title belongs to me," I said bitterly. "But don't worry, that's not a mistake I'm going to make again."

Silas's eyes met mine, and even though not a word passed between us, I understood the look in them well enough. He already knew what my choice was going to be. He knew it had been made long before I walked into this place.

It was the same choice he would have made if he were in my shoes, and I would've been giving him the same look, because Demon was right about one thing–it was pitiful when a monster fell in love. Everything and everyone else took a back seat, because once you opened up a black hole, it consumed everything. All else became meaningless in comparison.

I knew the moment Silas showed up at my office, ready to throw everything away—his life, his career, his freedom—for one man, things had changed. As impossible as it seemed, he had fallen in love. And the thing about men like him and me was that even love became a dark and violent thing when we touched it. It became an obsession, and there was no turning back. There was no falling out of love, because for us, it was never an emotion in the first place. That person—that unfortunate object of our fixation—became the central sun in our universe.

Enzo was his.

Valentine was mine.

I rushed forward, ignoring the look of dismay in Valentine's eyes as he shook his head. I wasn't sure how I was going to open the case, since I couldn't see any sign of a locking mechanism, and shooting it open would take more bullets and more time than I had to spare. There was no such thing as truly bulletproof glass, but by the time I succeeded at the task, Demon would've easily had time to kill them both in retribution.

It was a risk I couldn't take. Not even for Silas. My own life, I would give for his without a thought, but this wasn't just my life. This was my soul at stake.

Demon drew a remote from his pocket and pressed a button. As soon as the door opened, I rushed inside and tore the gag away from Valentine's mouth first.

"No!" he cried as I unfastened the ropes binding him to the chair. "No, it's a trap!"

He wasn't telling me anything I didn't already know, but this was hard enough already, and we didn't have a second to spare.

"Come on," I urged, dragging him off the chair.

I felt a sinking feeling in the pit of my stomach as I saw yellow gas filling the other box in the corner of my eye. When I looked over, Silas was already beginning to slump over in his chair, and I had just readied my hand to reach for my gun once more when I turned around and found Demon standing at the entrance to the open case Valentine and I were in.

His gun was aimed right at us. I put myself between him and Valentine, keeping my own leveled at the bastard's head.

"He was never going to kill Silas, Malcolm," Valentine choked, gripping the back of my jacket. "It's you."

I looked over at the other glass case in confusion. My brother was slumped over, and he looked fully unconscious now, but somehow, he was still breathing. I thought I saw gas seeping from the spot where I had shot the glass, but I couldn't risk looking for long enough to be sure.

"He's right, of course," Demon said casually. "It's a sedative. I'm not done with him yet. I have to admit, I am surprised at the choice you made. I guess nostalgia doesn't really count for all that much."

I prepared to squeeze my trigger, but he beat me to it, firing into my hand so the gun went flying.

I let out a strangled hiss, but everything in the next few seconds seemed to happen at once. Before I could go for my gun, Demon took aim again, and I prepared to tackle him, knowing I was going to get shot in the process.

And this time, it wouldn't just be my hand.

The gun fired, and at the same time, I heard a cry that made my blood run cold. Before I could process what was happening, I heard a thud and saw Valentine drop to the floor in front of me.

No...

No!

Even though it couldn't have been more than a fraction of a second, it felt like I was frozen solid forever, until I gained the presence of mind to lunge while Demon was equally stunned.

I realized then that Valentine was right. Demon hadn't planned on killing him, or Silas. They would've both been fine, if I hadn't...

I snarled in rage, grabbing the other man's throat and slamming his head into the floor hard enough that he blacked out. I grabbed his gun and the other one hiding in the holster at his hip before I turned back to Valentine, because I really didn't give a shit if Demon woke up and killed me right now.

If Valentine wasn't okay, if he was...

He was breathing. Thank God, he was breathing, but the wound in his right shoulder was gushing blood, and my attempt to hold pressure on it didn't seem to be doing much.

"Valentine?" I choked, looking down at him. He was conscious, but barely, and I could tell from the glazed look in his eyes he was in shock. "Val, stay with me, Kitten. Please. Tell me what to do, I..."

His eyes fluttered shut, and I felt my chest tighten as I realized I was losing him.

I looked around in panic, turning back to Demon, who was finally starting to stir.

"You," I seethed, taking aim at his head again while putting as much pressure on Val's wound as I could. "Get up. You're going to fix this. Save him and open that fucking case, or I swear to God, I'll tear you apart limbs first and feed you the pieces."

Demon gave a bitter laugh, rolling onto his stomach. Blood was trickling down the back of his neck from where I'd slammed his head into the wooden floor, staining his collar. If he was still himself enough to be a dick, then he could treat Valentine.

"How pathetic. I don't recall you being quite this emotional over Owen, and he certainly endured a lot worse than a relatively peaceful death."

"You heard him," came a familiar voice, followed by the sound of a gun cocking.

I looked up to find Silas staggering over to his former protégé. The bullet must have let enough of the gas out of the case, after all, but he was clearly still affected. He grabbed James by the back of the neck and hauled him to his feet. "Maybe you think he's bluffing, but you know me better than that. And I assure you, I will be *very* hands-on this time."

Demon froze, but Silas had called his bluff, and we both knew it. Even he wasn't crazy enough to want to be tortured to death, just to make a point. Especially not over someone he hadn't even intended to kill in the first place.

"My bag," he said through his teeth. "It's in the corner."

Silas hesitated, but he nodded, keeping the gun he'd picked up trained on Demon as he went to collect the bag. He returned a moment later, rummaging through the contents. He pulled out another gun nestled within the bag before dropping it at Demon's feet.

I could tell that was Demon's last-ditch plan from the look of irritation on his features, but he sank to his knees next to me, tearing Val's shirt open the rest of the way.

I pressed the barrel of my gun against Demon's temple and he froze. "One wrong move, bitch," I growled. "He dies, and I will make sure you spend the next sixty years wishing you were so lucky."

"You've made your point," he hissed. "Are you going to let me treat him, or should I let him bleed out on the floor?"

I narrowed my eyes, nodding for him to go ahead, but I watched him like a hawk as he worked while Silas called an ambulance with my phone. It seemed like forever until the sirens could be heard in the distance, even though it couldn't have been more than a few minutes. I was learning firsthand, though, that even a second could be an eternity of torment in its purest form when your entire world was hanging in the balance.

VALENTINE

I didn't think I was going to open my eyes again at all, so when I did to the familiar sight of the vinyl ceiling tiles I had worked beneath for hundreds of hours of my life, I was convinced Grandma was right and I had ended up in purgatory.

Then I felt the hand wrapped around mine, strong and rough and warm, and realized that wasn't possible. I had to be alive, because my version of heaven would have to include the Devil, and that was the kind of paradox that just couldn't exist in the afterlife.

But in my crazy, fucked-up life, yeah... it could.

"Mal?" I asked, my voice sounding weak and laced with confusion.

He appeared, backlit in a deceptive halo of light from the bulb overhead, looking like a nightmare come true. Dark circles rimmed his piercing eyes, and there was a faint smile on his face, but it wasn't quite as devious as usual. My head felt like it was swimming, so I assumed whatever they had in the drip bag above the hospital bed was a bit stronger than saline.

"Hey. How are you feeling?"

"Like I got shot in the chest," I mumbled, not really able to feel much other than pressure from all the bandages and the compression shirt.

"A few inches up and to the left, but yeah, sounds about right," he said, his voice husky with exhaustion. He looked like he hadn't slept in a week.

"How long have I been unconscious?"

"Long enough to scare the shit out of everyone," he answered.

"They're here?" I asked.

"Enzo and Silas are down the hall. We finally convinced Luca to go home to get a couple of hours of sleep," he said. "Johnny, too. They've been taking shifts to make sure you're not alone with me."

"Probably for the best," I said in a dry tone.

Malcolm laughed, but he cut himself short, giving me a strange look. "You know, when you get out of here, you're going to be on house arrest for the rest of your life. Just so you know."

"Why?" I asked, frowning. "Did Demon get away?"

"No," he said flatly. "I was referring to the fact that you took a fucking bullet for me. You know that's just an expression for most people, right?"

"I always have been a bit of a literalist," I said. When he continued to give me that furious look, which was at once unnerving and arousing, I muttered, "I don't regret it, you know. But you can relax. I know it doesn't change anything."

He frowned in confusion, like he had no idea what I was talking about.

"I hit my head in the accident, but not hard enough to forget what you said before I left," I told him. "What I don't get is why you chose me over Silas."

His brow furrowed. "God, you really are an idiot, aren't you?"

There was something affectionate about those scathing words that kept them from hitting the way they usually would have. "What are you talking about?"

He shook his head. "I didn't mean any of it, Val. Not wanting you, being bored... for once in my fucking life, I was trying to do the right thing."

"The right thing?" I echoed. "Maybe it's the morphine, but I really don't get it."

"Silas was right," he said quietly. "Protecting you was one thing, but keeping you? That could only end in disaster, and everything that happened is proof enough of that.

You could form an army out of all the enemies I've made in my lifetime, and until you, I never had anything I was so afraid to lose."

My throat grew tight as he spoke, but I had made the mistake of letting my guard down around Malcolm before, and it felt like someone ripped my heart out of my chest. He had done a hell of a lot more damage than Demon, that was for sure.

"You were trying to protect me?"

"Yeah, I was," he said. "Even if it wasn't for the danger, a decent man would keep you as far away from me as possible. You deserve better, Valentine. So much better than I could ever give you, and if you stay with me, I can't guarantee I won't corrupt you. Because if there's one thing this fucking life has taught me, it's that anyone who makes the mistake of caring about me either dies or becomes a monster, too."

I took a moment to process his words, smiling a little. "Well... what would corruption entail, exactly? Because if it's anything like the time we spent at the cabin, I think I can live with that."

Malcolm breathed a laugh, reaching down to cup my face in his hand, his touch uncharacteristically gentle. "It's a moot point," he answered. "Because I'm not a decent man, and I have no intention of ever letting you go again. Like I said, I was trying to do the right thing, and that turned out spectacularly, so lesson learned. Fuck the right thing. I don't give a shit what your brother, or mine, or anyone else has to say about it. And if I have to keep you locked up in a cage to keep you safe, to make sure no one ever takes you from me again, I'll do it. Even if it means you hate me. I can live with that. The one thing I can't live with is you being gone."

I stared at him, still half convinced that this was some kind of drug-induced fantasy, where he was telling me everything I wanted to hear. Or maybe it was pity. I would say guilt, but I knew perfectly well that wasn't one of his hangups.

"You know, all that sounds dangerously like you're trying to confess your undying love for me," I said pointedly. "And I could get the wrong idea."

His lips quirked at one corner. "Maybe it'd be the right one."

My face grew warm, because apparently, I was still a blusher. "Yeah, well... I love you, too, so I guess we're even."

Malcolm's gaze softened as he stroked my cheek. "That's another point for the cage." When he saw the confusion on my face, he added, "It's pretty clear all this hasn't awakened even an ounce of self-preservation in you."

I snorted. "I guess it's a good thing I have you to look out for me, then, isn't it?"

He leaned in, capturing my lips, and what started out as a chaste kiss became something that left me breathless and even dizzier than before.

"Like I said. You're not going anywhere." He paused, reaching into his pocket for something. "Which reminds me..."

I watched as he pulled out a small, slender black box with a red bow on top, setting it on the bed next to me. I looked down and saw his hand was still bandaged, but judging from the fact that he could still move it, the bullet hadn't done too much damage.

"I hope that isn't going to permanently affect your handjob skills or anything," I remarked.

"Just open the damn box."

I tugged one end of the ribbon tying the box shut until the bow came undone and took off the lid to reveal a collar resting on a satin pillow inside. I looked up at him, my eyes widening. The part of me clinging to the insecurity that maybe he was just saying all this to make me feel better melted away. He actually planned on keeping me as his pet.

It was a hell of a lot different from my last collar, since there was no flexible leather band. Instead, there was a solid metal band made of what looked like platinum with a silver tag hanging down from the center, surrounded by small diamonds and engraved with my name. On the reverse side, the tag read, "If found, return to Malcolm Whitlock," followed by his phone number.

And an address. But it wasn't his.

"Where is this?"

"I figured it was time for a new place," he answered. "One with a basement."

I looked up at Malcolm, blinking. Only he could make something so menacing sound romantic. "Is this your way of asking me to move in with you?" I asked.

"Of course not," he scoffed. Before I could fully cave in on myself, he added, "I'm not asking you shit. I meant what I said—I'm never letting you out of my sight again. You're coming with me, whether you like it or not."

I found myself smiling like an idiot, but I never really had been good at playing it cool. Definitely not when it came to him. I glanced back at the collar as he took it out of the box and noticed a tiny but clearly well-made padlock for the first time. "What the hell is that?"

He ignored my question and opened the collar by a seam in the back that was barely noticeable when it was shut. There were two thin metal loops that he fit the bar of the lock through before snapping it shut, giving it a slight tug as if to test its strength. When he was satisfied it wouldn't come open easily, he slipped it around my neck and clipped the lock into place.

"There," he said. "That should do."

"And exactly how am I supposed to wear this thing when I'm at work?" I asked, raising an eyebrow, even though my heart wasn't racing for any of the right reasons.

"You're not," he said, raising an eyebrow. "What part of 'cage' do you not understand?"

I blinked at him as it dawned on me for the first time that he was actually serious. "Malcolm, I can't just sit by the door all day waiting for you to come home like a dog."

"You're really more of a cat," he said, tucking a strand of hair behind my ear. Given how long I had been in the hospital, I knew I had to look like shit, but he was staring at me like I was the most perfect thing he'd ever seen.

He really was crazy. Lucky me.

"We're going to be talking about this," I mumbled.

"We can talk all you like, but you don't call the shots anymore," he said pointedly. "The fact that you literally stepped in front of a bullet the last time should be argument enough against that."

"You make it sound like there's ever been a time when you *weren't* calling the shots."

"You like it," he accused, capturing my lips again before I could betray myself by admitting that, yeah... I did. And I had plenty of trepidations about exactly what I had unleashed on myself, but they all took a backseat as his tongue slipped into my mouth, and I found myself enraptured in the bliss of his touch.

The door creaked open, and a familiar voice cried, "Fuck, can I not leave the room for ten minutes without you molesting my brother?"

Malcolm broke off the kiss, looking up at Enzo with an expression I had seen in Silas's eyes more than a few times over the years when I had walked in on them in a compromising position. It wasn't even like I hadn't learned to knock after the first couple of times, considering no room in the house was safe.

Now, I kind of understood.

"You'll live," said Malcolm, turning back to me to sweep his thumb along my bottom lip. It was a simple little gesture that made me shiver all the same.

Enzo walked over to the other side of my bed, giving me a tired smile. "Man, it's good to see you awake."

"Miss me?" I asked dryly.

"Yeah," he said without a trace of sarcasm in his voice. "More than you could possibly know." He glanced up at Malcolm, frowning. "I guess I should be grateful you brought him home, even if he does have more holes than before."

"There are a lot of places I could go with that, but in the interest of familial peace, I'm not going to," said Malcolm.

Enzo grimaced. "So I guess this is a thing now. The two of you."

"Yeah," Malcolm said before I had the chance to answer. His eyes traveled over to Silas, who was standing behind Enzo. "I'm afraid that's not up for debate."

Silas stared back at him for a few moments, unblinking, before he finally sighed. "About what I said before... I was wrong."

As cryptic as that was, it was proof that Malcolm was telling the truth, and his sudden shift at the cabin had been at his brother's behest. On one level, I was pissed, but on another, I was kind of touched that Silas actually gave enough of a shit about me to go against his own brother. Even if it was just because of Enzo.

"You are right about one thing," said Malcolm. "The way I live... the people I love are always going to be at risk. I'm retiring."

"You're what?" I asked, staring at him in disbelief.

Even Silas seemed surprised by his words.

"I've been in the spotlight for long enough," Malcolm said with a shrug. "It's time for a change of pace. And I already have an idea about my replacement."

"You're serious," Enzo said doubtfully.

"Absolutely," Malcolm said without hesitation, looking over at his brother. "I'm sorry, I know losing your connection on the force isn't ideal."

Silas smiled a little. "I think I'll manage. But what are you going to do?"

"Well, I haven't taken a vacation in about twenty years," Malcolm mused, running his fingers through my hair in that way that always made me melt, even if I was still reeling from his revelation. "And I've got plenty of contacts on every side of the law to look into after that. Contracting is pretty flexible."

"You could always join me," Silas said, folding his arms. "Make it a family business."

Malcolm paused like he was actually considering it. "Are we talking a fifty-fifty kind of thing? Because I don't do subordination."

"We can discuss it," said Silas.

"Are you sure?" I asked, finally recovered enough to speak. "I mean, it's your fucking career. You're really going to give that up because of me?"

"I wouldn't be a very good master if I asked you to do something I wasn't going to do myself, would I, Kitten?" he asked, tilting my chin toward him.

I melted at his words until Enzo reminded me we weren't alone.

"Master?" he echoed suspiciously. "And is that a collar?"

"Come, love," Silas said, putting a hand on Enzo's shoulder. "I think it's about time we got some sleep, and I'm sure they could use a moment alone."

"That's what I'm trying to avoid," Enzo said as Silas gently led him out of the room, and I could hear the sounds of their continued half-hearted bickering trailing off down the hall.

"I think they're taking it pretty well," I said, turning back to Malcolm.

"Spectacularly," he said, leaning in to kiss me again. "I'm sure he'll come around by the wedding."

"Wedding?" I echoed, my voice cracking.

Malcolm raised an eyebrow. "What, wearing my collar permanently is fine, but getting married is too much of a commitment?"

"I didn't say that," I mumbled, my face growing warm again for some fucking reason. "I just didn't think you were the marrying kind after what happened with Owen."

"I wasn't for a long time," he admitted. "But I find I'm open to new ideas where you're concerned."

"Oh, yeah?" I asked. "How about me being on top?"

Malcolm snorted, like it was a ridiculous question. "Maybe if you're riding my cock."

I paused to consider it. "I guess I could live with that."

He kissed me again, and it was all I could think about. I ran my hands down his chest, but when I got to his belt, he took my hand to stop me.

"You just got shot," he said in a scolding tone, like I would've forgotten that.

And okay, for a second, maybe I kind of had. He had that effect on me.

"In my professional medical opinion, it's fine."

Malcolm gave me a look, but his eyes were dancing with amusement. "Patience, Kitten. Rest now, because when we get home, you're going to need it."

When we get home.

Those words made my head even swimmier than the medication. To be fair, there was no high that could even compare to the shit Malcolm made me feel. He was my drug. My addiction. My complete and utter downfall.

And I didn't have a single fucking regret.

EPILOGUE

MALCOLM

As I stood in a sea of bodies with blood pooling around the soles of my boots, I looked around to survey the damage. Eleven dead on the upper floor, not counting the two runners my partner had gone off after, and sixteen on the lower levels combined.

It was probably safe to say that the East Coast branch of the Sigma Society's arms dealing ring was permanently closed.

The sound of shoes sticking on blood that was already growing tacky echoed through the vast warehouse loft, and I turned around to face Silas as he came toward me.

"Not bad," he remarked, looking around the room. "For your first gig."

"Seriously?" I muttered, stepping over a corpse as I unscrewed my silencer and re-holstered the gun.

He just smirked like the prick he was.

"Pretty big body count for a government job," I remarked.

"Are you kidding? Those are always the bloodiest," he replied, offering me a handkerchief.

I stared blankly at it. "What, am I a fucking Victorian maiden or something?"

He rolled his eyes. "You have blood on your face, and you're already going to be late for your own engagement party if we don't hurry. Something tells me your blushing bride isn't going to appreciate you showing up looking like Rambo. There's a fresh suit in the car."

Despite the fact that he was wearing the same gray one he'd been wearing when we came in, there wasn't a speck of blood on him.

I snorted, snatching the cloth out of his hand to wipe off the splatters on my cheek and jaw. "You're gonna have to tell me how you manage to do this shit without making a mess."

Silas paused, and his gaze traveled over me in judgmental contemplation. "That might be a lost cause."

"Oh, fuck off," I said, brushing past him on my way out the door. "Your cleaners are en route?"

"They're already here," he said, following me down the rickety metal steps. Sure enough, there were three black vehicles that hadn't been there before surrounding the warehouse. I watched as a team of men and women clad in hazmat suits and goggles slipped out of the vehicles and started carrying in a variety of equipment, from sheer plastic tarps to metal barrels and compact black kits filled with all the other shit they'd need to make this place look like it wasn't the scene of a massacre.

"Your new guys are pretty efficient."

"They should be," Silas said, opening the trunk to toss me a duffel bag. "Half of them worked for this evening's client a few months ago."

"And you're not worried about the clandestine alphabet organization you won't even tell me the name of getting pissy you poached their talent?" I asked, stripping out of my bloody clothes to get changed into the black suit I'd be wearing for the evening.

Some guy clad in white from head to toe came over and collected my discarded clothes, wordlessly slipping them into a plastic bag.

Killing was nothing new to me, but I could definitely get used to the concierge service.

"It goes both ways," Silas mused, before slipping into the driver's seat. "And you know what you need to know. For now."

"I thought this was a family business now," I quipped, getting into the passenger's side.

He blew a puff of air through his nostrils. "Consider this your training wheels phase, big brother. Besides, do you really want to take on so much responsibility this soon before your honeymoon?"

I rolled my eyes. "Yeah, whatever. When we get back, we'll talk."

"I'm sure we will," Silas said, keeping his eyes on the road. "Valentine seems to be adjusting well."

"To what?" I asked. "Life with me, or not working at the hospital?"

"Both," he replied after a moment. "It's been quite convenient, actually, having a doctor on demand."

I grunted. Having him go from working at the hospital to being the official mob doc wasn't exactly what I'd had in mind, but it kept him occupied and it meant Enzo could keep an eye on him when I was out on a mission with Silas, so I wasn't going to complain too much.

It was nearly a two-hour drive to the country club that was to serve as the venue for the party Valentine had been planning for the last two months, and when we arrived at an ocean of cars in the lot outside, I knew a good twenty of them at least had to be undercover security.

Demon was still buried in the deepest, darkest pit I could find, which happened to be the underground prison Silas was in charge of for "reasons." After a mere two months on the job with Silas after my retirement from the force, I had come to realize just how many occasions he had to use it.

Worked for me, though. But even if Demon was being monitored twenty-four seven from all angles, I still wasn't sure how I felt about the fact that he was still alive. Even if it did mean he could rot and suffer for the next fifty years, give or take.

"What's on your mind?" Silas asked, even though I could tell from his intonations he knew well enough.

I paused to consider my words for a moment before I answered, "I trust you."

It was the first time I had ever said those words to another living soul, and I meant them, but it was the truth. He had put his life on the line for Valentine, and that meant a hell of a lot more than if he had put it on the line for me. Valentine wasn't just my life, he was my soul. My entire life, I had assumed I didn't have one only to realize I did. It just lived outside of me.

"Just don't prove me wrong," I added.

Silas didn't answer immediately. When he finally did, he turned to face me, a look other than sarcasm on his face for once. "If I thought they would be safer with him dead, he would be," he finally said. He didn't even need to clarify what I was talking about, or who. "The fact remains that James has been out there for years, and he's had more than enough time to develop his own network of resources. Including a killswitch."

I nodded in acknowledgment as he pulled into an empty space in the lot. He was right, of course. There were a thousand different ways Demon could fuck us over from beyond the grave if we weren't careful, and he was just the kind of vindictive son of a bitch to go out with a bang.

"Besides, it's as you said before," Silas continued. "We both have more enemies out there than him alone. He has information. We can use him."

"Torture hasn't really been all that effective on him so far, has it?"

"No," Silas conceded. "But I know James. Better than he knows himself," he murmured. "If there's one thing he can't bear, it's boredom, and it hasn't even been enough time for it to set in yet."

He was probably right about that, too. And I believed he was right about Enzo and Valentine being safer with Demon alive than dead, for now. If there was one thing you could trust, it was a predator's survival instinct, and Silas had proved time and again that his obsessive protectiveness over his husband exceeded even that.

"We should go inside," Silas remarked, glancing at his watch. "Your 'Kitten' awaits."

I smirked at the half-hearted disgust in his tone. "You always were more of a dog person," I said, getting out of the car.

The club was lit up from the outside, but it paled in comparison to the extravagant layout within.

"He really outdid himself, didn't he?" Silas asked, looking around the various members of the crime world gathered to rub elbows and sip cocktails like we weren't all just junkyard dogs in suits.

"That's what I get for marrying a party boy, I guess," I said dryly, scanning the crowd for my pet.

I found him easily enough, since the people around him were keeping enough of a wide berth as he gesticulated wildly while telling some story that was probably half made up. He was with his brothers, Chuck, Johnny, and a few others I didn't recognize, which meant they were probably friends from college. I had already obsessively vetted every acquaintance from the hospital and the Family, because I wasn't above stalking my own fiance for his own protection.

Or my own possessiveness. But just because Valentine had changed me didn't mean I was fully reformed by any means.

Watching the others watch him filled me with amusement and irrational amounts of jealousy at once. Valentine was like a human bonfire, so full of warmth and vibrancy that people just kind of naturally gathered around him. I knew better than to think I was the only one who'd been enchanted by his innocence and the charisma he wielded like a weapon, even if I had come to realize he was completely oblivious to it. But that, too, was part of his charm.

One look at the way Johnny was watching him with a look of adoration he knew well enough to mask in my presence, and I knew I wasn't the only one who felt that way, either.

"He's family," Silas said, right beside me even though I didn't even know he was still there. Creep. "You can't kill family."

"Yeah, yeah," I muttered, grabbing a drink off a passing server's tray. I'd need something to take the edge off the green-eyed beast within if I was going to make it through the evening. Usually the one that thirsted for blood was the one raging against the cage, but that was yet another side of me Valentine had awakened.

I'd always been a possessive son of a bitch, but it had never extended to people. Not even in my former marriage. I could acknowledge now that in a way, I'd treated Owen like any other possession. I'd loved him as much as I was capable of back then, but mostly as an extension of myself. If he'd cheated on me, I would've been pissed, but mostly on account of my wounded pride. All Valentine had to do was look at someone else, and I turned into a fucking caveman.

And I really wasn't all that much of a civilized human being to begin with.

I walked through the throng of guests, trying not to look like a hungry shark circling its prey, even if that was exactly what I was. When I came up behind Valentine, I knew he hadn't noticed me, since he was still laughing so hard at his own joke he snorted.

"And then, he tore his stitches just like I said he would and you should've seen his face while I stitched him back up, trying to be all, 'Grr, I'm an alpha male, I don't feel pain.'"

He trailed off as the others fell silent and everyone but Enzo and Luca looked like they were going to piss themselves. Luca's lips were pursed, trying not to laugh as Valentine froze and asked, "He's right behind me, isn't he?"

"Yep," said Enzo, his eyes glimmering with amusement as Silas came over to slip an arm around his waist.

Valentine turned around and yelped in alarm when he saw how close I was. I slipped a hand behind his back and yanked him against me suddenly enough that his drink sloshed over in his hand. "Amusing yourself, Kitten?"

He flushed even more than usual, but he was going to have to get used to me calling him that in public. Just like he'd gotten used to wearing my collar at all times. It was subtler than the first collar I'd given him and was barely visible beneath the collar of his shirt, but I knew it was there, and that fueled some primal satisfaction deep within me.

"I was j-just telling them about that time at the lake house," he said with a sheepish little smile that would have mollified me even if I was angry.

"Oh, yeah?" I asked. "You tell them how I pulled those stitches?"

His face grew even redder. "Hadn't gotten to that part, no."

"And that's my cue," Luca muttered in disgust, patting my arm on the way past. "Congrats. Great party, but I don't need to hear in great detail how you railed my brother. Again."

"I thought we were bonding," I called after him.

He flipped me off before disappearing into the crowd.

"Yeah, I'll uh, probably duck out on that, too," Chuck said, nodding to us both. "Love the open bar."

Given the way he drank, I was probably going to regret giving the caterer my black card. At least until I saw the smile on Val's face as he leaned into me, and decided nah, I'd gladly pay any price for that.

Strangely, everyone seemed to split as soon as I arrived. Silas dragged Enzo onto the dance floor, and Johnny mumbled some excuse that seemed half-hearted before offering his congratulations and giving Val a hug. He eyed me warily the whole time before he took off.

"He seems nervous around me," I remarked once we were alone.

Valentine stared at me in disbelief. "Yeah, I wonder why."

I pulled him closer, kissing him hard, just because I could. I kissed him until he sank against my chest and slipped his arms around my neck, and by the time I pulled away, if only so I could get a look at him, his eyes were glazed and his lips pink from the rush of blood and the ferocity of the kiss.

"What was that for?" he asked in a daze.

"Because you're mine," I answered with a shrug. "And I missed you."

His lips crooked into a mischievous little smile and the light of the chandelier glimmered in his eyes. "You missed me, huh?"

"You sound surprised."

"Not really," he said, leaning into me as we happened to end up on the dance floor. I took his hand in my left and slid my other down onto his hip, leading him. "But you don't usually say it."

"I don't usually do a lot of things I feel compelled to do when it comes to you," I admitted.

"Oh, yeah?" The hand that was on my shoulder traveled up and his fingers played with the hair on the back of my neck. "Like what?"

"I can think of a few things right now," I said, my hand traveling a bit lower to cup his ass, just to see the sheepish look on his face as he glanced around to make sure no one else was paying attention. Not that they'd dare to comment if they were. "But it would be more fun to show you."

"Malcolm, it's our engagement party," Valentine mumbled.

"Is that a no?"

He hesitated, glancing around again. "Well... there is a supply room around that corner."

I took his hand, already leading him across the floor before he'd finished that sentence. Sure enough, there it was, even if it was small enough that it was more like a supply closet than a full room.

It would do, though. There was no way I was going to get through the night without losing my mind if I didn't have him, and I knew Valentine wasn't going to want to leave early from our own engagement party.

The moment we were inside the closet, I shut the door and pushed him up against it, kissing him hard enough to remind him that I'd been holding back before, if only for his sake.

"Malcolm," he breathed as I turned my attention to his neck. His hands found my hair, and he gave an enticing little whimper as my teeth grazed his throat.

I tore his jacket off and started on his belt, but I couldn't even wait to get his pants off before I slipped my hand past his boxers and palmed his cock. The feel of it hardening in my grasp was kerosene on a fire, and when he bucked into my touch instinctively like he couldn't control himself, it turned into a fucking inferno.

I managed to get ahold of myself enough to take his pants off, and he was already unbuckling my belt with trembling hands. I wondered if it was anticipation of what was about to happen, the thought of the last time I'd used it on his ass, or both.

"Oh, wait," he said, reaching down to grab something out of the pants pooled around his ankles. He pulled out a condom and I smirked.

"You came prepared."

I was usually opposed to there being any barrier between us, but it was lubricated, and something told me he was going to complain about my come dribbling down his thigh in the middle of such a civilized affair.

"I had a feeling," he said dryly, unwrapping the condom before taking my already stiff cock in his palm and sliding it on. He took his time, his fingertips brushing over the tip.

"Teasing me, huh?" I asked, grabbing his wrists before I spun him around and pushed him up against the door, face first.

He gasped, his fingers splayed against the door as he stood with his perfect ass half-exposed beneath the tail of his shirt, ready for the taking. I slipped my fingers past his cleft, brushing against the familiar base of the plug inside of him.

"Good boy. You listened. Must not have wanted to be punished tonight."

"I wouldn't say that," he mumbled.

A smirk tugged at my lips once more as I gave the plug a gentle tug. I felt him tense up automatically. I wet my fingers in my mouth before using them to lubricate the plug a little so I could get it out. He still whimpered a little, an enticing sound that made me want to comfort him and ravish him at once.

His hair was already pulled back, so I pressed a kiss to the back of his neck and replaced the plug with my fingers, gently rubbing his hole, which was still slightly agape.

"Looks like you're ready for Daddy," I said, my voice low and rough with approval against his ear.

Valentine shivered in response as I lined my cock up at his entrance and pushed inside, being swift for his sake since we had limited lube to work with. And also a little because I couldn't take much more waiting. I needed to be inside him now, and the sensation of his tight ass clenching down on me was more than reward enough.

"Fuck," he gritted out, his nails scraping against the door.

I put a hand on his hip for better control and gave him a second to adjust before I pushed the rest of the way into him. I clamped my other hand over his mouth to muffle the strangled cry that escaped him. The music and chatter of the party was too loud for anyone to hear us unless they happened to be right outside in the hall, and I didn't really give a damn if they were, but I knew he did. And it was also a turn-on. Judging from the way he arched back against me, he felt the same.

As I began to thrust slowly into him, I was about to pull away until I felt his tongue glide against my skin, slipping through my fingers. I moaned in approval and pushed two fingers into his mouth. He started sucking and laving them in a delicious little preview of what he was going to be doing to my cock later that night.

"Good kitten," I purred, my hands traveling around to the front of his body. I slipped one beneath his shirt and up to pinch his nipple until it hardened, and gripped his cock with the other.

Valentine's head fell back and he moaned in bliss as I started kissing the back of his neck and stroking him, all while thrusting into him harder than before. I enjoyed taking my time on most occasions. Savoring the sensations of his perfect body beneath mine, and taking the time to pluck all his strings to draw all the right notes of pleasure and pain from his full lips, but there was a time and a place for rough and fast, and this was it.

The night was still young, and once I had him home where he belonged, in my bed, we'd be going all night long until he begged for mercy or collapsed. Whichever came first. This was just the warmup.

No matter how many times I'd taken him though, or where, it never even came close to getting old. I'd explored every inch of his body so thoroughly with nearly every part of mine, and yet each time I fucked him, I felt the thrill of exploring uncharted territory. I'd already conquered him a thousand times, and still, I wanted more.

Judging from the way he was bucking desperately into my touch, so did he.

Valentine came with a tantalizing little moan and I wasn't far behind. I gave in to the temptation to bite down on his neck, almost hard enough to break the skin, right before I came, and his cry of pain pushed me over the edge.

"Son of a bitch," he said through his teeth, his cock still twitching in my palm as the last few drops of come slipped through my fingers. "I swear, you're like a fucking vampire."

I pulled out and tossed the used condom before taking my fingers into my mouth and sucking his come off them, salty and sweet. Just like him.

"You like it," I accused.

He gave me a half-hearted glare, his eyes still glazed with pleasure, but he didn't deny it. I watched as he struggled to catch his breath and pulled his pants up, his hands trembling as he tried to refasten his belt. I'd already taken care of mine, so I pushed his hands aside and took over for him.

"You're a mess," I remarked, taking in his newly disheveled appearance, from his rumpled shirt to the strands of hair that had fallen out of his low ponytail.

Irritation flashed in his eyes. "I wonder why."

I just grinned and took his face in my hands as I leaned in to kiss him, robbing him of his freshly caught breath. "When we go out there, you think they're gonna know? You think they'll be able to tell I fucked your brains out in the supply closet because you're such a naughty little slut, you couldn't wait until we got home?"

"Oh, fuck off," he muttered, but I could tell from the flush on his cheeks his irritation had more to do with getting turned on again than being insulted. He loved it when I talked dirty to him, but he also liked to pretend he didn't. Just another one of the little games we played both in the bedroom and outside of it.

I'd never really been big on boundaries, so it didn't make a whole lot of sense to compartmentalize that aspect of our relationship. Valentine was my pet, my boy, my best friend, and my lover. He was all those things and so much more, and I wanted him to be all those things whether we were in bed or out in the street. I wanted to own every part of him in all the ways I could, and I wanted the world to know it, too.

The ring on his finger was just another way of showing what the collar around his neck already did, and soon enough, we'd have a marriage certificate to prove the same. In the end, they were all just superficial symbols of an underlying truth.

"You're mine, Valentine," I whispered into another kiss as I pinned him against the door again. "Every part of you. Always. Forever. There's no escape."

He smiled against my lips and looked up at me with a wicked little glimmer in his eyes. "Only you could find a way to make that sound like a threat, you psycho."

"Oh, It is," I assured him, tucking an errant strand of hair behind his ear. "But you're marrying me, so really, which of us is crazier?"

"That's a fair question," he mused, slipping his arms around my neck and pressing his forehead against mine. "Guess it's just gonna have to be a tie."

THE END.

Printed in Great Britain
by Amazon